KAITLYN BANKSON

The Paper Pusher

To the memory of my mother

Contents

I

PART ONE

CHAPTER I

Routine dulls the edges of sickness—one that is festering inside a person's mind, leaving singed thoughts and ashes in its wake, a cerebral illness that shows no scars until the diseased person takes action.

When a person's routine turns the illness into an impulse it rationalizes all outcomes. The simple task of picking off crumbs from the table and placing them into the palm of a young woman's hand becomes a meager way of staying sane amongst the senselessness.

Lifting up an antique tablecloth, shaking out memories of childhood, a woman makes the illness leave, but it will not go. Routine only dulls the ache; it only softens the pain.

Sophia Weber brushed the crumbs and dust and memories from off herself, her modest dress rippling gently below her small knees. Heading toward the drawer of kitchen utensils that had lost their shine long before she was born, Sophia picked up three spoons, forks, and knives. She believed that to set the table was a matter of form and efficiency—a dance with only one dancer.

The speck of sunlight rising above the horizon this morning was more absorbed than reflected by the tarnished utensils Sophia held in her thin hand. One by one the utensils thudded against the wooden table that was designed to seat a happy family to their first meal of the day.

There was one spoon for mother, father, and daughter, one fork for mother, father, and daughter, one knife for mother, father, and daughter. Sophia then poured boiling water over unsuspecting tea bags, watching them blow up and fill themselves with tea dust. Bubbles circulated within the water and obscured the transparent liquid, and Sophia had to close her eyes in order to avoid drowning in it. Everything was already dark enough in her life.

The steam rose from each mug; all three mugs were appropriately-sized for their respective members of the tribe. Sophia watched the swirls forming and disappearing in the air, wishing, hoping, and pleading to be one of those wisps. As with every morning, being light as air would mean freedom from the dense wooden floor that she tread upon.

She turned sharply on her heel, scolding herself for such whimsical nothings, as she reached up to the highest cupboard to grab the napkins. The family's napkins were made of silk and never anything less. Her mother flaunted her belongings, though always putting on a show for no one. Carefully folding the utensils in the napkins, Gertrude felt that each family member's social status rose significantly. Breakfast was a time to remember what they had, who they were, and what they had to lose.

Sophia's mother dropped bacon, eggs, and toast onto each plate. Yet, she thought it a shame to share her favorite dishes. The bacon sizzled and continued to squirm on the plates as she moved them into the correct places on the table. Sophia's father always sat on the right of her and her mother on the left. Their positions had never changed since she could remember.

The eggs looked sad as the yolks drooped to the side and tore themselves open as they hit the bottoms of the plates, while the toast was severely burned. Her mother had made no attempt to scrape off the top crust, and the entire kitchen smelled like burnt popcorn.

Yet, Sophia was unsurprised. Routine reminded her that this was the way the world worked. The breakfast was always burned. She stared at her mother's seared and boiled things which seemed to be screaming in the pan. This was home cooking at the Weber household.

Carrying over the final piece of the table setup, Sophia held a glass vase with some plastic flowers sticking out of the pebbles filling it. In the evenings, per her mother's request, the vase sat by the window as if collecting the last rays of sunlight—like it was alive. Then, in the mornings, Sophia carried the vase back over to the table so that it might renew its rightful place as the centerpiece.

Sophia could see, and she was sure her parents could too, dust covering each fake petal. To her, the dust resembled the ashes of a loved one being thrown out onto an open field. The dust looked more at peace than Sophia ever could be.

Envy took hold of her heart, and she desired to smash the plastic thing to pieces. If she could not live peacefully in this house, then nobody could. Sophia could not handle seeing peace and contentedness in such a place. Peaceful behavior was foreign inside the shuttered windows and barred doors. Anything attempting to make a start in life would not survive until the end of the day because either Sophia or her mother would be sure to promptly end its peace.

Communication between each family member was nearly all through silent actions. Sophia more often felt her mother's glares before she heard her commands. Her father was never one to talk much anyway, so this method of communicating through mime must have felt normal to him.

Normalcy in the house was one of the family's highest values. To look normal to external eyes was all Sophia's mother desired. Routine was a way to lock in the expectations.

Sophia squeezed her nails into the inside of her palms. The little bites relieved her of her present need to demolish the centerpiece flowers. She looked down at her red hands and the marks she had just made.

The marks kept her from peeking underneath the carpets of the house, beneath the tablecloths, and inside the people running it. Not a soul should ever try to figure out the sickness' hiding places. For sickness morphs, it follows no routine of its own; rather, it sneaks up on a person and leaves them vulnerable to the next parasite.

Sophia had never read a textbook on the subject of illness, but she knew that if it was not kept in line it would win. No matter how much it took control, Sophia had to batter it back down with whatever was at her disposal. By washing the dishes and scrubbing the cold floorboards by hand, Sophia maintained the order her mother created.

Order created a silence just outside the reach of the disease. It was a loud, large squiggle of a disease that knew no bounds and fed off fear—Sophia's fear. But when the routine failed, Sophia knew her mother would always be there to catch her. Gertrude would carry Sophia over to a soft, warm bed and drape her weak frame over it. Her mother would heal the sick and mend the socks and shoes of the poor with her own two hands, if only they obeyed her commandments.

CHAPTER II

Sophia Weber was now twenty-two, and everything looked ugly to her—the hobo riding the bus, the rush hour traffic, everything that put the city in motion.

The bus to work took her from her house on Yardley Avenue to her workplace on 14th Street, which was much further downtown than her mother would have liked.

There was a peculiar woman that rode the public bus with Sophia every morning. This morning, a woman with black, stringy hair seemed to crawl on her belly toward a severe-looking Russian man at the bus stop. She carried a metal cart with her everywhere as she hobbled, while her black hair gave a slight quiver with every step she took. Sophia witnessed the awful tension between the two bus riders. The woman's eyes followed the gentlemen, causing him to become bewildered, but Sophia was more-so because she was behind a few people in the bus line and could barely see their unusual interaction. The only message available to Sophia was written in the black-haired woman's eyes. Her eyes seemed to command: "You! Boy! I love you for your dark look, your dirty hair, and your wild eyes. You make me stare and hunger for an answer. I love you! I want you! Do not waste your passion on these cannibals! Throw it on me in full force!" The bus stop line moved forward without noticing this odd scene. Sophia pretended to be one of the unobserving standing idly by.

One could tell she loved this man who had no idea who she was. As the bus driver released the air pressure and lowered the rusty, tin box of a bus for her, she shakily approached the first step with her spider-veined legs. Her short skirt revealed these veins to the innocent bus riders. Under her breath, she mumbled, "Pick up your bag. It might slip… Oh, don't knock on the door. I hate people like that. I hate bastards. …Cannibals. …It's freaking hot in here. …Filthy cannibals. …Ah! A psychiatrist. Good, just like my father. Need psychiatrists."

Sophia's heart rate increased as she strained her ears to listen to exactly what this woman was prophesying. The cannibals were a curious thing to mention on a bus full of professionally-attired and gadget-equipped people. Sophia wondered: What did cannibals signify? Why did she mention these creatures out loud?

The thought of being surrounded by people who want to harm her was not a new idea to Sophia, of course. She grew up thinking everyone was out to smother her face with a pillow.

Perhaps, there was a feeling of agreement and relief that what was known to Sophia about people was finally being said in public—even if what was known was just to the bus crowd.

At the next stop, and with the impending threat of rain, the professionals began to cram themselves onto the bus. Sophia was foisted up into a man's armpit, her face taking in the scent of sweat and deodorant that smelled vaguely of pine. "Oh sorry, Miss," said the man who would eventually step on Sophia's toes eight times, none of which he cared to apologize for at the end of the bus ride.

The next stop was in front of a new restaurant that had kept its "Grand Opening" sign out for months after opening. Sophia had low hopes for this place. She got pulled away from her thoughts about this restaurant, however, when the black-haired woman launched into a shrill squawking cry of "I need to get out! *I need to get out!*"

She pushed the wall of professionals in front of her until they collapsed as a unit. "Hey, lady! Relax!" shouted one of the men closest to her, yet she mortified all the others with her squawking.

Startled out of his morning daze, the bus driver looked in his rear-view mirror at the commotion-maker in the back. "All right already!" he shouted. The rest of the crowd was compelled to look up to see just how angry she made the one who was in control of all of their destinations that morning. The thought of him driving more slowly or crashing out of spite shamefully entered the minds of more than one of the bus riders.

The door flew open near the back of the bus and the stringy, black-haired woman, Sophia's new interest, fled from the doorway and out onto the sidewalk where the restaurant still kept their opening sign up.

Hobbling off, Sophia watched the woman move away from the bus, and she kept her eyes on her until she was obscured by the side of the metal box.

Scenes such as this one continued to happen on the bus in the morning. The bus was made for the public, by the public, after all, thought Sophia, who better to utilize these services than the public? Every day there was a monotonous tone to the strange chain of events which would happen on the bus as if a new bar was set for how strange and how dirty things were allowed to get. On the bus, there were times when it reeked of day-old chicken wings, urine, sweat, or some unknown smell that one could distantly characterize as used-diaper.

The bus harbored the homeless who shrugged at the pay box and moved to the back seats carrying their large garbage bags of belongings. The men often had worn-out sneakers pushed into worn-out boots, while the women had ankles that looked like trees shoved into shoes that did not fit them properly. Both smelled of sweat and grime which never left them even after they used the gym showers. During the winter months, they gathered themselves up in blanket-like fabric and slept as they splayed out over two seats. Sophia postulated that these may be the cannibals the black-haired woman spoke about. After all, they took up as many seats as they pleased while the professionals fit into each other's armpits and then had to tactically maneuver their way out of the bus at their stop. Typically, a person had about thirty seconds to get out of the bus before the doors slammed and they have transported away from their destination for good.

Before the bus got to the second-to-last stop, Sophia was already plotting her escape from the bus before the feelings of stress began. The time pressure of travel made commuting to work one of the most aggravating and taxing parts of her day, which was just another reason why everything started to look ugly to her.

***

Sophia tried to push her way into one of the window seats. She tended to prefer the left side of the bus, perhaps it was the driver side of the vehicle that made her feel a little more comfortable. No longer on the hook for needing to be on the lookout, Sophia eased herself down in the itchy bus seat, slinking further down as if to hide from everything.

Watching the buildings pass into one blur on the city's canvas, Sophia remembered back to those days on the swing at recess where she went as high as her body could swing her. When she was a small-framed girl of ten, her grasp on the world came in the form of a mother she hated and a father she never saw. She had sat on a swing and forcefully pushed herself as high as she could go to see past the playground and into the fields. The other children were running around, loaded with energy. But at recess, Sophia sat contentedly swinging, humming a lullaby while daydreaming about her dead cat and her quest to see the fields beyond the obstacles obscuring her view.

She even recalled, on one of those elementary school days, launching herself off the swing at its highest peak so that she felt for a moment like a bird. She desired to be a bird with wings that were broad enough to carry her over the school's fence and out into the town.

But then that bird grew older, and it seemed her sense of freedom shrunk with the progressing years. Sophia wondered what could have caused such fear to build up in her heart. Was it her age? Was it her schooling? Or was it something else? Her mother, perhaps? Regardless, the tightening of her mother's control and the growing sense of fear in Sophia began at the end of elementary school when the swing was no longer as appealing to her.

The swing only held meaning when a chance of escape was possible. There was no escape left—not for Sophia.

Her mother would never allow her baby bird to fly away. It became more apparent as Sophia reached puberty. The first

11

time she came out of the bathroom pale with blood trickling down her leg, her mother gave her a lecture about maturity, abstinence, and abortions that end in death for the mother-to-be. Menstruation was always seen as the enemy—a reminder of her womanhood and what her cycle stood for. It meant sex with negative consequences.

Sophia recalled one of her mother's lectures on the subject.

"Honey, I can see it must be that time of the month. You're unusually irritated," said Gertrude.

"I'm fine," said Sophia.

"All right, I must warn you, though, that you're looking rather pale again. It could be anemia. I'll make steak tonight; extra iron will fight that off. Sometimes I think that the first man on earth cursed the first woman with pain every month to remind her of the result of seducing and sleeping with a man. Yes, men never suffer anything, right? And let me tell you, they abuse that power all the time. They go and sleep with any woman they fancy and then leave once they're satisfied. It's disgusting. Meanwhile, the women blow up like balloons, suffer excruciating pains if they don't lose the baby before the end, and then die from complications in a cold, dreary hospital room. The baby becomes an orphan and wishes he had never been born before. There, that's life for a woman of pleasure for you. So, never do it. Okay, honey?"

Sophia did not have the strength to look at her mother. Struggling to say something, she blurted out: "But what about you and father?"

Gertrude's lipstick-shrunken lips twitched and curved into a smile. "Well, we were just lucky. I had you and I didn't die, though maybe I did in another way... Your father is never home, he hardly lays near to me in bed, and we never speak about anything intimate. You see, your father is done with me, and I have died." She drew herself up from her chair in the dining room before saying, "All I have left is you."

Sophia could not tell whether this meant anything positive. She could not tell whether she had saved her mother from death, or was just clinging to what was left. This fact remained a mystery to the present day.

The bus jerked forward and Sophia's purse fell to the floor. She quickly picked it up, wiping off the bottom with her hand. The idea of germs had not entered her mind because it was so full at the moment of memories.

Men were liars and cheats and babies were dangerous burdens that mostly brought death. Yet, Sophia saw a world that still seemed to move on. How could everyone function if they were always dying or being lied to? wondered Sophia. Could we have a functioning society otherwise? Perhaps her mother was exaggerating just a little bit?

She watched the man across from her offer a seat to a pregnant woman. Her face glowed as she thanked the gentleman who looked keen to give up his seat. The man looked like a shaggy thirty-year-old professional. He looked like he could fit into the world of technology gurus. Another woman was speaking to a friend as they laughed freely about a college party they went to the night before. All of these memories ganged up on Sophia, even when she tried to focus on her mother's teachings. It became apparent that something smacked of falsehood. But who was wrong? Sophia thought.

In her confusion, another memory came into focus in Sophia's mind: the scent of lavender in a hot cup of tea, while her mother told her about the latest abduction of a girl of just thirteen. The irony forged itself into a blade as it went down

13

Sophia's throat. The hot tea swept against her vocal cords, keeping them from closing too tightly in the effort to disagree. There was to be no disagreement in front of Mother.

Gertrude moved a little closer, her eyes growing larger, and a little white spittle formed around her puckered mouth as she told of the horrible rape of the abducted teenager.

"The girl has yet to be found. That's why she's all over this show, in the newspapers, even on our milk!" said Gertrude, a smile in her eyes. "She may be dead for all we know."

Sophia stopped drinking her tea when the anticipation of it coming back up made her put the cup down. No one could disagree with Mother, but one could retreat and turn the other way.

***

The window seat became more comfortable when Sophia was scurrying around in her own mind. Losing the feeling in her lower limbs, forgetting to switch legs, Sophia gazed at something she could not find outside the bus window. The shops all sped past but were in view just long enough for her to distinguish which boutique was which by their large, elegant signs.

Each shop window was festively themed. In the fall they were an orange and black mesh, in spring they were a jumble of butterflies and green, in summer they were a cacophony of sun yellow and reflective surfaces, and in winter they were a halo of lights and branches.

The shops usually held bold white letters above their doors, inviting all to enter indefinitely. The white mannequins reminded Sophia of her mother's own dress form. She always had pins sticking out of her sides and shoulders. Measuring ribbons were fitted so close to the mannequin's figure that she appeared to be sucking in the air just to fit the measurements her mother desired.

Sophia felt bad for these rigid things. They were touched by greedy fingers. The figures had no space and wore their clothes all day for people to ogle at in the window. The worst offenders were the lingerie mannequins that exposed their fabric bosoms or their plastic feet off for the public to see.

For a moment, the horror revealed itself to Sophia but was soon transformed into awe. It was as if the mannequin were a woman who could stand to be looked at, glared at, and feasted on by the eyes of the masses. A little tingle crawled down Sophia's spine because it was a risky game to bare skin.

Shaking her head, her hair whipped the man's face who had taken the bus seat right next to her.

"Oh! I'm so sorry, sir," said Sophia.

The man gave a curt smile as he looked back at his phone without a word.

Sophia returned to her musings about the world outside the ugly metal box. The mannequins in their windows remained an unfinished idea for her. The emotions behind imaging a woman barely clothed in front of a shop window were still an enigma. Sophia imagined one of the mannequins as a real woman.

A white, shiny hand wiggled her index finger in the window of a downtown boutique. The finger woke up the rest of the other fingers, and eventually the hand. Much like Pygmalion's statue, this mannequin turned into a real woman. Once most of the body had awoken, then a flush of blood colored the body from deathly white to tan. Her hard exterior became soft and fleshy. It became even more indecent for something so plush and warm to be standing in the window of a store in only a lace bra and underwear. Now that she moved, each movement created subtle waves in her flesh. She breathed.

No longer a mannequin, but a real woman, she backed away from the window and into the dressing room of the store, snatching some clothes off the hangers they resided on. She felt the need to clothe herself like Eve. Only a special person could see her as she really was—no longer just a pincushion for middle-aged women to stab, or for young men and women to ogle over.

Sophia felt exposed enough just sitting on the bus among all these professionals. These were the businesspeople of the downtown world. Meanwhile, she did not feel strong enough to even move her own feet one after the other.

Downtown was filled with vermin who fed off of the professionals, who kept moving without looking down. Sophia felt like she skated on both extremes; her own self-worth she rated as being among the vermin, while she knew that she was as educated as many of the young professionals. The mix of the poor and prosperous, able and unable, was all represented on the bus Sophia rode.

To gain the attention of her peers, it seemed easier to be like the mannequin and stand around with the most expensive-looking outfit on, allowing anyone to touch and stare at her for money. After all, Sophia was a pretty woman now. She could sense it in the way people smiled at her pleasantly or spoke less coarsely with her than with others. She enjoyed what her femininity could do for her. But as she grew up, her mother pulled her aside to warn her against showing too much skin, or wearing any makeup, or flirting with men. All led to abduction, rape, and death—usually in that order.

As Gertrude was folding some laundry one day she said,

"There is nothing innocent in a woman flirting with a man. She knows exactly how to drive them insane, and they will go insane if you play a game and then leave them dry. They will end up taking by force what you don't end up giving them. Now, would you like that, honey?"

Sophia remembered looking disturbedly at her mother. The only words that came out were, "No, mother."

It was reminders like those which made Sophia first see the bodies around her with horror, and then with interest. She earnestly wanted to make sense of the mixture of emotions. Everyone was a threat, according to her mother. But Sophia had never yet been assaulted by any one of her fellow seatmates. No one seemed to care that she was there on the bus thinking about each one of them. In fact, most wore a look of apathy toward everything around them. When Sophia pulled back, she found them all washed out in a dulled mass of gray. She, being the only one in color, was still was not of a normal hue either. Sophia was tinted a single pastel color with a shadow that she had to deal with before it expanded within her soul.

***

A loud popping sound arose before the passengers realized the back tire had popped. Sophia would have to walk the last mile to work today.

On any other day, this would have been stress-inducing to Sophia, but after watching other bizarre things happen it was no longer so stressful. It was an unlucky day and Sophia was preparing herself mentally for a cruel awakening while the bus slowly lurched to a stop on the side of the road.

People looked at each other blankly—not knowing what to do. They looked at each other as if asking: Was the bus really done for? What are we paying taxes for? Their eyes wanted you to say aloud back to them that it was okay. Comfort on any public bus was always lacking, so for such a convenience to be found among anyone at that point was unlikely.

In fact, no one had moved from their sardine-like proximity on the bus, they were unable to believe the bus may be out of service before their designated stops were passed. The professionals checked their watches, still hanging on to the germ-ridden, yellow hangers above their heads. Their arms stuck out like broken wings bracing against nothing. There was no momentum to fight against now.

Sophia shifted a bit, hoping along with the rest that perhaps the damage was not as bad as it sounded based on the pop of the tire. The bus driver hopped off and on the bus for several minutes, staring back at his passengers with a dreary, apathetic expression. Not a single person would lose out on his pay today—not one.

The wait was even more agonizing than Sophia could have guessed before this emergency started. She felt powerless when riding the bus: on this metal hunk of trash the driver could not be controlled, nor could the seats be adjusted, nor could the garbage littering the floor be picked up daily.

In ten minutes, the bus driver shouted, "Get the next bus!" The next bus he spoke about had just pulled up right behind the passengers and if they did not act quickly, then it would surely leave without concern. Sophia let go of the yellow hanger and raced over to the next bus, hoping to actually get a spot closer to one of the doors where she could find a spot to breathe freely, and not inhale someone else's sweat.

But she could not. Sophia lifted up her dress, hurriedly walked down the aisle, and nearly smacked into the man standing next to her at the back of the bus. It seemed even further away than her previous spot.

Maybe I should just faint here, thought Sophia, at least it would get me out of this god-awful situation. Actually, I don't feel quite so well…no, my heart is racing. Oh god. No, not here, I have to get to work. I'm already late as it is! I'm not going to pass out, I'm not going to pass out. I'm not going to pass out…

Shutting her eyes, Sophia imagined being back in her own room and in her own bed. She envisioned being served her mother's tea and hiding away beneath the oasis of sheets and their warmth. Breathing heavily, she tried to hold in her breath, only for it to come out in a strong cough. Oh god, thought Sophia, now I'm just drawing more attention to myself! She put her head down, trying to camouflage herself into the floor—the dirty, ugly, rubber-gray floor of the bus.

She imagined falling onto her knees and burying her head in between them, forcing the blood back up to her brain. The glazed-eyed people would look down at her in disgust. She could not take the city because only the strong lived here. Sophia did not belong among the healthy.

Finally, the second bus began moving and Sophia knew that it would just be a few more minutes until her stop and, thereby, her saving grace from this torment. Trying to focus on her body as it swayed forward and backward, Sophia felt a warm arm touch hers. She apologized profusely to the owner of the arm but did not dare look up to see who it was. When another sudden motion of the bus occurred, their broken wings touched again. Sophia tried to move from the hanger, closer to the even higher pole above her head.

But the body made contact with her again when everyone

shifted back for new people to get on the bus. Sophia looked up and saw the side of a man's face.

He had dark sideburns and long blond hair which accentuated his dark green eyes. She had never seen those colors before on a man. Was he moving closer to me on purpose? Sophia wondered. Was there a message that I was supposed to read? What did he want from me? I'm sick, I don't belong here. I must be fooling myself. Did he even touch me?

The bus turned a corner and Sophia moved to the side and back managing to hit his inner arm with her shoulder. He was so warm and firm, and Sophia's heart began to pound to the point of pain. She hoped he would not hear it. Sophia only looked up to see the end of his strong nose which she could tell was angled nearer to her head.

Starting at the base of her throat, an urge to have him hold her right there in the middle of the bus arose. She had to stifle it before she gave herself away. I must not be that easy, thought Sophia. Mother always says men only end up hurting you. I'm just imagining his interest anyway.

Coming to a halt, the bus slid up against the sidewalk next to Sophia's workplace; it was her second week at a law firm downtown, and she felt more energy getting off the bus now than she had getting on.

Sophia squeezed herself past a woman with an enormous purse, a girl with a full backpack, and a gentleman holding his lunch bag with one hand and fiddling with a newspaper in the other. In order to pass by unscathed, Sophia sucked in her breath and hurried past, also trying not to make any eye contact with anyone who saw her previous nervousness.

After leaping through the bus doors, Sophia began walking down the street to the high-rise building with the shiny golden letters of the street name, 14th Street, written across its entryway. The signage was sure to impress her parents when they would decide to visit her at work.

She saw the man with the dark sideburns enter her office.

CHAPTER III

S ophia's bus stopped at 14th Street in front of a six-story building that was wrapped with windows. The windows had a dark tint in the light, but from inside one had a perfect view of the city. Although the city was the most unlikely thing to grab the attention of the people inside the office.

The most beloved holiday of her law firm was St. Patrick's Day. There were drinks for everyone galore and the Christmas lights from many previous office parties were strung from the tiled ceiling. Sophia had once been offered cake by a coworker and she threw it down the garbage disposal. She did not know why it just seemed like the right thing to do when your office was attempting to fatten you up. Meanwhile, the drunken voices in a conference room escalated while Sophia headed to the bathroom to avoid being sucked into the party.

Sophia worked for a large law firm in the city. She managed to push a few papers forward, but most of them landed back on her desk because they had to be signed off on by just one more person. The days here melded into each other to the point where Fridays did not seem like the end of the week at all. It seemed, however, that the routine kept Sophia from having as many fits as she used to in her childhood. Still, she had her long, thin arms that tremored whenever a coworker asked her to coffee or lunch. Zack said, just yesterday, "Hey, would you like to pick up a sandwich with me at the new restaurant that just opened up across the street?" Sophia choked. Her throat closed as her mind became stormy. The thoughts launched against the sides of her head mouthing, "Don't do it! How, how do I get out of this? There is no easy way out! Wait, wait, I have an idea! Just say 'I'll think about it' and run to the bathroom! Yes, it's genius!" Within twenty seconds, the words raging inside her head poured out of her mouth and she sprinted to the bathroom.

The bathroom stalls were the only places in the office where she could hide from others' scrutiny. The four gray walls that kept her safe surrounded her snugly. To her, it was a place to recollect, breathe, and reenter the world.

On exiting the bathroom, Sophia walked back to the cubicle she occupied for forty hours a week. She had now swapped out the gray stall walls for these blue ones that had pins shoved into its fabric exterior, and these walls were only three. She had to fill the gap in her makeshift office with her body. The desk was made of cherry wood, and each fabric-lined drawer carried with it a faint scent of the previous employee. The chair was too short for her to lay her elbows on the desk, so a set of books were stashed underneath her bottom in order to get to the correct height. Sophia felt like a guest in this second home.

Her coworkers wore suits, but when the boss was gone everyone wore flip flops, jeans, and chewed gum. The pace of the office was usually fast, but when the boss was gone the pace became purposeless and slow movements comprised the entire scene. Of course, it was difficult to blame them in a place filled with small cubicles that blocked out half of the window light. But it was all right for Sophia because her cubicle kept her from imagining that the floor was moving underneath her—tilting her toward the windows so quickly she would crash through them to her death. Cubicles were necessary on this upper floor.

Every day was rigid for Sophia: she arrived, turned on her computer, took her seat, pulled up to the desk, and put her bag into the cabinet beside her. When the computer turned on, she checked her email, replied to several of the messages, and then dutifully followed her boss' instructions for the day.

Sophia had the same routine now for two weeks. But today, the same man who had entered her building was standing in front of her cubicle. He was a relatively tall man for such a small woman as Sophia. He had normal-sized wrists and normal-sized legs; he had much of what Sophia lacked.

He took a look at her emails over her shoulder before stating, "I didn't get your name as our boss walked me around earlier."

Sophia fidgeted, looking over her shoulder at him. He was wasting her email-checking time. Agitated, she said, "Sophia."

"Sophia. That's a nice name. Are you originally from this city?"

"Yes, I grew up in the suburbs. My family moved to this city before I was born."

The man paused, expecting Sophia to ask for his name, but she became quiet. "Well, I'm Damian. I'll see you around the office, probably when I need some paperwork filed."

He walked off slowly without turning his back on Sophia as if she were a queen who would chop off his head if he turned around.

After their first interaction, Sophia was able to turn around

24

back to her desk only to find a new email on her screen from Damian Voigt. Her heart plummeted; she was not allowed to speak to boys, according to her mother's orders. This was her job, though, and she had to respond to her work emails. It was written in her job description. After hovering with her cursor above the mysterious email for a while, she opened it only to find the words: "Testing. Testing."

Sophia calmed down because she knew her reply would be simple: "Received."

The rest of the day involved more phone calls and more paper. But Sophia enjoyed some of the paperwork. Her favorite was the indexing she had to do which meant placing numbered tabs from smallest to largest and the papers in date order. The ability to organize was ingrained in Sophia from birth. She worked just like her computer—in the most logical and effective way possible. Her coworkers said things like, "Wow! She's fast!" But to Sophia that only meant the others were not thinking hard enough about their own work. She could never take these compliments as real compliments.

***

Lunchtime arrived speedily today as did every part of the day when Sophia's routine changed. She had packed a few carrots and some grapes that rolled around the bottom of her lunch bag all morning: It was a poor man's meal, but her mother assured her eating modestly would help conserve her figure into old age. One of her mother's biggest enemies was age. She was not one for injecting poison into her face, but she always made sure to have her little makeup bag and hair curlers ready for every morning. She was a woman who had been raised to wear high heels every day and to maintain her figure and face even when no one was watching. She felt that

25

someone was always there in the mirror—watching her.

Sophia's chewing echoed in the nearly-empty office kitchen. Most of the employees made enough money to eat out for every meal. They even had their self-designated, social circles for lunch. But Sophia kept to herself in the empty kitchen left to her within the safe bounds of the office. In a few minutes, her chewing became entertainment enough for Sophia. She no longer felt lonely.

"Hey! I didn't see you there!" said Janine. She had decided to bring her expensive sandwich into the office today, rather than gorging on it immediately in the eatery.

There was not much to say about Janine. She was enthusiastic about everything. She loved all kinds of weather: rain, snow, sleet, hail, sun. Her favorite color was baby blue. She adored playing "Twenty Questions" with everyone she first met, including everyone in the office. Her maternal affection spread, and she quickly became the office mother. Janine adored everyone unconditionally. She had a surface-level affection for all.

Janine could wear you down with her sweetness though. Sophia felt a kind of pathetic form of warmth for Janine. Sophia liked her, even if Janine broke through her much-wanted silence at lunch.

Janine took a seat which made it feel as if she was halfway on top of Sophia. Oh god, thought Sophia, now I'm going to be up for "Twenty Questions."

"So, where are you from?" said Janine. Sophia thought: Yes, it's happening. Goodbye, lunchtime solitude.

Sophia shifted her seat just far enough away to not feel Janine's breath on her skin.

"I'm from around here, in the suburbs."

Janine's eyes opened wide as she latched her emotions onto a similarity she had with her newfound friend. "Me too! And why did you take this job?"

"I took it because it pays well and I'm interested in the legal profession. I suppose I also enjoy the fact that it's such a clean and organized environment. Hopefully, that doesn't sound too strange to you..."

"Oh, not at all! I used to work in the most awful place. Not to name names, but it was so crazy there, especially with the kids running all around you. It was impossible to keep them in their seats. I just knew I had to get out of teaching. I like that I'm with adults now."

"I think being a teacher could have its bright spots though," said Sophia.

"Sure, sure. But it takes a lot out of an adult, even the young ones." Janine was going to add to that, but she had to stop talking as soon as she bit into her sandwich because she could only roll her eyes at Sophia to signify how delicious her expensive meal was. Janine cut the questioning short and turned on the television to the home modeling channel while putting the volume up to blaring.

Sophia's heart pounded to the vibrations coming through the floor from the television set. She could not take it much longer. She nibbled like a rabbit through the rest of her food, chucked her water down the sink, and left as quickly as she came in. Janine was lost in an orgy of sandwich and fantasy homes.

Janine's fantasy was a life Sophia would never want, simply because she could not bear the thought of having a ton of empty rooms that echoed like in those newly remodeled houses. She would hate to clean them all when, in reality, she took up barely any space at all. She took up a tiny fraction of her mother's house and only a quarter of her own bed.

Her mother's house—that is what she always came back to when she thought of large, remodeled homes. The home her mother embodied had more rooms in it to fill with her spirit and watchful eyes. The house that held more darkness than light. The wooden floor grew darker with each year Sophia grew older. The wood absorbed any natural light that came in through the dusty windows, making the entire room stay at dusk all day. The air was stale.

That was another feature of her mother's house that she hated—it was stale. Sophia suffocated in a home that was impenetrable by sunlight. Her mother was afraid to leave the windows open too long because someone was sure to break in in the interval. The rooms stayed barred and dead.

Sophia walked back to the bathroom to try and beat these solemn thoughts out of her head. She needed time to think and put herself into a more peaceful place. A renewal had to happen for Sophia to recover her wits in between the four walls of the stall she designated to be her temporary womb.

The bathroom had never failed her. It had cold floors and toilets to soothe her aching head against, a cold bowl to lean on, and doors that gave her the privacy she never could get anywhere else. In order for her to survive the many hours ahead at work, Sophia had to be like a phoenix and emerge into the office as her best self until she could start nourishing her frail stress levels all over again the next day.

Sophia took some deep breaths, thrust her head between her knees, and contemplated something else besides her mother. The office had become a refuge for Sophia to grow and heal. Maybe someday she could venture out into the world without needing to compose herself anew in the bathroom every couple of hours. Maybe someday she would be free from her lingering fear.

***

Cubicles are a strange concept that lies on a foundation of cheapness and utility. No one below manager-level could afford an office with cherry-wood desks, executive chairs, and ergonomic keyboards. So why splurge on entry-level employees?

Yet, Sophia thrived in this limiting space. The freedom and respect each person gave to one another in the office was the most space she had been given in her entire life. Anything requiring more freedom and space would cause undue anxiety. She was so new to this world of autonomous adults that it frightened her to jump in.

The office work also became a way to hide from the curiosity other people held about Sophia. Coworkers, like Janine, were continuously asking about what made her choose this firm, this outfit, or this lunch. But the work proved to be enjoyable because she could escape from her own thoughts for a time.

There were little colored tabs and stickers all over her desk next to the stack of transcripts, exhibits, and other important documents that the attorneys handed off to her to organize. Sophia felt the inmost gratitude for the trust these people gave her. She relished in the chaos of the papers around her by her ability to create order out of the stacks.

By the late afternoons, Sophia began to see the entire alphabet in her mind. It served as a poster to refer to whenever she added a new document into the production line. She wrote notes about missing exhibits or duplicates in pleadings indexes.

29

She strove to correct any errors made in order to help the piles of paper move more quickly toward their ultimate destinations. Sophia spent any extra time inventing ways to work better to accomplish the tasks she had to do on a daily basis. Her mind's power was spent on perfecting her organizational skills.

Her work gave her what was like a new pregnancy glow. Each time she looked down at a stack of papers, she looked radiant. Sophia continued devouring the work until she was lost in between cases which filled her with joy.

This job gave Sophia hope. Perhaps they would keep her forever and she could just fall away each day into the work on her desk because the more there was to do the less she worried. The solution to her problem was an exact inverse ratio which was fueled by simply being given more paper.

Law firms are notorious for how much paper they use. Reams crowded their storage room and were gone within a week. The amounts of paper varied in terms of the attorneys' fields: litigation tended to have loads of paper, tax some, and intellectual property little. Sophia quickly learned that more depositions taken meant more exhibits, longer transcripts, and stronger binder rings to hold all of it together.

Sophia handed one of the attorneys his latest discovery binder, and she could not see him over the heaps of paperwork that lay everywhere in his office. The papers went back to his first case, and he kept them because he was too afraid to let go of his cases. His paper trail was laying all over his office floor.

One piece of paper near the doorway read "1983, Estate of T.R." The paper itself held nearly as much history as the man did. There was an old coffee stain on a corner, two clean folds running across the paper, and a yellowish tinge that carried with it its own musty odor.

This was history. He had a life that extended beyond Sophia's. This attorney had been devoting his life to the law before she was even conceived. Sophia thought he must already know everything there was to know about life.

But today she backed away from his office reverently and withdrew to her cubicle. She had to morph into a wiser person before she could properly talk to that attorney. Still, Sophia felt her growth in being able to talk with him as an equal to be steadily increasing as much as her daily work. Her work ethic gave her a crude sense of self-esteem. In the first couple of weeks in this job, Sophia was beginning to discover her own opinions as she read through the cases: a car accident was caused by this woman as opposed to this man, a divorce was hostile enough to cause even more trouble in court, a construction project was never completed due to a written agreement, and more.

Each case revealed a conflict and a resolution. The conflicts of each case were different from Sophia's and sometimes more tragic. For Sophia to notice such cases allowed her to wonder about how these people survived their situations. It comforted her to see them struggle and strive for their own lives.

An email ping roused Sophia from her daydreams. It was from Damian.

He asked, "Could I accompany you home on the bus today?"

Sophia paused. Taking a slip of paper out from the recycling bin, she jotted down a pros-and-cons table. In the "pro" table, Sophia wrote "seems kind," "is cute," "new experience," "more freedom." In the "cons" table, she wrote "moves too fast," "hardly know him," "Mother might find out." The "pros" outweighed the "cons."

Sophia redacted her own statements and damning conclusion with a black marker on the piece of paper she held and then shredded it up into tiny pieces. Then, she responded to Damian with a single word: "Sure."

Within a few minutes, Sophia had calculated a response that was not too committed, a bit standoffish, and yet in the affirmative.

Damian's head stuck up from his cubicle and he smiled at Sophia. She could have screamed "Yes!" to him then.

However, now the consequences of her response lingered in her mind and drew breath away from Sophia's lungs. She thought: What have I done? I have to show up now. I have to entertain him all the way home! That means no window, no contemplating, no deflating, and no space to breathe!

The panic was rising up in unison again and Sophia was familiar with such movement. This symphony took no time in building up to a climax as it changed from silence to the loudest crescendo in seconds, Sophia had to place her head between her knees while not hitting her head on the cherrywood desktop. There was no time to try to escape to the bathroom for the anxiety was already here. At least there were three walls hiding her diminished frame from the sight of her peers. By just taking three deep breaths, she regained some strength.

Sophia's thin fingers gripped at the stack of papers before her as she laid her head sideways on her desk. Out of the corner of her eyes, she lost herself in the next case. As soon as she could forget her situation back at home, she felt able to function again. Paper-pushing was a lifesaver.

***

Her work flowed smoothly for the rest of the afternoon.

Sophia accomplished her filing jobs with ease. Losing track of her own hands, she felt as if the papers traveled across her desk like waves—inevitable and constant. As the stacks diminished, the two-inch binders grew bulkier, stickers grew scarcer, and red ink grew lighter.

Sophia ended the day with a painful paper cut which she sucked until she managed to find a crinkled up bandage at the bottom of her bag. Half of the covering on the bandage had come off, but it would have to do for the moment. Seeing the blood trickle off her finger made her feel weak, so she quickly and tightly wrapped the bandage around her index finger hoping to close the skin with extra, loving force.

Blinking away her tears, Sophia held her hand close to her chest and finished up work, avoiding the paper that had served her all day. Instead, she went through some emails which had just arrived in her inbox, reading through them even though her mind was tired now.

The idea of having to go back home kept Sophia on edge.

Going home from school constantly felt like a recurring nightmare. On good days, home life meant being told by her mother to stay inside while also keeping safe. But the bad days were when Sophia could hear her mother slamming the dishes back into their proper places at five in the morning. She remembered those days in particular as a motley of cruel words and crueler glares.

"What are you standing there for, watching your poor mother put away the dishes by herself?"

Sophia's toes wriggled in her socks by the freshly-painted kitchen doorway as she said, "I'll help."

"I'm so tired of asking you to help before I get any," said Gertrude Weber, flinging the dirty drying-towel to her only daughter with such force that it felt like a whip tearing at her skin.

Stepping up onto an antique stool, Sophia began drying each delicate bowl with the disgusting towel. Gertrude rarely cleaned it. It annoyed Sophia that only particular things in the house were ruthlessly cleaned, remolded, and varnished. The doorway, for instance, had received a new coat of paint a few days prior; just yesterday the dinnerware had been hand-washed; every couple of weeks the bedsheets were put out in the sun. Yet, the towel remained soiled.

Gertrude tossed her another dish—not caring to share a word with her daughter.

Her childhood days reflected the many days passed similarly. Sophia never veered too far from what people considered to be "normal behavior" for fear of running into something far worse than doing chores with her mother.

Still, she resisted this bus ride back home now that it included the extra stress of having to take the ride back with Damian. Her mother ruled a house of doom and gloom—one that had an empty room, useless art hanging over gaudy furniture, and old-fashioned wallpaper. Her mother collected things she believed held antique and sentimental value.

The Weber home was made up of an armless statue, an unused fireplace, and a giant ticking clock. They each were the prime suspects of her mother's strange taste. Sophia thought the carpets were an undesirable blue, a fishy pink, and in other spotty areas, a depressing green. The lighter colors were paired with darker walls, which were featured most in the upstairs bedrooms; while the darker colors were paired with lighter walls downstairs in the living room, dining room, and kitchen areas. The contrast ended up making the entire home a dark hole.

Not only were the colors and decorations strange and unbecoming but so was the mother who filled it and the father who only teased the family with his presence. The mother wore her soldier-like uniform of short, chunky high heels, tight-fitting trousers, and a loose blouse. Her hair was always in curls that wrapped around her head. No one would ever guess her hair was thinning in any way from the care she took in shaping it each morning.

The father of the house also wore a uniform. His was simpler in that he wore his leather shoes, fitted brown pants, and a white shirt that usually made his skin look darker while his hair appeared whiter. He never cared to dye his hair; as a doctor, he had already made something of himself in the world, and colored hair would not make much more of an impact now.

Then there was the mouse in the corner of the house, Sophia. She lived there and left there in approximately equal intervals now, besides the dreaded weekends. The nights were spent at home, but the days were spent at work. Since childhood, her mother encouraged her to wear dresses and flats. This outfit kept her in her place as the family child. Only nowadays, she could add a work blazer on top of her outfit to give it a more professional look. But her childish attire was still there for all to see underneath her blazer. Many of her coworkers thought she could not be a day over twelve, but Sophia did not mind.

She kept to herself in that large house, only speaking when absolutely necessary. In fact, most of the communication that did go on occurred when she was sick—and only in the form of moans.

Sophia discovered that moans made more sense than talking

because her mother listened to her if she wanted her attention that way. But on good days she had no desire for her attention. On the days where she felt ill then the story changed.

Replying to some final emails, Sophia shuddered when she saw the clock near five. The office closed soon and she would have to leave, and not alone either, but with a man.

Damian was also sauntering around, seemingly impatient and ready to go home. In fact, the entire office exuded the sense of being hurried and tense. All her coworkers were eyeing their clocks and counting down the time. Pacing back and forth, chatting coolly with others, and scrambling to send out the last mail of the day, Sophia and the rest of her coworkers were closing in on the end of another workday cycle. Seeing the clock on the wall invigorated Sophia to finish up what she was doing, but at the same time, she wanted to slow down and stop the workday from ending. The workday ending meant more time at home.

She could not count on another workday starting again tomorrow when she had to head home every evening. Any time she was away from work, Sophia could be crushed under the weight of that house and its owner. Sophia was her mother's indentured servant. Her money went to pay for much of her mother's grocery expenses and her modest form of rent was handed over to her as well.

Perhaps, she would find a place of her own in the near future, but right now she was trapped. The strain from such circumstances made Sophia think crazy things that she would never tell a soul. She frequently thought: I should run away. Maybe I could pay cash for a small van. No, she would end up finding me no matter what I did to get away... But the thoughts were growing louder the older Sophia became.

Finally, the business day closed with the same set of established rules as the morning rules only now they were in reverse order: Sophia took her bag out from the cabinet beside her, pushed herself away from the desk, got up from her seat, turned off her computer, and left the office the way she came in. She could lose herself in the workday routine. Meanwhile, Damian followed her from a distance down to the main lobby.

Sophia could feel his presence behind her, but she would not turn around as long as she held the power, she would not turn around for his pleasure.

CHAPTER IV

E very weekday, Sophia left work as if she were never there, or was always ready to leave. She never left any photos stuck on her cubicle or an extra sweater in case it got cold—she left with her bag and returned the next day as if it was her first.

Leaving work meant waiting at the bus stop on 14th Street to go back to her home. The wait for a bus spanned from fifteen minutes to an hour. The buses were sometimes so full they drove right passed her stop to the next one. Or, she was running after the bus from her office only to get there and be told by the bus driver she could only be picked up at designated areas. With glee, the driver shook his head and pointed off into the distance to the next stop. Infuriated, Sophia felt trapped by the will of the driver who knew he had power over her. Inside Sophia's chest, her heart beat so quickly that she was not even sure she could control her body.

Managing to catch a bus was a feat which had to be won every single day, twice a day. But once on, Sophia found a seat, preferably on the left-hand side that she was used to and forgot for the time being the sights, smells, and sounds of the cramped bowels of the bus.

However, during the ride back home, an older woman with

a massive cross hanging from around her neck walked onto the bus which caught Sophia's attention. Every day was a test of faith—not for this older woman, but for *others*. The old woman trudged along down the bus aisle, passing the designated area for the old and disabled, and preferring the more challenging center of the bus. Her test of faith began now. She starting looking to her right with her hazy right eye without any takers. Then, she looked to the left and a girl with pity in her eyes rose and handed over her seat to this religious zealot. Pleased once again, she gave a final throwaway line, "Bless your heart," to seal the claim to her seat and sat down without another glance at the girl.

The girl who got up stood in the aisle with her phone close to her face, not daring to look back at the religious woman. Meanwhile, the old woman planted herself there gripping the seatback in front of her and gazing vacantly ahead at the streets beyond. Once in a while, her head tilted forward as if in prayer. Sophia bent down slightly to see what she was doing and it appeared she had fallen asleep.

Sophia waved her hand to the girl still staring into the screen of her phone.

"Hey, would you like a seat? There's one here," she said, waving her arm beside her.

The girl fumbled, wondering if Sophia was asking her specifically to take a seat. Her neck drooped a bit as she surveyed the spot for any suspicious liquid or crumbs, but the seat looked clean enough. She took the seat.

"Thanks," she said in a curt voice. Taking out her phone, she once again got lost in the screen that carried her away so effectively from this bus.

Sophia wanted to do the same, but a knot in her stomach

made her stay on watch for anyone dangerous. There could be someone following her right now. A stranger, probably a man, of large height with a shirt that did not quite fit over his stomach. This man would most likely have a beard that had been unkempt for weeks and dirty pants that barely reached his tree-trunk ankles. His hands were probably ready for strangling.

A cold sweat touched Sophia's temples while her heart pounded and her hands began to sweat. A wave of nausea held her thoughts hostage as they spiraled around about how she must not throw up here. Her whole body shook with fear as if in a high fever. The fever spread rapidly and suffocated her. She thought: I must not faint here! An escape plan was necessary or she would surely lose her mind.

Looking over at the girl on Sophia's right that she had invited to sit down, Sophia began to contemplate just how she would ask her to move the hell out of the way and stop the bus before it even reached its next destination. There was no way out for Sophia would surely be noticed by all and labeled as the next crazy person of the bus as she recalled the stringy, black-haired woman from this morning's ride. She wondered whether she would start whispering under her breath about cannibals the next day and openly feasting her eyes on boys she found attractive. Would she be the next crazy-looking woman to be all over the television screen for crossing social norms? There was no easy escape.

But waiting only gave her more time to worry and sweat. Her dress was soaked with sweat she could feel it squish under her arms, and her forehead felt oddly cool while she was feeling faint. The only thing to do in this situation was to bend forward like the old, religious woman on the bus and close her eyes—wishing for the anxiety to go away without further trouble. For a time, repeating to herself that this must disappear paused the negative slew of thoughts, but after a while, the thoughts came back and she grew more tired and weak battling a silent war on her own.

Yet, the only person who acknowledged this war was the one fighting it. She knew she must battle through until her street was spoken by the automated recording above her. Making a move to rise, the girl lifted her head from her phone, grimacing at Sophia for taking her out of her pixelated world and back into reality, while Sophia slid out from her seat and crept closer to the doors, trying to remain as unnoticed as possible.

At this point, Sophia did not have strength enough to care about a stranger following her. She felt as if a stranger had already gripped her body and given her a good scare from the inside-out. The only desire left in her was to get home and rest; other than that, she was numb.

***

That was how the first five minutes were spent traveling home. Sophia was completely ignoring Damian, and she was pleased he seemed to be content with merely sitting in her general area.

Their commute together was a quiet union in a world of chaotic feelings. Damian must have noticed Sophia's pale skin turn several different shades in the past few minutes. At least he was intelligent enough to know when she needed space. This is the saving grace of adults—they can read social cues. Sophia indulged in the fact that someone saw her, only her, and gave her the room she needed to start afresh, much like the office bathrooms. Yet, this time, there was a real person, an equal, reacting to her in the world.

She loved him from that moment of discovery.

Sharing with Damian in a serenity that spread over all the people on the bus, Sophia breathed in. Breathing came more easily as she sat close to Damian. For much of the bus ride she spent breathing and looking at his hands.

Damian's wrists showed from under his cuffs where the gentle hill of bone rides out into the palm. A few blue veins traveled up his skin and toward his fingers. White, youthful-looking skin was adorned with blond hairs on his hand and knuckles. The hairs emphasized this was a man's hand and accentuated the muscular grip his fingers had around one of the poles. His fingers were thin and dexterous, and they ended with short nails embedded perfectly into smooth fingertips. The hair on Sophia's forearm rose.

Sophia shook her head gently. This kind of daydreaming was of a new caliber. Damian and his hands kept her preoccupied for the rest of the ride. Did he sense I was boring through his hand on the pole? Sophia wondered. Could he know what I was screaming inside my head? His hands mean everything to me!

His hands spoke to her through the silence. They articulated a story about their strength which went back to the cavemen. They were the hands that took women and used them for their pleasure, hands that ruled a nation, hands that could fight and love with the same ferocity.

Fingertips are the part of a human body which have the densest areas of nerves. Sophia imagined them touching, sending signals to Damian's mind, awakening his senses further to her. She wanted him to see her, to focus on her, and to only notice what she wanted to be to him—a lover.

Sophia shifted in her seat as her body temperature had gone

up too much. Holding open the top of her dress, she blew down it in an effort to calm herself. Then she had to look down at the ugly, dirty bus floor to regain a sense of control.

Once having read a book of human anatomy for a high school class, Sophia now recalled a human hand consisting of twenty-seven delicate bones. All work together to help us create: There are the carpals, the metacarpals, the proximal phalanges, the intermediate phalanges, and the distal phalanges. All the muscles attach to each other to move these bones into a well-orchestrated dance.

To think a man's hands evolved from primates is utterly amazing. Primates have extremely long fingers for grip, which perhaps Damian shared. Sophia hoped so. She wanted Damian to grab her and never let her go.

With hands that could carry them through sickness and health, Damian would make her feel invincible, in control, and powerful. To worship his hands would be too little celebration for a grip that gave Sophia hope there was something outside her mother's grasp.

Besides, her mother's hands were hard and wrinkled. She had blue veins too but hers looked faded and squished underneath her folds of worn skin. Gertrude washed these hands incessantly as if always trying to clean the dirt from underneath her flesh. It never seemed to work: from the washing, her hands only grew dry and cracked after one too many passes with soap and scalding water.

Since Sophia's childhood, the days in Gertrude's house had always begun with dishes. The bone china's clanging even served as an alarm for little Sophia to clamber from bed to help in the kitchen. The volume of clanging helped her predict Gertrude's mood each day.

Sophia shimmied her dress over her head and through the armholes which were too large for her thin arms. Each day she was encased in one of many polyester dresses that fell below the knees and a chemise to hide her bare shoulders, as prescribed by Gertrude. When Sophia's black, pretty tresses became too long, Gertrude took her to the salon and forced her to donate them. To avoid the loss of even more hair, Sophia tied it up to hide its length.

Once dressed, she crept downstairs, avoiding the kitchen, and instead slipped into the dining room, where there was a cozy fireplace she liked to sit by—even when it was not lit. The firebox was cloaked in fine soot, and ashes settled at the bottom of the pit. The pillars and under mantle vaunted intricate nude figures. Some of the little white creatures had lost noses or hands over the years, but all the eyes were still there, watching this family's lives play out as if on stage. How intensely the beady eyes looked straight into Sophia's doe-like eyes… She felt camaraderie with these mythological beings, and she spoke to them of her troubles.

"Hello, my name is Sophia. 'Sophie' for short. Please tell my father to come home early today. I miss him."

The crippled figures seemed to nod.

"And…and please tell Mother to stop sending me off to bed so soon after school. I'm not even tired. Although, do you want to know a secret?"

They moved closer.

"I will sometimes stay up later than when Mother tells me to go to bed. I turn off the lights. I grab my flashlight and sneak under my sheets, and I read. It gets very stuffy and hard to breathe under all of those sheets, but that's okay. I forget about all those things when the stories are good."

Now in the evening, Sophia paid attention to the soap bubbles that avoided sticking to her mother's old hands unlike hers when they were washing dishes. Her mother's hands remained dry much longer and ruthlessly popped the bubbles around her. The suds ended up on Sophia's side of the sink and she often wound up the washer while Gertrude did the drying.

The older Gertrude became, the more shrunken and arthritic her hands became. At first, her aging was a slow process that sped up in recent years as Sophia grew up, almost as if Sophia's distance from her sucked the life from her mother's marrow. Sometimes, she actually worried about leaving for work lest her mother completely unravel.

Decay began in Gertrude's hands. Her hands became shaped, not by her own will, but by her body's failures; her callouses remained, her fingers curved sideways, and her skin became loose. Gertrude was no longer in charge of her hands—she may no longer be in charge of her daughter soon either.

The bus pulled harshly up to the sidewalk, and nearly over it, to stop at the next designated area. Sophia peeked over to see what Damian was doing. He was looking straight ahead now to see the next stop sign. His hands were placed into his lap, one hand was clenched into a fist and the other gripped his upper thigh. The muscles were flexed and Sophia tried counting how many were clearly visible to her eyes.

To any other young woman, having sensual thoughts was normal. But Sophia felt a need to fight thoughts of Damian touching her in various places all over her body. Yet, her mother's voice barged in with every thought telling her that this is the exact temptation that makes women weak, and according to Gertrude, weak women get killed.

***

Sophia could only be weak in the care of a protector, and she wondered who would take on this role if her mother could not. But, perhaps, with a new person in her life, Sophia would not have to learn how to be big and strong and alone to survive in the world.

These thoughts were swarming now at such reckless speeds that Sophia was getting jittery. The jitters could have been enough energy to re-exacerbate another attack of the nerves. Sophia forced herself to take air in, hold for three seconds, and release for four.

Observing the window of the bus, she saw streaks begin to run down its sides. The rain felt like a good sign. The sky understood that soon she would cry no more. Soon the world would begin afresh, a world in which Sophia could flourish under a new system. A system of muscle would suit Sophia well and would make her beg for more—not less.

To play right into his arms, no, to force herself in there no matter what began to be Sophia's sole objective. Her only goal was now to be taken in by another. Since relationships were all power-play, she saw more freedom in giving up her minute form of independence to a man. Her mother was cold. Damian was warm. They were opposites in their ruling styles, but both ruled over the same person—Sophia.

Peeking over once more at Damian, Sophia realized he had noticed her glance and she quickly asked, "Did you bring an umbrella?" A short, churlish grin on his face confirmed that neither one of them had expected this downpour. At least there was a bit more time left on the bus before Sophia had to walk the rest of the way to her house unprotected. Maybe the sky would clear up by then. It did not matter much now. The rain was not her master.

The window gave only a blurred image of a more open area, with fewer of the downtown boutiques and ritzy bars. The residential area became clear to Sophia by flashes of a blurry dog being walked by its blurry owner, or a blurry woman biking in a yellowish poncho, or a blurry restaurant overhang giving shelter to the blurry figure who forgot her umbrella.

The rain allowed Sophia to stay inside her own mind as thoughts concerning her slavery and freedom roamed. She gave in to the rain by staying with her thoughts and her breath. For the first time on this trip home, she felt at ease. As long as she thought about escape and renewal there came the ease in her body.

There had to be a plan that was so natural it could feel like the only choice for Sophia. Could such a thing be done? pondered Sophia. Was there any way to voluntarily leave one form of slavery for another? If an indentured servant wished to work for another master, then was it possible or was that too much of freedom for a servant to have?

It must have been the bouncing of the bus which snapped Sophia back to her current situation once more. Sophia reevaluated how she could escape and stay missing to her mother. If only she could run away from her mother and that wretched house and stay lost forever. Only Damian would know where she was and, maybe, they could live together in peace.

For the next few minutes, she gazed back at his hand and then slowly raised her eyes to meet his face. She stayed there beholding them without lowering her head too soon. Damian took note of her effort and did an ample amount of the chatting once he had established eye contact.

"Well, I don't actually mind the rain. It can be kind of soothing. Don't you agree?"

Sophia nodded vigorously, wishing she could convey all her plans in her head shakes.

Damian continued: "Rain sounds nice too with its pounding on the windowpanes. And I have many memories of playing baseball outside on summer days when sun showers cooled me down. Or memories of finding frogs and worms crawling out of their hiding spots to enjoy a shower as I was on those days. I could always be wild in the rain."

His eyes lit up as he spoke the word "wild" out loud as if he was casting a spell that released his inner wildness right there. Although it was a bit strange, Sophia found his excitement for wildness fascinating to see. She wanted to feed off of that glimmer of fire and suck down the word from his lips before it faded away.

He could be no good for her. Damian could weave together words that moved Sophia deeply. She was terrified to think of what he could do with physical touch.

Damian looked out the window. "Yes, I would take rain any day over the oppressive sun or sullen clouds. I want snow, I want rain, and I want wind. I desire movement and change in a world where I never get any change whatsoever. My parents are always the same, my work is always the same, and my hobbies are always the same. Sure, I may have voluntarily built up my life this way, but I still appreciate the weather making my life more exciting. The weather is the only thing I consider to be of interest in my life right now."

Letting his hand fall from his lap to his side, Sophia felt a need to get up and catch it from falling further. Like a flag being too close to touching the ground, she wanted to be underneath his hand to catch it if it fell. All honor at having saved his hands would lay with her. His hands were sacred and she felt he did not realize it because he used them too flippantly, whereas Sophia wanted to coddle them and keep them close to her body. She wanted to serve his hands.

**

The rain had slowed to a drizzle and the bus finally reached Sophia's stop. One more block and she would leave the bus behind and she wondered if Damian would follow her home.

"My stop is the next one. I'm going straight home. Do you live further out?"

"Yes, I live another mile or so away," said Damian. He adjusted himself in his seat to face Sophia better who was still standing by the center doors of the bus.

"Oh, well, that's nice. I'll see you tomorrow at work, then."

"Yes, I'll see you at work."

Sophia got off at her stop, somewhat relieved he did not seem to be following her home. He had no idea what kind of mother she had.

If Damian were only there at her mother's kitchen table a year ago when she asked: "Mother, will I ever be allowed to date a boy?"

Gertrude kept her head down, staring at the expensive wooden dining table, her eyes tracing the wood's story by its lines and dents.

"No, hon. I think, in time, you will learn to see it is not worth all the trouble."

Now it was Sophia's turn to look down at the table, her vision steadily growing blurry. The wood became bathed in tears, which it rejected and let the water pool up in angry circles.

49

Sophia bit her quivering lips and mumbled, "But why not?"

Smacking her hand down on the table, Gertrude said, "Men screw you and then they leave! And I will never allow my only daughter to go through any of the sufferings I endured. That's why!" She turned away from Sophia, rejecting, like the table, her daughter's tears.

Sophia coiled up into herself, feeling more alone than ever, while her future seemed lonelier still. She could not understand why her mother had a husband at all, or why her father stayed with a woman who seemed to hate him and all men alike.

Gertrude lived in a beautiful house with her husband and daughter. The exterior sparkled, while the interior was ugly. But Sophia's mother was lonely, she never slept intimately close to her husband nor did she have any friends to welcome inside their impressive home.

There were not enough bodies to properly fill the Weber household. If half of it were to crumble away the remains would still be too much space for such a small family. None of them would even know that the other half of the house was burning until the noxious air billowed under their kitchen doorway.

Sophia hoisted her bag over her shoulder and walked down the two streets that led deeper into the wilderness, away from the other streets and houses. Her house was hidden by trees and far from the main road. Being inside the house felt like Sophia was inhabiting her own island. If she screamed from inside no one would hear her.

For a mother who was paranoid about safety, this level of anonymity did not seem safe. The safer option, she thought, would have been to live near a street that went straight to a hospital.

Sophia had once counted the number of cracks in the sidewalk on her way home required to actually "break her mother's back." There were forty-three cracks before she reached the front door. All of those would need to be stepped on before her mother would answer the door bent over in half.

The thought of dishing out punishment to those who hurt her gave Sophia a secret pleasure. What would Damian think? she wondered. It was hard mixing something she loved now with a world that was the opposite. Inside one body, there was work life *and* home life.

The rain picked up, so Sophia speed-walked the rest of the way. Her flats were soaked through to her thin socks. She could feel the cold, damp rainwater slosh around in her shoes. Sophia believed that the punishment for prisoners should be to walk around in wet socks shoved in wet shoes for a week. The odor and sound of wet shoes could drive anyone mad after a day or two.

Water added to her shoes made Sophia feel heavy and ungraceful. Each step became weaker as she approached her house. She saw her house in the distance, yet she never wished to reach it. However, her wish never came true, the same ugly purple door since she could remember was there with its hokey sign of "Best Wishes." It was hung underneath the peephole.

The sign had been bought at an antique shop; her mother thought the sign had such a calming aura that it simply had to be brought home with her that same day. It had started out above the kitchen entrance, but then she decided its true home was to be outside in order to greet visitors. Sophia wondered:

What visitors? Only her mother knew what was meant by doing such things.

The color of the doorway and the rest of the house was also her mother's design. Each room had its own theme. She wanted the bedrooms to be calm and dark, the family areas to be bright and busy, and the rest of the house had to look cheery. Cheery for what? Sophia pondered. Cheery about how the sun was banned from the house, cheery about how the carpets and walls clashed, cheery about the family that was utterly controlled by a matriarch?

This kind of cheer was unwanted by Sophia and her father, and Gertrude could sense it. Nothing was cheery inside the house, regardless of what the signs told everyone on the outside.

Sophia was getting closer to her house now since she could read the sign from the sidewalk. She wondered what kind of drama her mother concocted for her today. Maybe Sophia would be able to have a discussion about her second week at work, or else she would be ignored until chores were completed around the house. Neither Sophia nor her father was saved from the lectures for always letting Gertrude suffer away at making the home a home.

Both Sophia's father and she were given those lectures a few times a week. In fact, Sophia no longer felt unfazed by such commentary. The lectures were long, but less biting now that Sophia could concentrate on Damian this evening. Her hands would be able to clean dishes or the table while her mind focused on his hands.

Damian would now bring comfort into a house that never knew affection. He had now already given Sophia hope without knowing it. She wondered: What could he do for her once he knew of her feelings for him?

Pausing before knocking, Sophia visualized for ages Damian's hand gripping his thigh and that grin of his which gave her goosebumps. She imagined the goosebumps were popping up in all the places she would like him to kiss. Sophia could say that regardless of whether he was a killer, rapist, abductor, or whatever her mother taught her, she would still want him to touch her. Even dying in his arms would be preferable than having to live another day in Gertrude's house.

CHAPTER V

Sophia's mind was turning in a whirl of thoughts and noise. She knew what could drive a person mad—their own thoughts—thoughts forming more thoughts and more and more until the heart's quickened pulse *makes* her focus on its beating. Walking toward her house, she asked herself, why do I waste my time on worthless anxieties? Does daily life worry me that much?

Upon reaching the front door, Sophia touched the knob, but it opened the rest of the way on its own. Gertrude was on the other side because Sophia could hear her clicking heels.

"I thought you would be home earlier. But then again, you're constantly dillydallying with something. Well, hurry up and get inside, I need to go out to check the trash."

Gertrude pulled Sophia through the door and into the kitchen, adding that she would be right back to start on dinner. Sophia cleaned off the table and set it with new forks, knives, spoons, glasses, and plates. The napkins were required to be folded into triangles which enveloped the utensils. Who was this show for anyway? wondered Sophia. No one was invited to our table to eat with us...

As the table was set up, Sophia could see her mother shaking her head as she stuck her hands into the trash cans. Being part of the local homeowners association meant that the community provided shared dumpsters. Her mother hated sharing. Fishing out one cardboard box and some plastic bottles, she threw them on the ground beside the trash can but not before checking the box label to see if she could track down the perpetrating neighbor.

Gertrude's thin lips twitched when she saw that the label once again read, Jim Keller, who was the neighbor one house down. The crow's feet around her eyes multiplied as her mouth curved into a slight smile. This was the third time in a month and the third offense meant punishment to Gertrude. She saw herself as the vigilante of the earth, saving it from the ugly people who created waste. However, her neighbors called her the "Trash Nazi" or the "Eco-Terrorist."

Ignorant of these names and only aware of her "mission," Gertrude threw the recyclables onto the ground, thereby saving them from the landfill. As with her many other neighbors, Gertrude's act of justice forced them into action. The neighbor who sinned that day had to go pick up their trash that was initially disposed of, was now littering the ground, and throw it into the blue bins. The same went for Jim Keller who woke up the next morning to an extra surprise: a cardboard sign in front of his door that read: "Is it that freaking hard to throw your recyclables in the blue bin?!"

After serving this justice, Gertrude felt better and rushed inside to cook some hard, dry tofu and instant rice. She had been meaning to try tofu for the longest time, though she was not quite ready to give up chicken, and now seemed like the right place to start. She was her own woman—her own superwoman.

Sophia recollected a day in which Gertrude had intruded

upon her confession.

"Dishes. Now," said Gertrude. She had on her apron, its great breadth underscored her authority.

Sophia went off to the dishes, longing for the day to continue. Since this was a weekend, school, Sophia's savior back then, was not going to save her.

Today was sure to be occupied with her sneaking around the house while Gertrude did what she did every day: clean, cook, sew, cook, clean, sew, cook, clean, and before bed, read. For Gertrude, the routine drove the woman and not the other way around. Gertrude was a sergeant and her daughter was a private: the routine made her feel needed and she loved it for that.

Gertrude wore trousers. Their beige hues made one think of a person feeling faint. A brass-buckled belt kept them up while a lilac-colored blouse hugged her postpartum belly.

A good part of her morning was spent in hair curlers and applying lipstick. After she removed the curlers, the tight, blond curls she sported commanded order. But it was her lipstick that drew the most attention since her thin lips were only emphasized by the faux color—they revealed a need for the order she felt was constantly slipping away.

Each morning while still tightening her belt, she hurried downstairs. It was as if she was racing against the sun's morning light to get down to the dishes in order to give them a brutal scrubbing. Each dish was meant to be displayed only in the china closet.

Unfortunately, though, her family had to eat.

To be the woman of the house meant unceasingly showing up for the job. Her husband worked away from the house all day and he, too, showed up for his job with fervor. Plus, having come from a farm, she warned Sophia that life was never to be easy.

But Sophia now sat at the table, thinking about how her mother was a philistine. She lacked knowledge about the actual process of slaughtering animals and of garbage disposal. The only content that filled her mind was the news reports on television. If the government dictated tomorrow that drugs were good and produce was bad, which one would she be consuming all the time? Sophia wondered.

Sophia despised her family. They made her stomach crawl with anxiety. She wanted out. The silent, agonizing meals made her mood more morose. Of all the people Sophia had shared a meal with the noises that came from her mother's and father's throats were the vilest she had ever heard. Their black sockets held nothing while the rest of their bodies were only walking imperfections. An ultimate agenda of conformity latched onto them like a shadow. Oftentimes, during the dinnertime silence, Sophia's head was muddled with lines for dramatic speeches she wished she could make to them, but she did not believe she ever would. Sophia imagined saying things like: I am not speaking to you unworthy maggots! I am doing this for me, not anyone else! Everything orbits around food, work, and sleep for you creatures. Well, my name is Sophia and you are not my blood! But the family continued to eat unaware of her brutal inner thoughts.

Unlike her father, Sophia's mother was always there but never in the way that she desired. It was a strange feeling of being stuck in the noose of her mother's ghostly umbilical cord. Sophia herself felt like a shadow of a woman. Gertrude had stripped her of all her womanly possessions. Sophia felt weak and sick. From the bus stop to work to the bus back home, the only time when she was physically away from her mother, she could almost feel the cord snaking out from underneath her knee-length dress and winding around her own neck.

The cord always hung above her head and was the motivation that dragged her back home. Her mother was always there.

Gertrude felt her little girl, her only daughter, was prey to everyone outside her home. In fact, last night on the news a girl Sophia's age, twenty-two, was abducted from her bus stop on her way home from work. Strange disappearances happen, thought Gertrude, especially in this dangerous country. What protective mother would not look out for her child in such a way?

In fact, such a mother would give her only daughter everything needed to fight off the bad guys, who on the news were usually men. Sophia was forced to carry a rape whistle, pepper spray, and an emergency beeper which was linked directly to her mother's landline. In addition to those precautions, her mother made sure her dresses went past her fingers because any shorter could send a signal to rapists. Gertrude checked the locks on her doors and windows every morning and evening to make sure they were bolted. Once a day, the security system around the house, the fire alarm, and the carbon monoxide alarm were also checked. Sophia grew so used to the sounds of the tested alarms in the house that she slept through the noise.

It was clear that Gertrude was the matriarch of the home and family, and she ruled with an iron fist.

**

Before dinner, the family had to gather to pray around the table before eating. Although, this only happened when

Gertrude remembered and wanted to punish her family's already famished stomachs.

"Bow your heads," said Gertrude. "Now, dear Lord, please take care of our family in its time of need. You see, we always aim to do what is right in the face of ease and comfort—unlike our ignorant neighbor who is harming the environment with his wasteful behavior. But, as we know and as I always say, his trash is the world's treasure. Please help him too to see Your light, or else Your lightning. Amen."

"Amen," said the father.

"Amen," said Sophia.

The tofu was dry and Sophia watched it further solidify in its hard cubes on her plate. It tasted like cardboard. The rice was cheap and stuck together, so it became hard to chew. Only gulping down two cups of water helped Sophia swallow much of her dinner.

The quality of dinner was normally at this state of plain food, but the level of dryness varied based on Mother's mood. Since she went through the ordeal again with the trash outside, the family's quality of food suffered. Sophia was sure that if Gertrude had her choice she would rather have dried the neighbor out like a raisin than her own meal. But such was not the choice this evening. She was so frustrated this evening that she even checked to see if his car was in the parking lot, but it was not. He was saved for the day.

Sophia watched her father mindlessly packing the food into his mouth. He made it appear as though he was not even chewing at all. Food, to him, was merely a requirement for human survival. The mind was the only tool that her father believed he had control over. For that reason, Sophia admired her father. He was an intelligent man, but he remained ignorant about the "private sphere." He ruled nothing inside the house, and no amount of intelligence could change the woman running it with brute force.

Clanks of forks and knives against plates were the frequent noises echoing in the house that evening. There was also a low hum of chewing sounds underneath the clanks and clashes. The monotony created in the kitchen could drive anyone to think gloomy thoughts.

Sophia imagined how someone in solitary confinement must hear this level of noise. The sound of his own breathing, his own swallowing, becomes the only constant reminder that he is still alive. The outside world stops behind iron bars.

At dinner, Sophia was battling the feelings of isolation. She had to swallow hard to keep from talking to herself. Even the comfort of a human voice could still keep her from falling apart at the table tonight. Instead, she tried to practice Morse code with her fork to her plate. If only someone were on the other side of the table to hear her plea for help.

Gertrude began giving Sophia concerned looks. She placed a piece of tofu in her mouth, swallowed, and then her eyes followed an invisible line from her plate to Sophia's face. Scanning from the top of Sophia's forehead down to her chin, Gertrude started over again as if searching out an illness she wished to discover. To add emphasis to new discoveries during meals, Gertrude often dropped her utensils onto her plate and gave a little inward breath.

"Huh! Oh, honey, you don't look so well. Let me feel your forehead!" Gertrude hopped up from her seat with more vigor than she ever had in her life to attend to Sophia.

"Oh, yes. You feel warm. Didn't I say to put a scarf around your neck? And now look, this is what happens when you don't listen. Stupid girl."

"I'm fine. I think I'm okay, at least." Sophia touched her own head wondering whether the heat emanating from her scalp was normal. This was the usual interaction between mother and daughter, but to Sophia it seemed like she was possibly right this time. Maybe she was sick after all.

"No, no, your head is hot. I'm going to have to call the doctor's and send you to your room to get to bed early. Goodness, if you would only listen! I work so hard to raise you right, and here you go not even caring about your own health!"

Gertrude left her own dried-out dinner to talk on the phone to the twenty-four-hour nurse at Sophia's doctor's office while Sophia and her father continued to chew their cud. In a slow, agonizing way, Sophia chewed and stared forward waiting for her mother to return with the verdict. Her father never opened his mouth.

"You are to try to eliminate milk from your diet. The nurse said that you are perhaps allergic. Tonight I'm going to pour all the milk in our fridge into the trash, so you won't be tempted. I will also just cook the rice in water, rather than mixing it with water and milk."

"But mother, I drank milk this morning for breakfast and I was—"

"I don't want to hear it. Stop. The least you can do is follow your nurse's instructions if you don't want to follow your own mother's."

Sophia knew this would continue for as long as she resisted. It was easier to give in. She had lost her appetite with the dry tofu and rice anyway. Sophia slid up from out of her chair, pushed it back in, and slunk back to her room.

Gertrude sat down to eat the rest of her meal.

"You know, I cannot understand why that girl is so rebellious. Did I not give her everything, my life, my soul?" She looked at her husband whose eyes were set on the clock in the kitchen. He was waiting for tomorrow when he was in his office at work.

Gertrude stood up and collected the leftover food while her husband was still finishing the last scraps on his plate. He was usually the only one to finish his meal in full, no matter what condition the food was in.

While her husband kept eating, Gertrude clanged the dishes together to warn every living thing in the house of her wrath. It was an all-consuming, all-encompassing fury which, when honed in directly onto a subject, would burst into ashes and never rise again.

***

From her room, Sophia could hear the way the lid of the pot slammed together like a gong. Her mother was fuming. After twenty-two years of hearing her upset about something, Sophia had grown accustomed to the violent and morbid atmosphere Gertrude created in the house before bedtime.

Home never felt calm nor cheery. To Sophia, "home" did not bring with it images of comfortable furniture and warm fires. "Home" did not carry out its promise of warmth, rather it remained cold.

Sophia thought about what "home" actually meant to her; it meant a mother force-feeding her medicines she did not want to take. "Home" was a father who only returned to eat. The rest of the world was locked and left outside the doors of this prison.

But, for Sophia, the most aggravating aspect of the situation was that her mother feigned that the house was in ruins because of Sophia and her "condition." Gertrude believed Sophia was always sick and, in particular, mentally sick.

Gertrude saw her child as weak-willed, weak-minded, and weak-everything. She blamed her husband for this weakness. When Sophia was a child, Gertrude used to say, "If only your father took me like a man, then he would have produced a stronger child." Over the years, Sophia's father recoiled deeper inside of himself, waiting for the next day's office work to be in front of him already.

This was strange behavior for a woman who was so very pleasant with the other people she came into contact with outside the house. She patiently waited in a long grocery line, or tipped extra at a restaurant, or even helped a stray animal find an owner. It was as if her mother imagined herself to be the saint of the world and she suffered for it in her martyrdom at home.

The family sent the obligatory holiday cards of a perfect family all dressed in the same outfits. Her mother was the orchestrator of the entire ordeal. She even signed the cards with everyone's name on them, and the gifts from her shopping were lavish. The gifts were meant to show just how much she loved her family. Her family was special, at least according to baggers at the shopping centers. Gertrude was a saint.

Sophia heaped curses on her mother's head. She wanted to stomp on all of those cracks in the sidewalk on the way home from work and break her mother's back for real. Inside Sophia, there was a vicious desire to see her father finally divorce the vile creature. Or else, she imagined learning a spell that would make her mother just as invisible as Sophia felt oftentimes, or she would create a curse that would make her mother weaker and iller than her. That would be justice.

She thought up crazy, intricate schemes about other ways to punish her mother.

One night, perhaps, Sophia would join a group of witches out in a dark forest. She would take drops of her own blood, a dead frog, and any kind of willpower that she could gather together to cast into the cauldron. The night air would be thin and cool. A crackling fire would lick the outer edges of her cauldron. The concoction would give Sophia the fuel to say all she desired about her mother.

She imagined the witches' chant began with her mother's name. They whispered, "Gertrude," "Gertrude," "Gertrude," three times into the night. The sound of the whispers vanished where the flames met the pitch blackness of the night. The chant echoed: "Fire of the night, hear our prayer. We ask that you call on a great demon to come and cast a dark shadow over Sophia's mother, Gertrude. O damned spirits, punish those who harm us. Be the judge of our own inner toils and carry out a vengeance over all those who have yet to pay for their injustice. Fire, fire, fire hear us! See us! Work for us!"

They danced. Twirling, circling the flames in wild glee and kissing each other as if it were their last day on earth. Sophia believed that this must be what justice feels like. She wanted nothing more in that dreamlike state than for the magical chant to be true. She wanted someone to make the moment real. Staring into the fire, Sophia watched it form shapes akin to an old woman. The old woman would writhe and turn to ash when the fire was done. It would be a sign.

The clanging plates brought Sophia back to her room and back to its dark walls and sickly-looking carpet. Gertrude was shouting at the plates now. Sophia tried to bury herself underneath her covers.

If Sophia was weak, then there was no way *except* by magic she could use force against her mother. The only harm she could do without a spell would be to herself because Gertrude may notice her once she was no longer there. The realization made her nauseous, but her desperation with each passing year made the fantasy seem less crazy.

Besides, she loved her mother when she was feeling ill. Her mother gave her head massages, fed her homemade soup, and took her to the doctor's office whenever she wanted. She could feel a kinship with Bernini's *Pieta*, in which Jesus lies dead in his mother's arms. Sophia wanted to let go of life like that. When life became too much of a struggle and the anxiety attacks grew longer in length, Sophia wanted to die in her mother's arms—just to stop feeling anything at all.

Dying had come to mean to Sophia a long sleep where no one would bother her anymore with life's worries. It would be an anxiety-free zone. Sophia knew it would be wrong to give up the fight too soon, but how much did she have to struggle before giving in?

***

The dinner ended in only fifteen minutes. But that was an agonizingly long time for Sophia. She had eaten her meal without relish in five minutes, and the rest of the time was spent fuming and jiggling her fork around.

Gertrude normally dismissed her husband and daughter when she rose from her chair and violently clanked her fork down onto her plate, foisting the plate and fork up, and then dumping them both into the sink. After that freeing noise, Sophia usually launched up and out to her room for bed. Gertrude gathered the rest of the plates and showed her husband how, once again, she had to wash the dishes by herself.

"I just want you to see how I cooked this entire delicious meal and now since the girl ran out, I am stuck cleaning these dishes by myself again. She is ungrateful." Gertrude took the wet towel in her hand and scrubbed away at the plate she held.

"Well, she does have a full-time job, dear. She must be tired by the end of the day."

Gertrude shook her head and finger at her husband as if connected by a single string. She refused to believe such a young girl, so full of motivation to leave the table, could be tired after her paper-pushing job.

"I just can't see how that girl holds down that job with her kind of behavior at home. Really."

Gertrude's husband understood arguing was futile. He kissed her goodnight on the forehead and left in silence.

Gertrude reached for the sponge once more with a bitter pout.

"Humph! This family…" she mumbled.

Worn like a mask, Gertrude's martyrdom allowed her to freely nag her family every evening. But when Sophia offered to help the outcome was always the same. It began:

"Mother, would you like me to help wash the dishes?"

Gertrude thought about it and studied her daughter for a moment. "No," said Gertrude, upon coming to the conclusion that her daughter only slowed her down.

Sophia backed away and went to her room without asking the question again.

Is that what I taught her? Gertrude wondered. Not to be persistent in her requests? To just leave without a second thought? She clutched at her dish towel and scrubbed roughly at the table a second time as if it were her daughter's face. That would have taught her a lesson, thought Gertrude. But she's sick. I suppose I should be a bit more lenient for that reason...

To Gertrude, her family consisted of two loafers who needed to be commanded to accomplish anything in life. Her husband was probably sick in some way too, but most prominently he was just weak-willed. He knew nothing about how to raise and discipline their daughter or take control of the household on a daily basis. That left the lifeblood of this family to Gertrude's care. She pulled up her trousers every morning, put on her best blouse, and the most uncomfortable high heels and repeated these duties with militaristic vigor.

Her family was to be the best on the block. Her husband must be the best doctor and her daughter the wealthiest young adult in the area. Meanwhile, she planned on remaining the unnoticed housewife who made all of their success possible. It was her mission in life to outshine her neighbors through her family members.

There was a particularly special moment when Gertrude chose to dedicate her life to outperforming her neighbors. It was the first time she had found a cardboard box in the shared trash receptacle when they had first bought the house. She hoisted herself up and into the bin, while the guilty culprit watched from her window and motioned for her husband.

"Hey! Randall, come over here! Look, look at what she is doing to our trash. She's pulling it all out and moving it into the recycling bins. She must be crazy!"

Randall looked outside beside his wife, a pit of shameful rage growing deep in his stomach. "Well, Nancy, I guess someone cares about enforcing social policy about what constitutes trash and what doesn't." He pulled on his collar which he felt to be creeping too far up his neck.

"I just can't believe that someone would dirty themselves up for…well, that!" said Nancy. She wiped her delicate fingers down her expensive dress and grimaced at the thought of garbage debris touching it. "I'd have to wash three times after that kind of dumpster diving."

Shaking her head, Nancy signaled the show was over and the two could leave their spots in the front row of the shared trash bins. Gertrude still had her legs hanging out from one of them.

But Gertrude had briefly noticed these two in the window, and she would use that to her advantage. She would make them feel sorry for having caused a wealthy woman to get dirty due to their laziness and her own good heart. She performed this duty at every chance she could get.

It almost became a hobby of hers. She had committed herself to make her neighbors look as vicious as she felt they were for harming the earth.

Not only were her neighbors not recycling, but Gertrude also noticed they parked their big, oil-guzzling truck too close to her property, they used disposable plates, and they kept having a new baby every year. The worst offense, to Gertrude, were the babies. This world was already populated enough, thought Gertrude. More babies meant more waste, more screaming, more chances for her lawn being ruined or her property being stolen by babies who would grow up to be hooligans.

Babies were meant to be molded and controlled, but the more of them you had the less control you had over each. There could be no way her neighbors remembered their fourth child's name or age by now. They were just another part of a clan, following their parents blindly and stupidly.

Gertrude pulled another recyclable out of the garbage, a rush of anger coloring her face. She wondered: Is this what martyrs feel like? It had better be because I am not doing this for nothing. I am doing this for the planet and for myself.

She thought back to the first days when she was pregnant with Sophia. Her desires for mineral-rich foods and her growing belly followed the waves of intense nausea. Every day was unpredictable. On some days she felt prepared to bring a child into the world and shield her from the toxicity in it. On other days she felt too weak and angry to deal with a child who would spit in her face and would betray her one of these days.

There was no in between for Gertrude and her baby: Either her baby would learn to fear all, or she would force her back to the womb. Gertrude felt utterly in control of this thing growing inside of her. The baby was using her body after all: using her tissue, her nutrients, and her umbilical cord.

The older Gertrude became, the more she believed babies should not be born into the world. The world was a place crawling with perverts and polluters. It was full of apathetic people who behaved more like animals. Gertrude was revolted by her neighbors. Could they not see what they were doing? she wondered. They were adding to the landfills with everything they touched.

This is why Gertrude committed her household to the strictest of rules. If the Lord decided she was a chosen one, then she must honor her house and family, at least. Her house remained spotless. Her items remained minimal, though expensive. Her meals were simple and made by hand. Her daughter was not allowed to produce waste like the other people in the neighborhood, nor was her husband.

Keeping the quarters clean required immense discipline and willpower. So much so that any deviation made Gertrude scream. She once caught her daughter wiping crumbs from the table onto the floor.

"What are you doing!" hollered Gertrude.

Sophia froze there like a startled deer. "I…I just…I'm sorry, mother."

Gertrude placed her hand over Sophia's shoulder, squatting down to look her daughter right in the eyes. "Never do that again, young lady. There are rules in this house you must follow as long as you still live here. You just fed a million bugs by wiping those crumbs onto the ground. I hope they come and feast on you tonight."

Thinking back on it now, Gertrude felt she was a bit too hard on her daughter, although, Sophia did increase the risk of an infestation in the house after her little shenanigan. It was only fit to tell her the truth about how she made her mother feel.

All things could be controlled inside her own property line. As to controlling the rest of the world, Gertrude treaded cautiously and only reprimanded one neighbor at a time. She vowed to pick out every piece of cardboard she could find and rescue them—to save the trees that gave us the air we never deserved, for we are all sinners on this earth. But Gertrude promised to be better and to drag along the dumb and blind, whether they wanted to go along with it or not. She would force the sinner to recognize their sins. To coerce the sin from out of people before it was too late, Gertrude had to act quickly.

Sin was committed by all, not only the obviously sick. In fact, Gertrude believed the maimed and the sick who acknowledged their sin were more redeemable than those who were healthy and happy. She dedicated herself to the sick and promised the Lord to act as a servant to the happy ignoramuses of the world. Gertrude knew that someday she would be forgiven of all sin, wiped clean of all that was unholy, and given a seat next to God himself.

Before her passage into the next world, she wanted her family to rise to power and fame. Everyone would want to socialize with her, fawning over her charitable acts, and wish to be accepted into her circle of goodwill to mankind and the earth.

The tears would form on command as she preached to her crowds of followers. She would explain to them that a woman was meant to have only one baby and to raise it up right. The mother would care for her child, and the wife would feed her husband. Her reward would be fame, attention, love, gratitude, and undying worship from the other people of the home.

But in her current situation, Gertrude felt like a dirty washcloth her family used to wipe themselves with and then throw by the sink when done. She felt discarded and forgotten when her husband left in the early morning for work and her daughter not much longer after him. The house felt too quiet to Gertrude than when they were silently eating together at the table. At least the chewing and clanking on plates kept up a musical charm that, she felt, validated her existence. Her family was fed and now they were obligated to bring her riches.

It did not matter to Gertrude if her husband never touched her anymore, nor did it matter if her daughter stopped saying

"I love you" to her. Their distance was a small compromise to make for the wealth and attention that she was determined to obtain from hundreds of adoring followers, maybe even thousands. Eventually, though, all her current pains would melt away when the Lord saw that she had been good and had worked so hard to steer the world right. She felt vindicated if she was biting instead of kissing her family.

CHAPTER VI

Gertrude was finished with the dishwashing and had now moved on to wiping down the kitchen table. Her strokes against the wooden tabletop remained unthinking and constantly moving clockwise. They revolved around the table as plate spinners do at a circus. The table had a waxy, buffed glow by the time she finished.

Gertrude had sent Sophia to her room and she had pushed her husband out to watch television in the living room while she continued to slave away after dinner in the kitchen. The same process occurred every night. Mother and daughter at the dinner table barely ate, the husband scarfed, daughter and father left, and mother stayed to clean up the rest.

Meanwhile, Sophia stayed in the only place in the entire house where she could feel comfortable—her own room. The room was not big, more of an average size, but it could fit her full-sized bed, a standing mirror, and an immense oak dresser. There were white curtains hanging off of rods that hung over two small windows. In the summer, they fluttered about from the mini fan. Beige carpet kept her feet warm in the winter. The only thing that bothered her were the dark walls. The walls were of a forest green paint that absorbed so much of the light that came in through the windows, and it became utterly black in the room at night. Sophia still felt like the room was invaded by her mother. A prisoner's cell was what this room passed for at night. At least, it carried the label of "Sophia's room" with it to her parents. Shutting the lights off, Sophia crept into bed.

Similar to her workplace bathroom, Sophia loved her bed because it felt like a place to hide. Under the comforter that heated her body, she could be sure no one was underneath with her. She was alone with her thoughts.

Sophia knew that Mother did not see her as disciplined. Sophia, Gertrude felt, was more corrupt than "the worst welfare-stuffed pustule in the United States," as she liked to declare while ticking off her daily chores.

But Sophia did not think herself all that undisciplined since she required routine and order to keep sane. Perhaps it just was not her mother's kind of order. Regardless of whether Gertrude or she had it right, Sophia kept to herself, consulting only with her fireplace friends from childhood who, she believed, had always sided with her. For these little figures knew nothing about time, nor were they ever busied with work or any other adult-related matters. Their tiny ears seemed open to anyone who might happen to need a confidante. This service was exactly what Sophia craved.

"Hello, again. Can you please make sure I do all of my chores right today? I really don't want to get in trouble again." Sophia laid her pinky finger on the nymph's pointy ear believing that this act could determine whether or not it had heard her plea.

She could, however, feel nothing. A loss of control felt imminent, for she was unsure of her status among her group of fireplace confidantes.

Perhaps, though, wiping the dust off the figures may win

their marble hearts in her favor. Thus, with a napkin lifted from the dining room table, Sophia rubbed the figures clean. The polishing made their beady eyes look more animated. "If only," she thought, "a wish could be granted by each one. I'd have two, four, six, twelve wishes! I could even wish for control over my parents, protection from them, too, and gold, and jewelry, and...and..." More than anything else on her wish list, it was the power to escape she longed for.

In this, the Weber household, all were aware of who wielded the most power. Although her father's income supported them all, no one listened to him. Just yesterday her father had asked for some quietude, but Sophia and Gertrude continued to argue around him. It must have been Gertrude's trousers that propelled her to the head of household position.

When chatting with her fireside friends, she saw them nodding along as she relayed her thoughts; but even if she were not to speak out loud, she was glad they would still, she knew, understand her soul. On the right pillar, there was sculpted a curious nymph who appeared to be reaching out against its marble tomb, as if to touch the living warmth of Sophia's hand. Perhaps, though, if the nymph could just touch the girl, then, she too would become living. For years, Sophia had wanted a human friend, one who could do more than remain forever trapped in the same pose. Although she valued the statues, their contorted limbs made her uneasy, but she ignored this feeling as best she could.

Later that evening, Sophia dreamed that it was winter, and she was looking from her window out onto the front street. She imagined seeing a thick layer of fresh snow that had just fallen and the rising sun glistened on the upper branches of the trees. The previous night had frozen the snow for Sophia to go out and frolic in. She wished that she could touch the snow piles without getting her hands cold and wet.

The snowy hills wanted her to come out to play and the trees' icy branches seemed to drip in sorrow for her not being there yet. Sophia imagined herself getting up, changing into her warmest clothes, pulling on her snow boots, and checking her window again to make sure the snow was still there when she saw *it*. The giant snow plow for her block was raging down the street toward her paradise. She wanted to shout: "No! Don't clear a pathway through the snow!" But the truck raged on. Sophia wanted to say to the driver: "Let us play outside like children and remain lost in dreams of safety and warmth!" But as the pathways were all cleared the chance of a snow day vanished.

Sophia's dream of winter changed after the snow was forcefully removed by the giant claws of metal. Sophia grew nauseous and then she turned around from the window to lie down. However, she knew that feeling; she had had it before, and she knew it would not go away for ages. Then, the quiet arrived which switched her brain into depression mode. Tears began rolling down her cheeks as she began crying for herself, her mother, and her father. Sophia's gagging reflex kicked in and the stomach cramps came in agonizing waves only to lull her into a steady rhythm of sobbing. Why do people have to add to the excitement and fear I see all around me? Sophia wondered. Could life really be that boring to them? I lacerate myself when these crises happen…all I can think about is: Will I get cancer? Will I get robbed or raped? Will I be around for my children? Am I going to start having panic attacks? Will I get very homesick if I ever leave this place? Will I ever be able to fall in love? Worries raced through her head; she felt as if her heart would explode with its rapid beating. Could it stop? she pondered. How easily she could cease to exist at any moment.

She shot up in bed. Sophia felt her wet skin rise with goosebumps from her own sweat. Her heart intensely beat as she realized she was panicking. But nothing could be done about it tonight except to wait until the anxiety passed. It was the middle of the night and even in her own room, alone with her own thoughts in bed, she was not free from her mother's power.

***

Her mother was everywhere in the room. She was the light carpet, the dark walls, and the floaty drapes. All the design choices were Gertrude's, not Sophia's. Sophia was simply a guest in someone's beloved home. She was another piece of furniture in the house.

Sophia pushed her pillows up against the wall and leaned back into them similarly to when she had been sick in bed as a child. She was either propped up or leaning over her crossed legs preparing to vomit into a plastic bucket.

There were many days when Sophia was stuck in these positions that her childhood reminiscences mostly consisted of—those same bodily feelings of sitting up or bending forward to heave.

When Sophia was eleven years old, her mother's power over her started to become clear. One time she was told to go upstairs to bed after breakfast, and she ended up missing a week of school due to this illness she had.

Eventually, her mother had a nurse come in to examine her in that same prisoner's bed.

"I see your daughter looks awfully pale and weak. Perhaps

she's anemic. Let's take some blood and then I can examine it for anemia and other tests may be run for possible allergens."

Gertrude nodded her head up and down vigorously, saying "See, Sophia, I knew you were seriously ill. Didn't I say that? I'm glad this nurse here knows a thing or two about a sick child when she sees one."

The nurse smiled at her and grabbed a large syringe out of her case. Sophia's face grew paler.

Gertrude could tell what Sophia must have been thinking as she gave her a glaring look while the nurse was tying the rubber band around Sophia's arm. Sophia swallowed, staring uncomprehendingly at how she got here. She wondered: Was she really that sick? Was this normal? Was she normal?

The needle sucked its fill like a hungry leech, and Sophia cried. The act of having something taken from her was new and alarming. There was no way now to get it back, to stop the power her mother was building from this checkup.

A vision bubbled up of her mother using the blood of her daughter to keep herself young. Sophia had read a story like that about a year ago and had laughed at it then. But now it no longer seemed so funny. She glanced at her mother's face as the nurse was sticking that long needle into her vein; her mother's eyes seemed brilliant. A light she had never seen before shined as it went from the tip of the needle to her daughter's thin, pale arm. This was like watching a lion being thrown a giant portion of raw meat by a zookeeper. There was a ravenous excitement in her eyes. Feeding time was near.

Sophia hated seeing her mother's face at that moment. She felt confused too for she wanted so badly to please her mother and this was how: just bleed for her. But at the same time, her own suffering must have been meaningless to her mother.

Sophia wished she was well enough to spit in her face. She thought it was disgusting how much pleasure she was getting from her only daughter's pain.

"You will get the results in a week, Ms. Weber," said the nurse, closing her case and walking toward the front door.

"Thank you so much, nurse. Really, I hope I can finally discover why my daughter is always so weak nowadays," said Gertrude. With that final and gracious goodbye, she closed the front door, sliding the bolt into place. She stomped up the stairs rapidly.

Stepping up and peering down into Sophia's face, Gertrude said: "You didn't look very sick to me. The nurse didn't believe you had anemia, even though that may be exactly why you are ill. What's wrong with you?" She slapped a cold, hard hand on Sophia's forehead.

Tears gushed forth anew. "I'm sorry, mother. I don't feel well, I just showed her how I really felt."

"Well, that's not good enough. The nurse won't take you seriously unless you're on the floor puking. So next time, I suggest you do so," said Gertrude, as she backed away from the bed to go downstairs. But pausing by the handrail, she turned on her heels and clicked back to Sophia's sickbed: "I promise to give you the best head rub yet if you only show the nurses and doctors how sick you *really* are tomorrow. Okay?"

Gertrude dropped further down to kiss Sophia's furrowed brows. Sophia was just so confused.

"Yes, mother. I'll try, really." Sophia decided turning over onto her side toward the wall would be the best thing to keep her mother at bay for now.

"That's my girl. Now, I'm going to make you some delicious chicken broth soup. Then I expect you to sleep early. You need all the strength you can muster for tomorrow."

Gertrude left.

The room remained silent for a few more seconds until Sophia opened the floodgates. She wept aloud and ripped her fresh bandage off and threw it onto the floor with all the hatred she harbored toward her mother.

What was she supposed to do? she wondered. Die? Live? Stay perpetually sick, or perpetually well? What?

Her mother positioned herself in such a way as to make Sophia feel like her life depended on her, but that she was not following through on her part—as if her mind was too callous to realize her body was malfunctioning, and when her mother was not doing well, neither was she. Sophia's feelings were directly linked to her mother's feelings. If her mother was upset, then Sophia was on the verge of death. If her mother was elated, then Sophia was getting better and a renewed hope of living for a long, long time arose.

The movement from this roller-coaster was enough to make Sophia nauseous whether she was really sick or not. She wanted off the ride that she never paid for to get on. Every day the diagnosis from her mother was different and kept young Sophia on edge. The safest thing that she could do was to lie in bed and stare at something without stirring—a living doll for her mother to play with.

***

It is much harder to make yourself still than not. The more Sophia told herself to remain still in bed, the more difficult it became. She had an itchy nose here, a loose hair there. Even her stomach was protesting her order to remain still. Perhaps if she practiced the art of staying still long enough, then she would disappear into her sheets and her mother would no longer be able to find her.

Freedom was a commonly used word that was kept inside a box, inside another box, inside Sophia's mind. The idea of it was addicting, but even a little more than normal could cause her to suffocate now. Sophia always put the box back in her mind, because she still needed her mother.

Sophia could hear Gertrude clicking back up the steps in her high heels. They clicked all the way up to her doorway.

"I brought you your soup, dear," said Gertrude.

"Thank you, mother." Sophia took the lapboard out and helped set the soup on top. "Hey, mother? May I spend the evening with you?"

Gertrude nodded her head, pleased to see her daughter still wanted to be around her own mother. They could still bond.

"Of course, love. Your father will probably be downstairs watching television until about ten tonight anyway. I could use the company. But first, finish your soup." Gertrude got up and headed to her bedroom.

Sophia slurped up her soup, she was craving feeling close to someone tonight. In a twisted push-pull scenario, the more her mother was displeased with her, the more she wanted to win her love back. When Sophia was pampered she felt ecstasy, but she was afraid to lose the ability to hold her mother's love. She threatened Sophia or herself with violence, and the distress caused Sophia to crawl right back.

Tonight Gertrude was winning. Sophia would skulk into her arms seeking forgiveness.

Sophia rose from her bed, weak-kneed from having lain in bed for so long. She stumbled down the hall toward her mother's king-sized bed. First Sophia had to pass her mother's mannequin stuck with pins and her amateur paintings that adorned her walls. The little television box was constantly on, replaying documentaries on serial killers, assassins, and any other gory occurrences of the last decade.

"Come sit on the bed. What would you like to do?" said Gertrude.

"Oh, maybe look through your button or shoe collections in the closet," said Sophia, as she eyed the wooden doors.

"Dive right on in." Gertrude was laying on the bed watching the television while crocheting what looked like a square piece of toilet paper.

Sophia slid off the bed, keeping a hand on the side of it for balance. She approached the closet where her mother kept her finest things: jewelry, hundred-dollar shoes, handbags, and stylish suit jackets.

Sophia stuck her feet into one pair of high heels that were jet black, not a scuff on them, and they had deadly points at the toes. Although Sophia was her mother's foot-size, her mother had large bunions that had become permanent casts in the shoes she owned. Sophia's feet slipped in the front due to the extra space. She foresaw breaking an ankle attempting to walk in them for much longer.

Still, to Sophia, this act of dressing up in her mother's clothing was a tradition. Ever since childhood, Sophia picked out her favorite high heels and pretended she was as womanly as the shoes made her feel. Her mother had various colors from brilliant red to autumn brown. Her makeup, particularly the lipstick, matched the heel colors. Her mother was the ultimate color coordinator.

The shoes Gertrude owned gave her the extra height and boost of confidence that she desired in order to prove her control over the Weber household's affairs. They clicked with such precision when she walked that every step she took was as if she had hit your hand with a ruler. Her shoes shaped her unshapely toes. The feminine form was forced by the slenderness of the toe box and the lift of the heel. The high heels formed an image of grace and power without having the wearer of the shoes do anything special.

Gertrude wielded this power nicely, and she knew it.

After trying on the most beautiful of her mother's heels, Sophia tried to find her bag of buttons. Since Gertrude was always haphazardly pursuing creative projects, she frequently ended up collecting an assortment of buttons.

Spilling the bag all over her mother's bed, Sophia amused herself like a child looking at a newly discovered treasure. The television droned on about rape, murder, and mayhem as Sophia brought a garnet button up to the lamp. It could have passed for a real gem by Sophia's standards. There were also tiny, plastic elephant-shaped buttons. There were blue bow buttons.

As a child, Sophia categorized her mother's buttons on the bed like she was now. The task kept her hands busy while her mind was free to create new patterns and notice new features of each button.

Buttons and high heels were the extents of the material love shared between Sophia and her mother. The rest of the tenuous bond between daughter and mother was buried deep under something that weighed a ton. Sophia still could not understand if it was guilt that sat on top of the other emotional bond, or whether it was something more sinister. Either way, the heaviness of her connection to her mother was sinking deeper down into the muck with each passing day.

This evening, however, Sophia focused on the buttons and

the little lines that could be made with each one. She sorted the buttons two by two or paired the animals together or the reds with the blues and the grays. The most ornate buttons were kept closer to Sophia so that one day she may be able to understand where they each came from.

***

"Where is this button from, Mother?"

"That button was from an old prom dress, I believe. I bought it from a thrift store a few years ago for its beautiful color; it was like a robin's egg blue with white flower shapes lining the hem. I used up the material for a dress I made and took the buttons off to keep. Aren't they just lovely?" Gertrude took one of the buttons and rolled it around in her palm. The button revolved with ease and glittered under the lamplight with a pearly sheen.

Sophia found those buttons mesmerizing. She wanted them for herself. A little wave of jealousy hit Sophia as she watched the buttons, which were not really hers, in her mother's hand.

"Mother, may I have one?"

Gertrude closed her fist around the button in her palm and thought for a moment before saying, "Why don't I make us each a necklace out of them? We could be matching!" Her eyes brightened with excitement at the thought of owning something her daughter wanted.

Sophia thought she was much too old to be sharing matching jewelry with her mother, but she wanted to possess that particular button badly enough to say yes.

Gertrude quickly pushed herself off the bed to work on her newest creative project. Nothing made her feel more alive, aside from taking Sophia to the doctor's office, than being needed for a creative project by her family.

Meanwhile, Sophia began placing the rest of the buttons back in the bag into their rightful home. With her mother's closet doors closed, Sophia decided that it was time to go to bed. Or rather, her body kicked her into motion, because the television was still droning on about murder and her mother was facing away from her anyway. She felt like it was time to leave.

"Well, goodnight, mother. I need to get some rest. I've got work tomorrow." Sophia slinked back out of the room she adored and loathed. She soaked in the mellow lighting in such a spacious bedroom, while the pincushions she passed seemed to be bleeding from their wounds.

Gertrude swiveled on her chair by the television. "Goodnight, dear. I'll have these matching necklaces done tonight. They'll look great on us!" She winked at Sophia which made Sophia run out of the doorway. A wink meant that all was fine in this instant, but her mother's patience was wearing thin. She was not affectionate then as much as she was when her happiness never seemed to end, instead, a wink kept her at a distance, a happy distance, but one that became the signal for impending doom.

Sophia was brought up to read these signals. She had to read them for her own survival. A head nod out in public was equivalent to a wink in that it meant trouble; Sophia made sure to remain at a happy distance, at least for the time being. A grimace meant to run away from a prickly situation. Clanking dishes at home meant it would be the worst day of her life.

Walking down the hallway, Sophia entered her own room once more. She turned on the little lamp next to her bed, drew the curtains, and stopped in front of her body mirror. It was another thrift shop find her mother came across last weekend. It had an antique look with its golden rim of swirls. The mirror itself was not perfect and some specks stayed on, resistant to any type of cleaning spray.

The mirror was the equivalent of a black and white picture with graininess and black holes in the film. Part of Sophia's body was always marred by the mirror's own imperfections.

Tonight Sophia looked hard at her own body. A line of goosebumps was brought on by her mother's wink. They were still on her skin as she entered her bedroom. Sophia noticed that there were two hip bones sticking out through her nightgown. They made her look skeletal. She looked like a ghostly beauty.

It was an odd thing to feel so sickly on the inside and look so eerily beautiful on the outside. Perhaps the mirror reflected more of the truth than a normal one would. Her mirror left spots on her face and distorted places on her body. Her elbow, for instance, stuck out too far. It nearly made Sophia jump at the awful sight of it. One of her calves looked double the size of her other calf in the mirror.

How much information could truly be gathered from this image? Sophia pondered. Is my idea of beauty strange? She looked at herself and could not tell. Her thinking went as follows: I'm sick and weak, therefore, I must not be pretty. If I was healthy and strong, then I'd also be pretty.

Maybe it was possible to be pretty in a sick way. She could be too thin, but it was better showing off the symmetry of her bones, veins, and muscles. Her body was not plush but defined. A man could feel more of her insides than a woman who had filled out. He could get closer to her physically.

Sophia kept staring, trying to determine an argument for why Damian could accept her and find her beautiful as she was—sick.

She still had a stick figure. Her hips were small, her breasts were small, and her backside was small. Everything was packaged up nicely in this tiny body that had not matured yet. Even though she was weak, she felt limber. When she was around Damian, she desired to drape herself over his body and allow herself to fall limp in his arms. She wanted to give up all the rest of the strength she had to him.

Sophia wished more than anything to give herself to him to allow him to take control. She desired to become a vessel, a receiver, a giver, a submissive lover. Her soul was more than ready to be carried.

II

PART TWO

CHAPTER I

The next morning Sophia woke up feeling weak. The night was too filled with troubling questions to allow for any meaningful sleep. She rolled out from under her sheets onto carpet fibers that deadened her footsteps as she drew near the dresser to grab fresh clothes for the day.

Dishes were clanking downstairs. Sophia felt guilty for her mother's bad moods, yet she could never tell why.

Sometimes she played the therapist with herself when she felt a certain way.

The internal therapist asked, "How is your home life?"

"Guilt-ridden," she replied internally.

"And why do you think that is?" asked the internal therapist.

Sophia lifted her head up toward the ceiling to see if she could find answers there. After a time she responded with only "my mother."

"Your mother? How is that?"

"My mother is not a woman. It is like she is a machine who only coddles me when I am ill. It's like she is my enemy and not my caretaker. I don't know why she dislikes me, but I can feel it when she looks at me. But the strangest thing is that whenever I admit defeat by feeling weak in front of her, she wipes away my tears, serves me a meal in bed, and gives me foot massages while I lay there. I want that version of her all the time though, and not just when I'm weak.'

"I never thought about it, but I am drawn to her while I am spurned by her. How did I get this way?'

"Yesterday, we went grocery shopping together and I remember growing envious of the bagger who kept looking at my mother. I know he was not even attracted to her! He was just checking to see what she was putting on the conveyor belt as it was headed toward him. Still, my eyes followed his fixed look on her hands as they hovered over the produce items and then the dairy products.'

"A fire blazed up inside of me while my hands shook and my head pounded. I began grabbing onto my mother's trousers and staring back at the bagger. I grabbed his attention for one moment, enough to make him look down at the groceries in front of him. I won.'

"But then, I let go of her trousers and wondered, what am I protecting? This woman who tells me not to fall in love with men, watches bad soap operas on the television, and just wants me all to herself. No, I hate her.'

"My mother makes me feel incapable of living in this world without her. I can no longer feel free, or at least less susceptible to anxious thinking, without her being there. I require another person to give me a stable ground to walk on. Any more or less freedom might be intoxicating...and dangerous.'

"That's why I feel old mentally, but I am physically young. I am afraid of the unknown, of losing control in this world. I desire to live in a world full of hope, but my mother is slowly killing it. Every day, I wake up feeling more cynical about the world and the angry thoughts become a giant mound of words inside my body that are dangerously expanding. I am afraid one day I may explode.'

"I have no sense of balance. My own voice, the one I will eventually need to confront my mother with, is quieted by my fear. It is covering up my drive to actually do something more with my life than be a paper pusher. I'm better than her. Death is too easy—life is hard.'

"I mean, I struggle every single day with accepting the moment and my situation and overcoming it, it's so hard to beat the crushing feeling that I will always need help. Today, I will have to coax myself to overcome the nauseous sensation I get after breakfast, get on the bus, and silence the voice that's saying 'hurry up and get from point A to point B.' I am waiting for the moment when I will burn out from all of this pressure.'

"So, you see Ms. Internal Therapist, my mother is the problem. She has caused me to lose sight of my priorities. I want the freedom to live on my own, I want to date a man, and I want to enjoy myself while I am young. Yet, I still live with her in my twenties, I still have my old room from childhood, I still take the bus, I still have to prepare the table for breakfast and dinner, and I still have a bedtime. I'm lucky she even let me go to college. I convinced her to let me go by telling her that students with degrees get higher-paying jobs. She agreed to let me go but only to a school that I could commute to. The same rules apply to my working at the law firm. I am her perpetual child. But when I'm healthy I'm even lower than that, I'm her placemat. I'm something to step on and wipe her filthy shoes on. If she wants me to love her jealously, then all she has to do is rub my head. If she wants me to hate her deeply, then all she has to do is not talk to me once during a meal.'

"I am beginning to see that manipulation is a mighty force

in our home. I believe my mother's lust for power started when she married my father and then her need for power honed in onto me. I'm weaker and, therefore, I make an easier target for her manipulation. Every morning when I arrive downstairs, Mother will complain that I am not doing my part to keep the home running. The sound of her voice screeching unsettles my heart. My back hunches every morning I walk into this kitchen that smells of soap and the prior night's meal. On getting to the sink, she thrusts the dishes into my hands and I know that the day has begun. This solidifies her power because when I get on the bus to work I feel like a fool. How long will I remain the fool?"

***

Sophia stepped away from the mirror and her internal therapist, heading down the stairs and pausing with a breath at each step. She tried to calm herself and stultify the inevitable longing to scream when she first saw her mother's face that morning. Besides, it was a new day and perhaps life outside of these walls did not require the routine which currently existed in her mother's home.

Someday, her mother would die and the routine would cease to continue. Sophia would be free to create her own habits, her own lifestyle, and her own daily routines. Her breathing came more easily with that thought of destruction and rebirth as she descended the stairs.

The handrails reminded her of childhood when she had feared splinters more than anything else. The fears were still large, but the scope was small. Now her fears were much more complicated and less well-defined than in her childhood; she feared her mother's wishes more than the splinters on the handrails. The splinters only stung if Sophia moved incorrectly, but her mother stung without reason.

She could see herself back then kneeling by the fireplace, talking with her nymph friends, while her mother raged through the house with clicking heels. Every step was a hammer to Sophia's head, forcing her deeper into the floor of her childhood home. When she heard the heels she wanted to hide and wait until tomorrow or however long it took for her mother to regain her composure; at least in this state she was less likely to attack.

The clicking neared the fireplace. Standing above her and looking down, Gertrude towered over her young daughter.

The next question did not match her expression.

"Oh, honey," her lips twitched, "are you talking to your little friends again?"

The shame rose up into her cheeks. "I am eleven years old now," she thought, "and I know better than to talk to things that aren't alive."

"Well?" said Gertrude.

Sophia got up from her crouch and wiped off her dress with a hand that turned numb from sitting on it for so long.

"I think it's fine, dear. A mother always senses what their children are really about. It's okay if you don't have many friends—you have me. Let me make you some tea."

Tea is her way of lulling me back to her, Sophia thought, to her baby powder smell, back to her warmth, back to her clean kitchen, back to her order, back to her home...and every single time, I give in.

"Yes, mother. Let's go," she mumbled.

Now, Gertrude was bustling around the kitchen again. She reminded Sophia of a bee, flying from one flower to the next, her stinger always at the ready to emerge and threatening. She even had English ivy that reminded Sophia of the five fingers of her hand.

"The only things that get 'free housing' are the spiders living in my kitchen," said Gertrude to her husband, turning around to see Sophia in the doorway. "There you are, finally. Get the table ready or the pancakes will get cold!" Gertrude threw open the drawer with the silverware to give Sophia a good head start on getting the table ready. She briskly walked toward it. Sophia had made the mistake when she was younger of lazily walking toward the drawer. Then, her mother promptly gave her a kick in the backside or spanked her bottom forward with whatever kitchen utensil she had in her hand at the moment. Sophia made it a habit of scurrying like a rat around her mother. Turns out that it made her a rather good, obedient employee at work too.

"Scurrying is a skill all young people should learn. Are you finished with your work? Make it up! Just keep scurrying on! It makes your superiors like you more and then they feel like you're worth their money," said Gertrude.

Sophia's father had just reached the table and interjected during Gertrude's lesson: "Yes, I always look like I'm doing something at work." He gave a quick wink at Sophia.

Sophia smiled and stated: "Well, I think it's important to always have something to do, and not just fake it. My job never slows down. The papers stack up exponentially on my desk."

Gertrude nodded. It was the closest to approval Sophia had gotten in a long time. She nearly drooled with the expectation of praise.

"Yes, and I'm always running around at work trying to keep up with it—returning and receiving signed documents here and there. I like the filing and organizing of all the paperwork that flows in and out of the law firm every day." Sophia glowed with pleasure.

"I'm glad you enjoy it," said Gertrude, "but don't go overboard. Those people at the very top don't even know your name and could fire you in an instant."

A stone fell in Sophia's stomach and it forced her to sit down. The thought of getting fired had never even occurred to her. The consequences would be even more devastating for Sophia than for anyone else; if she were to lose this job she would be forced to stay at home again during the day. She would be ridiculed by her mother even more than she already was now about her job. On top of all that she would lose the chance to get to know Damian more. He could be the very key she needs to escape her mother for good.

This speedy calculation caused an equivalent loss of blood to her head, and Sophia nearly fell forward onto the floor.

Falling forward allowed Sophia to come back to reality and the fact that she was good at her job and liked it. This was normal for her mother to put her dreams down, even if those things she said were often distorted or unrealistic.

It was circumstances, usually tragic, Sophia's mother would create and dwell on. She would say things like: "Oh, no, I don't think you have enough muscle control to work as a receptionist. Remember when you peed on the playground? Receptionists never get to leave their seats!" Those reminders crushed anything that looked like a way out of the house and it infuriated her. In those instances, her hatred for her mother could be seen in the way her veins pulsed furiously under her thin skin.

The hatred did not leave either. It festered inside the bodies of each of the family members of that house. Nothing her mother could say or repent for later would likely erase the many fragments of lies and bitterness that remained as shards of hate beneath Sophia's skin. The entire family remained fragmented.

When her mother got into these moods of verbally stabbing anything with ears, her eyes looked darker and the wrinkles around her mouth ran deeper. Her streak of cruelty astounded Sophia because it never felt to her to have an end. It was like a well that she could lean over and stare down into without seeing a bottom. There was only a pitch blackness and a cold echo from the bowels of a great hole in the ground.

The house reverberated that hatred too. Even at breakfast when the sun had just arisen, the house remained a dark web of hallways, fireplaces, and rooms. Some of the corners were darker than the turned-off television screens.

Sophia was so tired of the darkness, which weighed down on her. Each successive day seemed to weigh more heavily on her. She slept an excessive amount, yet by morning she was still tired. In a never-ending cycle, Sophia moved her limbs that constantly felt limp and unmoving. Her body mirrored her sluggish mind which only jolted back to life when she was either lost in work or contemplating Damian's hands.

This was yet another reason why Sophia could not afford to lose her job. She would lose hold of the only two things that made her feel alive anymore—work and play.

The pancakes were about to be served with the obligatory butter and maple syrup by the side of the hefty platter. Sophia and her father often heaped syrup onto their pancakes to mask the flavor of charred flour and hard pieces. Since becoming a wife and mother, Gertrude resented cooking meals and made it a point to have others suffer for it. They did.

***

Sophia's jaws became sore as she tried to gnaw her way through the pancake, the up and down motion set her hinges on fire, and she winced throughout breakfast. Her mother and father both noticed though they ignored the reasons for her pain. The chewing continued to be the only sound imbuing the kitchen, besides the stove fan that was still hustling to clear out the smoke continually rising from the frying pan. Thankfully, the fan this morning gave a calming white noise to the background of their loud, cow chewing.

There would come a day, thought Sophia, when she would escape the aggregate loneliness that haunted the meals of the house. There would be a day when the freedom to have a real discussion with another person full of laughter and high spirits would become the norm for Sophia. She desired to have some kind of normalcy in her life, which is why she asked: "Mother, what is your greatest fear?"

Gertrude looked like Sophia's head had just exploded all over the kitchen.

"Now what kind of question is that to ask at breakfast? How unpleasant. Shame on you."

Sophia felt herself blush and cave into herself. "I was just trying to start a conversation at the table with you. Sorry."

"Sorry? My goodness, you should apologize more than that. If you are so curious though, I'm afraid of a fire burning this whole house down and us becoming a heap of useless ashes."

Sophia was actually surprised to hear this answer since her mother watched so many crime shows about rape and murder. She thought it must be some horrific combination of the two.

"But you always turn off the gas stove diligently and we

have working fire alarms in every room. Why would that still worry you? Isn't such an event typically rare nowadays?"

The father of the house stepped in to say: "Well, actually, house fires occur frequently. There were nearly four hundred thousand house fires last year."

Gertrude's hands and face stiffened. "See? That's why it still makes me paranoid about turning off the stove and checking our house for anything flammable. Can we move on to another subject? Or can we just drop this entirely? I'm all wound up now."

Gertrude stood up, forcefully pushed her chair back in the table, and robotically made her way to the sink with her dishes. The morning breakfast was deemed officially over when Mother was upset.

Sophia's father knew Gertrude would never abandon them for what they had said though. He knew she was just as dependent on them as they both were on her. In a twisted and tormented chain, each member of the family whipped the other in a circular fashion. It was a family that fed off of pain to keep their love chained closer to their bodies.

When Gertrude shot an awful glare at her husband you could see him retreat into his turtle shell and come out only when the path was clear of her rage. Sometimes he took her verbal beatings, but let them roll off his unseeing eyes and deaf ears. He learned early in the marriage to tune out the first sign of verbal abuse or nagging. That may be the only strategy to keep him sane. Sophia was often observing him and trying to mimic his behavior when he was in Gertrude's line of fire.

But Sophia was young, and she could not seem to shut off in such an effective way. Her turtle shell was too small and every word hurt. Her mother's words still wounded and she took them personally.

Only maturity, age, and enough abuse would allow Sophia to kill all of her senses in front of her mother. But she could tell she was getting better at it each day. Like this morning when Gertrude took her by the arms, looking deep into her eyes. A few tears welled up in Gertrude's eyes as she said, "I love you." But Sophia recognized that moment from the many previous times she had been fooled into saying, "I love you" back.

The last time this happened Gertrude had ordered a new dress in the mail which she had been talking about to anyone she could. She said, "I'm going to look just like the hottest celebrity when I put this piece on! I may even look younger than you, Sophia!" But when the dress arrived that morning, Gertrude tried it on and it was too small, fit too snuggly on parts Gertrude thought it better for the dress to hide, and, if anything, made her look older than she already was. Her youthful, cheery vision of herself had disappeared in an instant. To grow her self-esteem back in seconds, she decided to see if her daughter still needed her and loved her—even if she was old and ugly. Sophia back then had said "I love you" believing that maybe her mother was realizing how she had treated her family all those years, but later she found the new dress tossed on the bed and a new pair of shoes placed carefully beside the bed.

Today, Sophia knew better and withheld her "I love you." She would rather have taken a punch in the stomach than a lie about love spoken to her face. The fact that her mother used and abused the phrase made her hate the very thing. "I love you." Sophia thought it was disgusting.

Sophia knew she needed a plan to escape from the fake "I love yous" and the constant manipulation. She was tired of being the person her mother leaned on and used when she was feeling awful about herself. There was no room for any more falsity. Sophia's heart grew cold in her home where the fan hummed, the television threatened, her father hid, and her mother maimed all for nothing. It was a home that made life itself appear absurd.

***

Gertrude continued to clean up as she decided to weave a story to tell Sophia about her own family—which was a rare occurrence. She was a woman fond of hyperbole. But this time it was a story Sophia had never heard before. She sat back down at the table to fully listen while her mother handed her the rest of the dishes.

With a clearing of her throat and a glance at her seated audience, Gertrude began:

"I grew up on a farm, as you both know. But what you didn't know is my father was a war hero and my mother was a pinup girl. She met him at a USO show. They fell in love and had me, and then they had my younger sister.'

"Simply put, I was always the moody, devilish child; my sister was considered the outgoing, angelic child. We were as different as could be, and I hated my sister. That's why I never invite her over to our Christmas dinners. She walks with an embellished step intending to say she's better than everyone else. It still gets to me.'

"Anyway, my parents found a stray kitten that had made its way onto our farm. It must have smelled some of the farm animals' food. The poor little thing wobbled on its legs. My parents said it was half dead by the time they had found it.'

"For a few weeks, my parents' bottle-fed the kitten and allowed it to sleep all day. In only a few weeks, the kitten had filled out nicely and it started growing normally. Its life was saved. And that kitten seemed to know it. It would rub itself against our legs, curl itself up on our laps when we sat down, and butt its little head against our cheeks whenever it wanted extra love and attention. That kitten made everyone's heart melt.'

"But as the kitten got older, it started to prefer the youngest among us. Maybe it felt a kinship to the youngest one of the pack; the one that was most like itself. I'll never know, but once again my flawless sister stole that kitten away from us.'

"The kitten followed my sister nonstop. If she napped on the couch, the kitten joined her; if she watered the plants, the kitten joined her; if she talked to our parents, the kitten joined her. Well, I let this go on for about a month before I hatched a plan.'

"Granted, it was not a very well-thought-out plan, but I was determined to do something. I would toss the kitten and my sister over the edge for all I cared. So, I followed my sister around without her noticing. I watched her habits and took note of the times when she was alone with the kitten.'

"One day, when I felt ready, I followed my sister to the barn beside our house. A few days prior as I was figuring out how to execute my plan, I noticed my father had a shed with a lighter in it—one of those long stick lighters. I grabbed that off his desk from the shed and headed toward the barn with vengeance on my mind.'

"I called out to my sister, 'Hey! Irene, do you want to see a magic trick?' Her face broke into a wide smile, a foolishly wide grin. I brought the lighter out, which I knew she had no idea of what it was. The kitten was rubbing my leg but once my sister came over it quickly circled around *her* legs instead. I gave that kitten the evilest look I could muster and I pulled the trigger on the lighter. I lowered it down and swiftly caught the kitten's tail on fire as it danced around my sister's ankles. The kitten meowed as soon as the flame had burned through the hair to the flesh. My sister panicked and ran toward the house to get my parents, while I watched with a smile.'

"But the flame was so small that after the kitten had rolled over a few times the fire went out. It was a bit of a disappointment, but I thought the lesson had already been learned. My sister was never to steal away from me anything I loved again.'

"After the flame went out, the kitten ran far away out into the fields to recover and lick at its burns. Meanwhile, I began to sweep up the ashes caused by some of the hair that had burned off, and maybe a bit of skin. A tingling sensation went through my body. In fact, I would almost say that I felt exalted. I replayed the scene in my head many times as I lay on my bed with my stomach growling; my parents had denied me dinner that night.'

"I was the naughty child and I was learning to love my place; that's all. I took pleasure in the power that force brought me. And I can still vividly see and smell the ashes that came from the kitten. I was never allowed near the animal again. But you see, it was not the kitten's fault, it was my sister's. I love animals, but I hate when other people steal them away from me.'

"I kept those ashes I had scooped up that day from the barn floor. I had a gold locket I dumped them into and kept it at my breast for the rest of that year. It served as a reminder to myself that no one was allowed to take from me without punishment. Sophia, I believe you've held that locket before. It's still full of those ashes.'

Sophia squirmed in her chair. Her mother could have gone to jail for animal abuse. But her next thought was that this might all be a lie. She had made up stories before. Although, Sophia did remember that golden locket. She wondered: Was it really filled with that poor kitten's fur?

Both father and daughter cleared their throats and gathered their items together before heading out to work. It was a normal day in their crumbling house, and yet this story reached a new level. Perhaps her mother was finally wearing down. The stories, the lies, even the truths she would divulge over time would be her undoing. The stories she composed would unwind and she would disappear back into the frame of this doomed house.

CHAPTER II

Breakfast ended with the smell of lemon-scented soap and coffee. Sophia left as quickly as possible to the bus stop. She could barely hold back the disgust that she wanted to express during the meal; sometimes only leaving the environment could keep the gates closed. Not yet, not yet, Sophia told herself.

The bus arrived and she squeezed herself in just barely past the magical yellow line the bus driver used to keep people out of his space. Standing on her tiptoes, Sophia tried to see if Damian was on the bus. But it appeared that Damian had not taken the bus to work today.

Sophia felt like cattle being taken to a new farm. It certainly smelled like a barn full of cattle, especially on rainy, hot days. The humidity trapped the odor inside the bus and held it there.

Some of the people on the bus smelled of sweaty gym socks which they probably did indeed have on them to use at their office gyms. Others had on a strong perfume or cologne that reminded Sophia of high school locker rooms and sore muscles. A few had less competitive smells. Sophia would probably include herself among the ones who went sans spray-on smell and only hinted of the deodorant applied freely underneath one's armpits. She smelled like a fresh shower, but it was really just the powder that kept her from sweating in the most embarrassing areas.

Even the objects on the bus had their own distinct smells: the rubber on the door, the dirt on the floor, the paint on the walls. The living were the smelliest, but the lifeless remained high up on the list. The world became a stirring pot of odors. The pot loomed and boiled while producing different smells for Sophia's nose. Her nose experienced the rise and fall of new paths where each second a new neural pathway was carved out with the thoughts that concerned this one sense.

Sophia closed her eyes to focus on the symphony of smells. It was no surprise to Sophia that she became overwhelmed in such a stimulating world. She had a sensitivity to change, and smells were no exception. All of life was in constant flux; Sophia saw subtle changes in expressions, placements of the body, movement of the garbage on the ground. She witnessed the sounds from the outside that passed the bus and the ones on the bus each varied in their intonation. She tasted the sweat that formed around her lips and traces from breakfast this morning. The way the seat felt underneath her shifted with every movement in her weight. At any time, not a thing was still. Sophia wished she could find a stillness in the world that did not involve death as the only answer to solving her problems at home.

Looking around, Sophia saw the upper sides of the bus contained ads for the homeless, for charity, and some sort of stickers were applied about the golden gates to the lord. The windows on the bus had scratch marks on them with curse words—usually from teenagers or the homeless who thought God was telling them to vandalize. The bus floors were littered: peanut shells, the daily newspaper, and chicken bones. It was always different and yet everyone defined it as the same thing: garbage on the city bus. Nothing was new about this problem, so no one figured that anything could be done about it.

The garbage lay there, the vandalism remained there, and the inappropriate stickers stuck there. The bus ecosystem would never change. Yet, Sophia needed to get used to it in order to keep using the buses. Once she said to the bus driver, "Hey, there is some offensive stuff written on that back window. I just wanted to let you know." The bus driver just shook his hand and said, "Okay, later." The next day the bus had a different window. Sophia thought: Maybe I can change my environment on the bus. Only she realized later the bus had an entirely different number and she saw her old bus passing on the way to work which still wielded the same offensive window. No, thought Sophia, I can't change it alone. As if I'm the only one offended by that window...

Then, Sophia closed her eyes on the bus which allowed her at least some distance from the ugly environment around her. She began to think about earlier that morning.

The story her mother told her was frightening. Her own mother taught her to fear the world, yet she was the one causing violence to others. It was an unusual twist which made Sophia despise her mother even more than before. There was more of a valid reason, now that Sophia began to see inconsistencies, to distrust her mother. Was there always a boogeyman out in the world who was waiting to get his hands on her? Sophia wondered. Or did her mother make all of it up just to keep her daughter tied to her for good?

A sudden and intense smell of smoke and tar forced Sophia's dark eyes open. An older gentleman sat down next to her and reeked of cigarettes. His gnarled fingers were yellowed and his beard carried even more of the odor wrapped in each thick hair. It was like he was made of the ashes from his past cigarettes.

Sophia scooted closer to the window to escape smelling this man, yet it was impossible, and if her nose was not taking in the fumes, then her pores were. His scent was being absorbed by her body and she hoped that no one at work would notice. Smoking killed people. It would take even that large man down one day. A tiny stick infiltrating a full-sized man. One could only stare in awe at such power.

The bus went over a bad bump and Sophia's thoughts jumbled up like puzzle pieces in a box.

***

The bus made headway on the road, while Sophia was still piecing together the fragmented thoughts in her mind.

A decision was forming inside Sophia as she was gathering evidence. It was weighing the facts against the fiction. Ever since Sophia took this job and began living outside of the home, she felt her decision blossoming. Now, the thorns were growing out of the vine and Sophia was less and less comfortable in her body.

Damian seemed trustworthy. He did not appear to be a werewolf like her mother said all men are in this day and age. Still, Sophia felt so at ease around him. Even while her mother's voice was warning her to back away, her internal dialogue started becoming less loving and more cautionary in its tone. It was as if her mother's concern was starting to rot. It smelled expired and soured. The putrid leaking came through in Sophia's mind when she was conversing with Damian. It shouted: Sophia, get out of there! Get away from him before

109

it's too late!

Gertrude once told Sophia a story about herself and a boyfriend she had once had. Sophia could never tell what parts of the story were accurate and which parts were fabricated. When she started her story, Gertrude was still living on the farm, but now she was sixteen. Her school had been closed that day due to heavy snowing.

However, that did not stop a boy who adored my mother at that time. He trudged through the snow piles up to her parent's front door to ask for Gertrude. She came out, shocked a boy had come this far to see her.

Her mother noted at this point in her story how her heart leaped with excitement and joy, believing that he would only do this crazy act for her. But she said the crummy boy had gone to a few girls' homes beforehand to see "how intimate he could get with them before they ended up calling their parents for help."

This boy had a crush on about any developing girl.

That boy had gotten up to Gertrude's neck and the top button of her blouse before she shoved him off her after seeing a fresh hickey welling up on his neck. According to Gertrude, he also had the faint smell of another girl on him. She screamed from the back porch and her father came running in with a bat to chase the boy right out of the house.

The boy never so much as looked at Gertrude again.

But Gertrude started to tell Sophia that story as a way of teaching her to never feel special when a man does something one thinks is absurd. They will go to unusual heights for the lowest girls in town. "Men just use flattery as a game," she said. "No man really sees a woman individually, men have a checklist of goodies. They only desire and take." Gertrude pursed her lips as she spoke of men and rolled her eyes into the back of her head.

Men were the enemy. But Sophia always wondered about how her father seemed to have bypassed her set of standards. Sophia had dared to ask the question before, but her mother gave an unsatisfactory answer of "well, I wanted a child and the only way to do it in those days was to marry a man. Your father was a necessity, and I don't think he's ever minded being in that position. He treats his work more like his wife or lovely mistress than he ever has me."

Sophia felt repulsed by the idea of her father knowing and accepting such a low rank by his spouse. Yet, he never cheated on his wife. Did he ever desire anything more loving than this hostile porcupine of a woman? pondered Sophia.

If only an answer could appear from above. Instead, it was as if some shard of bone was tearing at her bowels, shredding them into slivers. Sophia leaned forward in her seat, holding her stomach. She felt an urge to hold her head, her breasts, her arms, her legs, and everything in her body began to feel the conflict forming. A battle raged in her mind, but the blood continually circulating back to her heart marred her ability to solve the problem now. She could not continue to live this way.

One path had to be chosen soon, one single path that made her feel at peace. At the end of whichever path she chose, Sophia would rather be alive than dead.

The paths divided into two: one path led back to her mother and one path led to Damian.

The path back to her mother seemed like the safest trajectory. Yet, she had a feeling of being run down all the time at just twenty-two years old. The days felt numbered with this path. Sophia did not know how much more of this tension she could take.

Whereas, the path to Damian seemed like a frightening and yet exciting one. The path of Damian could yield love, sex, happiness, freedom…or rape, unhappiness, abuse, and death. Sophia's choice depended on how he responded to her presence. Her decision was a chance draw. Was Sophia willing to take the riskier path which may hold a happier future?

It appeared to Sophia that either path led to death eventually. The difference was in the amount of time it took. Would she rather die happily in Damian's arms or die unhappily in her mother's? If death had to come, then Sophia wanted to gamble.

***

The bus dipped and jostled over potholes in the downtown streets. Sophia's commute was always unpleasant since there were more holes in the road on the way there than on the way back. It caused ripples and made Sophia quickly forfeit the idea of bringing a hot beverage with her to work, even if it had a lid. It seemed even the streets dictated how Sophia behaved. With this frustrating realization, she slid down in her seat with her arms folded heavily across her chest.

The gentleman smelling strongly of cigarettes slid down in his seat too. The similarity of their postures further inflamed Sophia and she sat back up. Her head had to stay above his to get any fresh air.

She bet he would not sit back up in his seat, and she stayed upright for the rest of the trip. She was gambling. The ashy man stayed slumped taking a nap. A long string of drool trailed down onto his jacket sleeve. Sophia cringed. It was clear and wiggly with an unnatural strength to hold together inside of his mouth down to his sleeve. Every breath made

112

the saliva furiously wiggle around. Sophia was prepared to scream if any of it ended up on her.

Her heart rate accelerated staring at the line of drool. In fact, she lost track of the other people around her with their faces grinning at the horror marked on Sophia's face as she stared at the man's only product. His drool was a danger Sophia had to pay attention to until her stop.

She moved all the way up against the window, keeping as much distance as possible between herself and this unconscious man. The next small gamble she would make that day was to peripherally watch and stay as far away as possible and bet that no drool would land on her. She made it her mission to make the odds turn in her favor by staying hyperaware of her situation.

Picking up her bag, she reached inside and pulled out a tissue that she draped over her left side as a makeshift shield. She kept her bag on her lap while attempting to cover up as much space as possible. It was a defense system that hopefully would protect her until her stop. The principal challenge would be when she had to pass this man in his seat. He was blocking her with more force than he realized. The power of his drool confining her to her seat was enormous.

Once or twice he moved further and further down in his seat. In fact, it was at a depth Sophia believed no man had ever gone before. He was near to the floor with his knees grazing one of the discarded chicken bones left underneath the seat in front. Sophia thought: Now I'll have no way around him but over.

The mission to leave the bus appeared grim, but Sophia kept thinking of this as a work-up against her own fears. Besides, this gentleman was a stranger whom she would hopefully never see again. Who cares if he walks away from this offended, thought Sophia, or bruised? Sophia was trying to survive in this city.

Her decision rung true in her head as she kept her eyes on him and the impending threat. The number of germs living up and down the wriggling thing made her shiver with goosebumps. Feeling pale, she watched as her stop approached. The man was still in the same low position, and Sophia rapidly was calculating her next moves.

In her imagination, she used all her strength and grabbed the pole and the seatback in front of her and hurled herself right over the drooling man. But in actuality, she poked him hard and politely asked him to sit up so she could exit the bus at the next stop.

Moments of imagination like these often occurred before reality became the unsatisfying truth. She was always polite to other people. According to her mother, any show of emotion in front of the public was a great mistake. "All people should have their public persona on display and become angels" she constantly said. It bothered Sophia that she had to be fake in front of people, but she had been trained so well it became impossible now to assert herself in this kind of situation. Perhaps someday her learned behavior would pay off.

As the driver approached her stop, Sophia picked up her bag, pulled on the yellow call line, squeezed herself in between two round individuals, and waited by the front exit. The door had carved out a shape in the dirt around itself from opening and closing all day. Two dirty, half-moon shapes carved out by the doors amused Sophia until they opened once more and she stepped off toward her office building.

The bus ride was finally at her work stop and Sophia leaped

through the doors before they closed on her. She had seen so many people get their sleeves, bags, legs caught by them. The infamous "closing doors" and rude drivers were nothing new in this city. In less than thirty seconds they closed and Sophia was out in the chilly weather where her clones were pacing around in suits and business skirts.

The city was created for a workforce. It swallowed up and spat out the young, the old, the sick, and the poor. The only people who seemed resilient to the mass crushing were the poor who laid down and slept through the day. Meanwhile, the employed sprinted from work to lunch to work to home to work repeatedly. They scurried far and wide to places they were supposed to have been yesterday. Each day was never long enough for the workers to finish work and for the hobos to start looking for work.

Sophia treaded somewhere in the middle of the morning ebb and flow. She was a worker, she loved her paper-pushing job, but she also took the time to look at the buildings around her. The world was teeming inside of her, and her conflicts at home were floating up to the surface even now. It made Sophia walk on the sidewalk cracks on her way to her office.

***

Late autumn was the perfect season for a warm cup of tea. Whenever she did grab a cup on her way to work, she inhaled the scented steam, enhancing the air filling her lungs. On some days the air smelled like fresh lemongrass. On other days the air smelled like an exotic black tea or a spicy mix with an overpowering cinnamon scent. Sophia's world became much more beautiful when it was filled with such colorful scents.

The walk to the office was where Sophia felt the calmest. This was out in the fresh, chilled air. Taking in deep breaths, she felt that at any time she could turn back and run away. It was this sense of ultimate freedom that put her at ease. Outside the trees stood tall, the grass was frosted still, and the wind kept Sophia contracted in her jacket.

Yet, interwoven within the delightful smells and chilly air arose the memory of her mother's bribes. Whenever her mother asked, Sophia went to have tea with her mother. Her childhood was scattered with memories of tea with Mother. The offers were most frequently made on Saturday mornings and Sophia would follow her mother into the kitchen with her head down.

One memory, in particular, blew away the comfort of a cup of warm tea. When Sophia had given in to her mother's offer of tea it was more than just a mere admission that day, her acceptance was a confession. Sophia thought she would die if she refused the tea. Perhaps the dying would be slow at first, but day by day it would wear her down until she became nothing but dust.

A deal occurred in the kitchen while the teapot was singing at its highest pitch. She watched the vapors hitting the ceiling and dispersing. Sophia tried to breathe in the steam. If only someone will come to take me away, Sophia thought, even if I meant little to them.

Gertrude turned the stove off and asked, "Milk and sugar, love?" She poured the boiling water into cups that were as old as her.

"Yes, please."

Gertrude set the cups by the milk and sugar, next to a teaspoon that was aimed at her own heart.

"You know, dear, I've always thought you must be popular in school. You do seem to thrive there. I don't understand how everyone could *not* love you. You're smart, you're pretty. I just don't get it. Maybe I could help somehow?"

Sophia knew what was coming next.

"I'd like to make you a dress for the dance, Gertrude said. It will definitely turn heads."

Sophia felt Gertrude was going to sew this dress out of chainmail. In fact, she had felt the same way when Gertrude had sewed her a dress for last year's school dance. During the whole summer leading up to the dance, her mother had upbraided her for the labor she had to put into the dress, for the blood drawn by the sewing needle, and for the pain that had come with fitting a dress on such a "thin, sickly-looking girl."

By the time fall arrived, Sophia looked at the dress with malice and guilt. At the dance, her dress felt like it weighed a hundred pounds.

On that day, however, she had to pass on Gertrude's tea. The bus route had been taking longer than usual. She had walked quickly, still making sure to stomp precisely on each sidewalk crack, willfully hoping that her stomping was doing something very bad to her mother.

Out here when she had a mission to get to and from work, Sophia felt more in control of her life. Perhaps that was also what had caused the sense of relaxation she had felt earlier. She was in control here and hardly anywhere else. That day was no exception to how she felt, even if she was behind on executing her schedule.

She had sped up the pace but noticed she passed a thin, graying man who paced back and forth in the urban patch that the city called grass. She had seen him every day, yet the only thing that changed was the layers of clothing he adorned—on hot days it was a cotton shirt, on cool days it was a sweatshirt with the hood tied snugly around his face. As he walked, her thoughts whirled around trying to find a reason for his pacing when there was none. She could not grasp what was not there.

Still, it made her wonder about how she could feel freedom while on a mission but nowhere else. Could this man feel truly free without purpose? Sophia pondered. Why did he pace like an animal in a cage? What had happened to him? A few weeks back, Sophia had caught him opening the zipper of his pants and relieving himself on one of the public trees. Grimacing at this vulgarity, Sophia had hoped a policeman would catch him in the act. But no police officer was around. Even so, it would not have changed his path. The hobo turned away from the tree and continued his fickle march from one end of the patch of frozen grass to the other—back and forth and back and forth without any reason at all to continue or to stop at that point. His pacing was the epitome of absurdity to Sophia.

She had shivered at the thought of becoming a mindless creature—a bundle of sensations and stimuli—though even that looked dulled in this man. His eyes were red and blurry, his beard was unkempt, and his skin was baggy and sallow from lack of food. A layer of dirt clung to his hands and face. The dumpster dives kept him alive, but only physically.

Sophia wanted to talk to this man on one of her commutes. It was possible he might be conducting some kind of experiment for science. Maybe he was purposefully homeless. But it was hard to imagine that the two ways of life could coincide with each other. It was in that moment of intense wonder about this hobo that she suddenly stopped and turned.

Walking back about a block, Sophia approached the pacing hobo. She wanted to understand more about his constant laps, and whether they meant anything more than proving to himself that he was still alive. The only thing that she could to think say to him was, "Hello. May I ask what you're doing?"

The hobo kept walking. Was it possible he didn't hear her? she wondered.

"Hello. May I ask what you're doing, sir?" Sophia said a bit louder.

On his returning lap, the hobo glanced up at her face but did not look her in the eyes. One thing was definite, he would not stop for her in his pacing. So, Sophia adapted and followed in his wake.

"I was just wondering how you can stand the cold out here. Do you visit a homeless shelter when winter comes?" Sophia tried to look into his eyes as she asked this but failed, her eyes awkwardly searching for something on the ground. She felt as if she had no right to ask him why he did what he did because she never asked anyone else the same questions.

The man said gruffly, "Yes, I go elsewhere in the winter." With this answer, he stuck his dirty fingers out to Sophia for money.

"I'm sorry, sir. I don't carry cash on me, only cards. May I ask why you pace like this? What do you think about all day while people are cooped up in their office buildings?" Sophia got a glare from him this time for half a second.

The man kept walking in silence with Sophia following ridiculously at his side. Finally, the man said, "I drank and I ended up here. I walk to keep myself alive. If I sit on that bench with a bottle in my hand now, I'll for sure never rise again. Happy?"

Underneath the agitated exterior of his voice, he sounded ashamed to be in this rut.

"My brain is also fried, I think. Again, too much drink. I walk it all off which keeps me as sober as I'm going to get these days."

Sophia started to get nervous around this man. He was not quite there. He was somewhere in between the Living and the Dead. He continued his laps back and forth. Sophia also stopped feeling well from having to sharply turn so often on this little urban patch of greenery. She was also surprised that the grass had not died where his feet were crushing it all day long.

"Well, thanks for being honest," Sophia said. She had no idea what else she might say.

The hobo did not reveal any secret genius underneath, but he certainly did reveal what life married to the drink will do to a man. Sophia made a mental note as she continued on her way toward her office. She thought all the while about this man. Maybe his purpose was to out-walk his alcoholism. But Sophia had to let go of this idea that seemed driven by fear. A purpose could only bring a person, ultimately, joy. Sophia wanted to satisfy that craving for a purpose by achieving something positive in her life, and she walked forward.

CHAPTER III

W alking up to the tall glass doors, Sophia threw them open and the cool air inside woke her from her reverie. She took a deep breath as she passed the front door's security guard and took the elevator up to the sixth floor. This elevator was cramped—even for one person. It had ugly dark blue carpet lining the entire inside to where one felt like they were drowning. Sophia was drowning.

She was deep down in the water with her memories of school dances and hokey music floating up like bubbles from those nights. Visualizing occasions, like those dances, made Sophia feel small.

Her mother had worried about her all day, while Sophia worried about her own appearance all night. She desired to be fawned over by the boys in her school, but each time an opportunity to shine arose, Sophia ran to the bathroom to check on her dress or makeup. Some sneaking thought that her underwear was showing or that she had lipstick on her teeth nagged at her enough to take yet another trip outside the dance room.

When the dance ended, Sophia went home feeling hungover with worry. She was exhausted, not from dancing with friends or boys, but from anxiety. These nights never ended well. As soon as Sophia got home, Gertrude asked her questions that made her stomach tighten even more than before.

"So, how did it go? How many boys looked at you? Did you win anything for my dress?" asked Gertrude.

Yet, all Sophia wanted to do was take a shower to rub off all the makeup and, hopefully, drown some of her shame down the shower drain. The fact that she spent most of the time alone in the bathroom made for an awful impression on everyone there, and the last person she wanted to know was her mother: for her mother, failure socially meant failure totally.

Gertrude pressed on as she usually did: "You haven't answered me yet, dear. How many boys do I have to send away tonight when they come crawling after you?"

She gave a little sigh and picked up her tea and further interrogated Sophia.

"Well? I need to know just how many there are to fend off. You know, I still think you are too young to have a boyfriend, even if they all adore you. You're my daughter after all. When I was about your age my father asked, before every outing, for the names of the children who would be there and the address of where the party was being held. He reminded me that I was a farm girl and should not be taken by just any boy. I had to ask my parents for permission in those days to see a boy."

A few drops of tea flew out of Gertrude's swinging cup at the emphasis on "permission." But Sophia looked down at the floor, trying to keep her stomach from tying itself into knots.

"I should have gone with you. Boys these days are even wilder than in my day."

Sophia threw up.

The memory from that moment vanished as soon as she

remembered what color the kitchen floor was after she had thrown up her unfinished tea. Sophia cringed as the elevator doors opened and she began to walk toward her designated cubicle. However, Damian barred the way.

His hands clenched the door trim around Sophia's head.

"Oh, you're bleeding! What happened?"

"No, it's dried." Damian's eyes darted to his recent wounds.

"But what happened?" asked Sophia, her face cringing as she stepped out of the elevator.

"I…well, I needed to take back what was mine."

"What do you mean?"

"Some bastard took the paint off my nice car, so I took some of his."

"But shouldn't you just have called the police?"

Damian screwed up his face while attempting to stifle his laughter. "The police? Here? Are you kidding? This country is so soft that there are no real policemen anymore. Besides, I know how to take care of myself. That man won't try the same stunt again, I can tell you that."

Sophia dropped her blushing face to stare at his poor hands. They were inflamed with angry red mounds of skin surrounding new cuts. If only she could get down on her knees in the office and kiss them. Hopefully, her healing kisses would bind up his wounds and erase the pain he must be feeling.

"Taking paint off a car still does not explain your hands… I don't mean to be so nosy but—"

"I punched him in the mouth too."

"Oh." Sophia was afraid of saying anything else.

"Don't worry, it's not like he's in the hospital or anything. I'm not even sure he needed stitches. It was just a warning.

Anyway, my hands will heal just fine. My car, on the other hand, well, my car might need a new paint job." Damian kicked at an imaginary stone on the floor.

Sophia kept her eyes on his hands. He must have driven to work today which explains why he was not on the bus, she thought. She felt that perhaps her focus by itself could heal some of his wounds. She felt uneasy that he was violent toward others, but he had nearly convinced her that the other man was in the wrong and Damian was in the right.

"Would you like me to get you something for your hands?" Sophia asked.

Damian's face softened as he said: "No, but I would like to get lunch together today."

Shock stole Sophia's voice away momentarily. "No, I really can't. I've got so much work to catch up on today that I'll probably just end up eating my packed lunch at my desk... again." She could no longer look him in the eye. She looked at her blouse instead, hoping there was not a stain from breakfast which had gone unnoticed in her haste to leave.

It appeared as if he wanted to say something else from the way his mouth twitched slightly, but instead, he merely said, "All right, I will ask Tim to join me today then," and he walked off with his hands buried in his pockets. Sophia could tell that his hands were clenched into fists.

He walked faster to open the door for her, but then she felt his breath on her ear and shivered. Her skin pricked up a bit and he must have seen it because Sophia blushed as she turned around to confirm her suspicions. He would ask her again to lunch.

Sophia quickly rubbed her shoulders to eliminate her moment of weakness in front of Damian. Today, was unlike yesterday when his hands were the only object of interest for Sophia. Today, her mother's voice was louder in her head and Sophia knew it would fade by the time work was over, only to ramp up again on the way home. This was a cycle Sophia did not know how to break. How could she bring the vision of his hands back into her mind where in the same cooped-up space her mother was lurking to bite his hands off? Yesterday, he was the one and only man on the horizon. Yet, today, he was the most threatening object in Sophia's sight. But she reminded herself of the pact she had made with herself. Now was the time to break from her mother and jump into the abyss. She would force herself to swim in its murky waters and drown if she had to. Sophia began to believe that she would drown for Damian and *only* for Damian since he seemed to be one savior in sight.

Sophia placed her bag in the cabinet, pulled back her chair, turned on the computer, sat down, and read her latest unopened emails. The pile of papers next to her was the obstacle to conquer afterward. Another paper, masking the others beneath it, lay on top; it had Damian's name and phone number on it. When was this placed here? she wondered. Then she snatched it off, crumbled it into a ball, and threw it into the recycle bin. The dangerous phone number returned though before the day was over in various places around her cubicle. The only way to rid herself of the information was to incinerate it, but the office only had sinks and microwaves at her disposal. She grew resentful of this man imposing himself on her. Sophia could try to forget his hands if only he would let her. Finally, Sophia grabbed the piece of paper with her to the women's restroom and threw it in the trash bin there. The knowledge of having a way to contact him and have his voice right against her ear was too agonizing to dwell on.

When she arrived back at her desk, her cubicle remained empty. She breathed deeply and was finally able to get lost in the paperwork which lay before her. Papers that had to be signed by the boss went in one pile, papers that needed to be filed into date order went into another, papers that were to be filed in alphabetical order into another, and, finally, papers which were to be shredded went into a fourth pile. This was her sphere, the place where all of her work was controlled and where her designs were followed.

Sadly, no one followed Sophia's desires based on the questions she regularly received from coworkers, such as, "Hey, where are those documents I have to sign?" or "Nice pile." Sophia did, in fact, move around papers all day, and she did it swiftly. What little power she had in the world was based on her job of moving the company's papers to the proper locations. They all lined up properly for her, and she made them stand at attention before she marched them off to the right files and desks. Pleasure was the only word she could fathom to describe her daily tasks.

There was a distinct pleasure in touching each piece of paper, which Sophia knew came from the pulp of a tree. People used trees to make beautiful tools. She saw words more clearly when they were laid down with black ink on a white background. Handling each individual piece made Sophia feel the gravity of the words written on it. It was as if the words were jumping off the page to be noticed by Sophia. "Hear me! See me!" bellowed the letters from the clients to their attorneys or to the estate plans that laid out one's most intimate final requests.

Paper was a product and a gift to Sophia. She was allowed to handle one person's work in order to then perform her own. Each sheet was just a tangle of fibers, strong enough to catch Sophia when she fell. Like a spider's web or a strand of hair, paper fibers acted as support. Strength laid in the mountains of paper covering her on all flanks.

Shifting through another stack, she laid her eyes on an interesting case. It had all the common legal jargon used in a motor vehicle accident, like "objection" or "misstates testimony," except for one detail—the driver was supposedly following another driver up ahead. A man was following a woman after a fight. The argument continued even while the two were in separate vehicles. It was no different than the chase between Apollo and Daphne.

The man in Vehicle 1 was chasing after the woman in Vehicle 2 until she stopped suddenly and stood like a tree rooted to the spot. Refusing to step out of the vehicle until the police arrived, the woman used her car akin to the bark of a tree to protect herself from misuse. Only when the red and blue light reflected off of her car door mirror did she crack open the door and breathe in the cool, night breeze.

She knew she had escaped from the worst of it. Sophia knew a restraining order would be sought in this lawsuit. Daphne would be safe from harm once more.

Sophia began to wonder: What if Damian ever caused her pain or suffering? Would she be smart enough to run? Sophia put herself in the scenario. Damian desired something Sophia could not give. Of course, she may crumble before him but first beg to be saved. He must listen to a crying voice. If tears could not get to him, then she was determined to seek out her mother...

Yes, Sophia knew herself well enough to know she would

probably crawl back in shame. Her mother would know what to do. Her mother was still wrapped in her tree bark. Her mother would always stop anything or anyone from coming between her and her daughter.

Young, strong Damian would have to stop running. A barrier of mother, house, and rooms within the house would keep out all things unwanted. Maybe Sophia could spend her time inside dreaming about changing into a bird, and then she could follow Damian without being seen. She could love him from afar.

Sophia imagined dipping her little beak into an open inkwell and using the paper from her office to write love letters to him. She would wash off her beak, dry it in the sun, and then take the letter up with the power of her wings. Flying over to his cubicle, she imaged dropping a love letter once a day on his desk before heading toward the open air.

The ink from her beak would dry on the paper slowly, filling in the dents like little rivers. Black rivers flowing and absorbing into the paper, digging down into the fibers of the paper, they would travel for ages. Touching the paper, Damian would be able to feel the texture of each letter impressing upon him the significance of each word.

Paper was a whisperer for the trees they came from. All the women who stood tall waiting inside of them wrote on the rings of the trees. The rings became mashed and battered into pulp, mixed with water, and rung out to dry. A quiet hum stayed trapped in the fibers. It was the hum of stories being told to a deaf audience.

Sophia knew she may very well become one of those Daphnes, whispering to the person cradling her in their arms, not noticing what is beneath her boss's coffee stain or the latest work schedule, but solely focusing on the rings of the tree.

Sophia's boss could be difficult to deal with. He sat in the same position every morning with his newspaper and his rude manners. He occasionally looked up at you when you were telling him your tasks for the day, but usually he hid behind his paper. Eric was a tall man of about fifty with features shrunken from smoking and a wizened face who carried his experiences in his wrinkles. He commanded power from others and he knew it. He tested people with just a look to see if he could get away without speaking to the entire office for the day, while still keeping it functioning. Eric drank with his board of executives while talking stocks. Sophia felt worlds apart from this man, but she preferred it that way since he gave her the space to work in peace.

However, Damian would not allow her that space anymore.

***

Damian came into her mind involuntarily throughout her time among the masses of paper. He was there inside her head, asking her to lunch a thousand times over again. Sophia would be fully prepared when he asked her again in reality.

The paperwork was moving along nicely. The A files were done and the B files were well on their way to the right desks. Sophia worked through them expertly. She trained herself to work efficiently and fluidly to the point where her mind could travel to other worlds while her hands made the mountains of paper move.

The proper documents were stamped and signed where the sticky notes pointed. Her suppleness extended from her arms to her wrists to her fingers as they swiped and whirled around the file folders and their corresponding documents.

But the whole time Damian was there with her. His presence made Sophia keep checking over her shoulder to see if he was actually there. Yet, every time she glanced over her shoulder that morning it was just in her imagination. When she turned around at around eleven o'clock to take a quick break, Sophia saw him again.

"Oh, hi, you startled me." Sophia launched back into her chair as if presuming to continue working. She had only gotten up for a stretch anyway.

But Damian had caught the bluff, and even if he had not, he did not seem to care. Damian was going to go on with his plans once he had put them into action. He pulled a chair over from another cubicle, hoping to hide for a time behind her three blue walls.

"You did not seem very chatty on the bus home yesterday. Can I ask what's on your mind? You look like you to have more interesting thoughts than Eli or Jerry around here." He smiled and looked right at Sophia.

His eyes were green like a swamp or perhaps he was the alligator in the swamp who would come and drag Sophia down into its murky depths. Either way, he was dangerous.

Sophia choked, "I'm not really that interesting. I just come here and go back home to my parents most of the time." She glared at the floor now in shame.

Damian knew better. "No, I can see right through that. You think and I like a thinking girl." He lightly took his finger and put it under her chin lifting it. He just kept looking at her, intensely. "I see a sheltered girl who's about to explode. I see her glancing over the precipice each day awaiting the moment when someone will push her over. You're even curious to see where you'd land." He chuckled. "Yes, I see you hiding behind your own skin. You're waiting to hatch from your egg. Well, let me tell you it's about time to break that shell. Poke through it and see what you find. There are no villains out here, just a world filled with people striving to survive in it."

Sophia was hearing his words, but it was hard to believe they were really being said out loud, in the office. She had had variants of these thoughts such as how many ways he could call her beautiful. But she did not record her thoughts on paper, so there was no way for him to know...unless he was really looking.

Sophia no longer felt so lonely. She placed her hand gently on top of Damian's, careful with his wounds, and a tingle of pleasure coursed through her body. It was pure electricity between them both.

Damian moved closer to Sophia until his knee was touching hers. "You know, I'm an outsider too, cast away from my fellow men. I want a companion on this lonely island I inhabit."

He spoke so strangely, thought Sophia. She had never heard someone say such enticing things. It made her forget herself and her situation.

"Damian, how are you so sure?"

"So sure that I know who you are as a person?"

"Yes, I've never really had a long conversation with you."

"I've watched and observed you. Everything about you is subtly different from the others like the somber note in your eyes. Yes, they are the others, not us. You and I are one, Sophia."

His eyes flashed as he spoke those last words. Sophia was hooked.

"You mean like soul mates?" asked Sophia.

"Yes, like that and I mean to prove it to you as soon as I can.

No one needs to push you off the precipice, Sophia. You've already done it yourself."

"And how is that?"

"You've allowed me to touch you." Damian grasped Sophia's hand in his and squeezed like a viper.

A piece of his dark hair fell out of place and grazed his cheek. It made him look more angular and less kind.

"Yes, yes, I suppose I have," said Sophia. She did not remove herself from his tight grip.

"I will teach you more about yourself than you've ever dared to see. I may even become a mirror for you. I can tell that you are intelligent. But you could know so much more if you just follow me. Allow me to be your Master, your God, and your Lover."

Sophia nearly dry-heaved hearing such a strong proposal on such an ordinary day. It was too much to hear all at once. Damian must have known this would be too much for her to handle. She needed some time, just a little more time to consider.

"I know what you are thinking," said Damian, "you wanted more time."

She nodded her head, dumbfounded.

"It's too late. You've already committed yourself to jump off the edge and into my arms. I've caught you from a horrible fall. And I want you all for my own, Sophia. There is no more time to dawdle—prancing around the edge and waiting for something to finally happen. You are twenty-two years old and life is much too short for our kind. Let me take you by the hand and I promise not to drop you even deeper into the fray."

He gave her his other hand to take and to hold. Sophia

grabbed it with all the strength she had left.

***

"Now, would you like to go to lunch together?" asked Damian. His hand twitched around Sophia's as he said it.

Sophia knew she was not being given a choice any longer. Time had run out, as Damian said. She was either all in or all out.

"Yes." Sophia exhaled deeply as she felt his grip loosening like a snake that was finished killing its prey.

Damian checked the insufferable office clock ticking on the wall across from Sophia's cubicle.

"Ten minutes past noon. Looks like we are already late for lunch." With that Damian helped her up, heading swiftly for the door, as she turned to grab her bag of lunch. Damian already had his meal wrapped up in squished tinfoil, which, yet again, meant he would not be deterred from his forward progression.

"We're going to be taking my car just a little bit outside the city."

Sophia panicked. "Wait, I thought we would just be going to some restaurant across the street from work. We don't have time to travel anywhere far!" Her face burned and her hands began to slide through Damian's with sweat.

Damian let go to wipe his hands on his pants, and to glare at Sophia. "Trust me," was all he said. Sophia followed.

After a few minutes' drive, they got out of his car right near a little pond. Sophia had never seen such a delicate spot so close to the city. She marveled at how green the grass still was in this area and that the pond had not frozen over yet.

"Wow, this is a gorgeous little spot. Will anyone find us here?" That was her mother's question. Her nagging voice grew louder, reminding Sophia that if she screamed no one would hear.

Damian gave her another murky stare and said, "You're safe with me. Who cares about others? Now come here." Damian opened his arms just to hold Sophia. She went into the space that was meant for her, afraid of what would happen next.

"Get down on your knees," Damian said.

Oh, god, he's going to shoot me execution-style, thought Sophia. Maybe he did something worse to the man he claimed he only punched in the mouth. Please, *please* Damian, I trust you. Don't let me die here. I'm so young. I've never had sex, or gotten married, or had a real family. Tears welled up in Sophia's eyes as she shut them tightly.

"Keep your eyes open, silly girl."

Then, Damian walked over to the pond water, dipped his finger in the water, and approached Sophia again. He took his wet finger and drew something on Sophia's forehead. The water dripped down and coated her eyebrows. They felt so cool when the wind picked up. Sophia smiled.

"There, now you're mine forever."

"What did you write?" she giggled.

Damian knelt down now with her and took each hand in his. In all seriousness, he said, "Property of Damian Voigt."

There was a silence as Sophia grew faint. She had been part of a ceremony that Damian had devised, right here and now. It was overwhelming. Her mother's voice was beaten out of her, and her body was filled with *his* voice—*his* promise.

The act was stronger than any superficial ring or tattoo. But Sophia was still unsure if she could uphold her end of the unspoken promise.

Damian kept silent until Sophia spoke: "I don't know what

I should say."

"Well, you can start with 'you trust me.' I'm not here to kill you. I want you."

"I know, I'm sorry." She looked down. Sophia was raised to think that men kill first, and love later.

"I want you to start fresh now. Forget everything you were raised to believe. Live now. Live with me."

Sophia stumbled for words. Is he asking for marriage? she wondered. For her to leave home? What? "Damian, what do you want from me exactly?"

"Exactly what I said. Leave home to come with me. I'll take you away from that hell to my own."

"Your own...hell?"

"My existence is hellish without you. Come home with me."

"I'm not sure I'm ready yet. We have only known each other for a couple of days, and not as lovers."

"Fine. I'll give you some time to be with me—then you'll get out of that miserable house."

"I never told you my house was miserable..." said Sophia.

"Look at you! You come into the office as a thief would. You crawl in unseen and leave as if you were never here. I can tell your parents have messed you up somehow."

"Oh." Sophia's face grew hot.

"Now, let's get to know each other," said Damian.

"Yes, Damian." Sophia glanced up for just a second before quickly looking down again.

"I think you mean, yes, *Sir*."

Sophia did not understand what had just happened. For one moment she was trapped under her mother's reign and now it was Damian's turn. But she had chosen. She gulped, but her saliva had to bypass a lump forming in her throat.

"Yes...Sir."

The lock was sealed and the key hidden. Running away was impossible. But do I really want to run? she questioned. Is not this exactly what I want? An unsettled stomach was giving her no signals. Sophia felt the need to curl up under her covers in her bed and think through this whole day. After her unplanned baptism, Sophia felt as if her weak self had shed from her and now stood like an apparition in front of herself. Yet, she felt the weakness radiating from her to this ghost. It was revealing to her that it was still connected to her body even though it was prevented from entering again. The weakness pulsated, causing the panic to reach up and take hold of her heart, squeezing it to its own chaotic rhythm. Sophia thought she might fail on her promise to live for Damian, and before this workday was even over. Her heart hurt.

"Good. Let's eat some lunch." Damian helped pull Sophia up to attend to the lunches they had dropped under a tree by the little pond. Without speaking, they sat there for a half an hour shoving bits and pieces down their throats, got back into the car, and returned to the office as completely different people.

Sophia was entirely his now.

***

Without another word, they walked back separately to their desks. Damian looked like a hungry animal. He kept his fists clenched in his pockets, and he did not seem inclined to go back to work when his own business was unfinished.

There would be no taking of his "property" during the workday. Yet thoughts were swarming like flies in his mind. He thought that she must be just as distracted.

Sophia's papers were piling up and she moved dexterously,

shifting the paper stacks from one side of the desk to the other without slicing open her fingers, but the only pounding words in her head while moving were: What happens now?

She was still alive, which was a pleasant surprise. She had not been abducted, beaten, or raped on her lunch break. But her heart was beating as if she had gone through something as traumatic; it was thumping up into her throat. Taking deep breaths, Sophia tried to push her fears back down into normal-sized breaths which was the kind of breathing she could control.

Sophia tried to focus on where her papers needed to be, and this gave her enough space to calm down. Besides, it was clear Damian was in charge now. She had to trust him because he was the only one to help her now. Trust would be the most challenging aspect yet. Sophia trusted her mother once before without any good results. Rather, Sophia had suffered under the ones she thought she loved. Her parents took her trusting nature and crushed it under heel like a celebratory glass. But this was a person of her choosing and a man who she believed knew what he was doing.

At the end of the workday, Damian sauntered up to Sophia's desk. He had come with a new question already on his lips, but he was waiting for her to acknowledge him first.

Sophia pushed her chair back, turned off her computer, and pulled her bag out of the lower cabinet just like every other day.

Damian took a step forward and said, "Follow me. I have a question."

Although she knew she had to obey, Sophia still had a thought that if this was the only way to avoid going to do something more adventurous than coffee or lunch then she would follow him. As she walked to the elevator and pressed the big arrow button down, Damian leaned forward and said, "If I had to guess, you want a strong man who can protect you from harm. Is that correct?"

A tremor went down Sophia's legs. "Yes, but I'm not so sure this is an appropriate conversation to have so close to the office."

Damian smiled and grabbed Sophia's wrist as they went into the elevator together. It was only six floors, but it felt like hours since he then asked her to say "yes" again.

"Yes. I've been waiting for someone strong…" Sophia blushed.

"Good. That's what I thought."

The elevator doors opened and Sophia walked straight out the doors to the bus stop as she always did. Her reflexes kept her moving forward.

Picking up speed, Damian left her with one more question: "Do you like handcuffs?"

Sophia's mouth gaped for two seconds before she could recollect herself. "W-what do you mean? Am I in trouble?"

Damian smirked, sighed, and added, "No, I meant for sexual use. I'm not a cop." He lingered by her at the bus stop and she noticed his clenched fists shoved into his pockets again. The sun was unbearable today, even with the chilly fall air, so they both were cornered together in the shade that the bus stop sign gave to lustful criminals like themselves.

"I've never done anything with them before. Sorry." Sophia looked down.

Damian suddenly placed his finger under her chin, lifting it up, and looking at her with eyes that burned her.

Damian knew he was planting the first seeds of his idea of

pleasure in her mind. He could afford to leave Sophia alone now to think about his offer. He dropped her chin as her face glistened with perspiration from the heat and the situation.

She watched him walking to his car, while she was stuck waiting for the bus like a little girl. Her blush rose again to her cheeks, but inside a new feeling of desire was emerging.

As soon as he drove away though, thoughts of Gertrude reminded her of all the male rapists, serial killers, abductors, mass murders, stranglers, sadists, and whatever other evil lurks out in the city. Sophia envisioned several scenes of men in cars luring hitchhiking girls inside only to end up bludgeoning them to death and shoving them in their trunk the rest of the way to their house where they would then dissect them bit by bit. She began shaking. She continued to imagine being poisoned by Damian, smothered by his chloroform-drenched rag, or being punched hard in the face with his clenched fists until she gave in to his lustful desires. She could feel the rope being tied around her hands and feet with her chest exposed to his rough hands and tongue. Her heart did backflips and her face grew too hot, her hands started to sweat, she felt faint—another anxiety attack was on its way. Sophia sat on the bus stop seat, its metal top burned her thighs, but all she could think about doing now was to put her head between her knees.

The spiraling thoughts continued to obsessively return to images of an ax, a rope, and a dirty old rag, and blood, lots and lots of her *own* blood all over everything: the walls, the floors, the ceiling, the ax, the rope, the rag. A new wave of nausea overtook her. She would never be able to see Damian again with this new feeling associated with him. The last thing she felt before the bus arrived was the noose of her mother's umbilical cord wrapping itself around her neck and pulling her back in the direction of home. Her mother would never, ever let her near a man.

CHAPTER IV

Weakly opening the door to her house, Sophia smelled gravy as it wafted in through her nose. She went straight into the kitchen to set the table. Meanwhile, a war was raging inside her head.

She thought: I get fed and sometimes it's even good food. I get mostly free rent even though I should be out on my own right now. I am even given money for clothes and jewelry. So, what right have I to complain?

She watched her shadow of a mother scurrying around the kitchen trying to identify the weak points of her domain and where they came from. The searching was all a game with her. The exterior of their house looked perfect, but inside her and her parents' minds, they were screaming.

That evening during dinner was the same as usual: newspapers out, silence, the clanking of knives and forks, and the sound of every bite. Sophia imagined a grand speech she wanted to tell her psychotic, life-sucking family.

First, I would jump onto the table for effect and then I would shout:

"I hate this family! What is wrong with you all?! Thanks to you all of my teenage years went to hell! I want my life back! Do you know I have moments where I have anxiety attacks? I only get that feeling when something reminds me of this place: the smells, the faces, the places…it is pure torture and that side of me will always be there. I hate you both. You, father, for staying silent, and you, mother, for being too loud. I'm never coming back."

After my speech, I would get down from the table with a wrenching pain as if my heart was being squeezed through a meat grinder.

Instead, Sophia pushed her fork aimlessly across her plate as she thought about her days. They seemed stretched out ahead of her without end. She thought: Now, I can't eat without the feeling of vomiting, but I sure as hell can sleep. I can sleep because the darkness, depression, and silence of this house remain untouched by noise. My life now is death or like an uneasy sleep—a sleep that lasts for days, and slows the hours down to minutes down to seconds. My days feel like ten, and each silent meal is as horrific and awkward as the next. I have begun counting on the meals to tell me when it is morning, noon, or evening. The sun refuses to shine through this house. It does not want to look upon nature's mistake. My mother, in particular, is a crazy, dramatic person who will not get her head out of the novels and soap operas she thinks we are living in, and my father is never home. No, the sun cannot see my parents as living anymore with their monotonous conversations, motions, meals, awkwardness, aloofness, melodramatic fixations, grieving, and uneducated ways of living. How do you tell your family you absolutely despise everything about them?

Sophia continued to think about how she would run away from her parents. What would she bring with her? Would she leave a final note? What would it say?

She excused herself from the table after she had had enough of the gravy on her meat and potatoes which smelled better than it tasted. The gravy had chunks in it which were unidentifiable and the meat was overcooked again and the potatoes were probably already sprouting new shoots that got mashed up into the rest of the dish anyway.

Heading up to her room, Sophia managed to pull her thoughts back to what happened at the office earlier. Damian came back to her as he was—not as a mass murderer. He was attractive and seemed brusquely kind. His possessiveness over her was exactly what she wanted. In order to trust him, she had to believe that what he was doing was right and safe.

After thinking through the whole scene again, from the baptism at the pond to the question of a strong man to the one about handcuffs, Sophia began to think about what a strong man with a pair of handcuffs would do for pleasure. Perhaps he would handcuff her to the bed? Perhaps he had some other strange rituals to perform on her? Perhaps he needed a sacrificial lamb for an orgy? The image of a serial killer in control clouded her fantasy. The killer had her in his power and had gone to go grab his chainsaw. Sophia shook her head hard to redo the scene. No, Damian did not seem like a killer. But then she heard her mother's voice in her head say: "Killers never seem like killers at all. In fact, they are usually handsome men who are extremely persuasive."

Her mother was the expert on the kinds of plots where a handsomely dark man uses his looks only to deceive and maim. But that was fiction. Damian really seemed to want her the way she was because he took the time to lift her chin and look at her. Damian was preoccupied with her mouth, and her hands, and her eyes. It seemed unbelievable to think there was more to those looks. Besides, all of the men that Sophia knew were never as complicated as her own mother. Her mother could beguile and drag men into her web, but Damian? Sophia refused to believe it.

Anyway, it was already too late. Even Damian had acknowledged that. Since that first bus ride home with him, Sophia had given herself up for his hands. His hands could crush her beneath them if they really wanted to. She had given up her own freedom to him.

Taking a deep breath, Sophia closed her eyes and replayed the day with Damian. She weighed the pros and cons of accepting him. She played the scene out as if he was a good guy and if he was a bad guy. She tried to guess what the first signs would be if he was a killing machine. Maybe it would be his persistence? she pondered. Or his mention of sexual objects at work? Could it be nothing more than a hard handshake?

His possible intentions kept forming new patterns in Sophia's mind. She wanted the hero, but the villain kept bursting in—her mother's voice. Sophia kept wavering between a passionate kiss and a violent blow to the head.

***

Her chewing slowed down as she sat at the table lost in thought. In fact, she had forgotten she was eating at all until she swallowed and nearly choked.

Molding her being into his every shape and desire, Sophia was learning to accept committing herself to Damian and his overpowering will. He could do anything with her and that would feel so much better than the life she had here at home. He could even beat her, kick her, and she would still cling to his shirt in tears when he was finished. He was a god, and she was starting to think that she would die without him.

Sophia looked at her mother and then her father whose faces were staring down into the depths of their plates as if waiting for some kind of magical eight-ball answer to appear to them.

"Mother?" Sophia asked.

"Hmmm?" Gertrude was still chewing and staring intensely. "What is it?"

"Why are you and father so quiet at meals?"

"That's just what we find the most comfortable, honey. We like our silence." That final sentence reeked of a lie. Sophia pushed further:

"But you don't seem to spend time together like normal married people." Sophia looked up from her plate to see her mother's countenance shrink.

"And how would you know so much about how couples behave?" This was war.

"Movies. Television. I don't know, maybe I've picked it up from books." Sophia tried not to back down. Her mother was no longer in charge.

Sophia's father kept looking at his plate, allowing Gertrude to do the answering as she usually did when they were both directed a question.

"Dearest, your father and I are content and comfortable with the way things are now. We have some money saved, a nice home, and a precious daughter. We spend each day thankful for it." Gertrude showed her front teeth, the very act being a rarity in the Weber house. Sophia knew this was the trophy-wife answer she gave our neighbors after berating them for not recycling.

Sophia sat up straighter, deeming herself the psychologist and her mother the patient. "But mother, you sit at the table and always seem to want to be somewhere else. You hate cooking for us and father is always taking the brunt of the verbal beatings with me following closely behind."

Gertrude gave Sophia massive bug eyes. She looked like a sea creature who lived in the darkest depths of the ocean.

"How dare you! Did I ask you to sit here and judge our family? Good god! You have no idea what I've done for you over these long, hard years. But no, that's not good enough. Am I the evil disciplinarian of the house? Can't I enjoy my efforts yet or, perhaps, does my daughter think it's not enough? Do you imagine my sacrifices weren't grand enough? Huh?! Speak up!" The entire time Gertrude had been slapping her hand down on the table and flapping her arms around.

Sophia made a sudden shift downward into her chair. This questioning would have severe consequences. But she felt free in knowing only Damian could harm her now.

"Mother, please. I'm not afraid of you anymore. You don't seem happy and neither does father. You've raised me and now I can take care of myself. Why don't you two do something to salvage your marriage now?"

"I will not be told what to do by my child! Don't ever tell me what to do! We are doing fine as a family. I have enough going on now as it is. Isn't that right?" Gertrude made eyes at her husband who shakily nodded his head. "Right, so don't you dare, young lady, get any ideas about taking charge of this house. I'm in charge, and you are not well enough to leave. This is just so clear by the way you are misbehaving right now. You're sick. *Sick!*"

Sophia felt those words pierce her. She felt sick, too. For she was indeed Sophia, the weak daughter, Sophia, the poor daughter, Sophia, the *sick* daughter.

The sickly feeling reminded her of when she threw up after one of those awful school dances.

Her mother had said after she threw up that night: "Oh, good lord! Honey! Clean yourself up. Are you all right?"

Sophia raced to the bathroom to cough up the rest of her dinner. She pressed her head to the cool basin of the toilet.

"Are you listening to me?" screeched Gertrude.

But Sophia had no words for her mother—only venomous drool.

Gertrude launched into her infamous mode, which everyone in the Weber household recognized, where nothing got in the way of her caring for her child. When Sophia became ill, Gertrude dropped everything to pamper her—unless her favorite soap opera was playing or unless her cooking would burn.

After straining out the excess water from a towel, Gertrude placed it on Sophia's forehead while she escorted her up to her room. Water from the towel dripped down Sophia's face into the tresses around her chin, but that was barely noticeable since she was transfixed on her next trial—to get well again as quickly as possible or perish.

After experiencing the word "sick" twist her insides, Sophia could feel her own bones being small and her arms being slender, and sloping down to easily breakable fingers. Her hair felt thin and damaged, her eyes tired of being open, and her legs felt weak and shaky. A fever made her skin pop up with goosebumps. Suddenly, fear of fainting overcame Sophia and she rested her head on the table.

"Ah, there see? This has excited your weak frame and now you must get to bed! Come on." Gertrude lifted Sophia up and put her arm over her shoulder as she helped her up the stairs to her room.

Her room which meant safety was now transforming into an inescapable chamber. Her room where the mirror was to expose her sick soul to herself. Sophia was wasting away now more than ever. She was not eating as much and her soul ached for Damian to come and rescue her in any way he cared to—whether it was to kill her immediately or later—it did not matter now. But this slow death was tortuous.

The slow death was like a court sentencing Sophia to life in prison without parole. She was wasting away in her mother's cell. The odd thing was she still had an attachment to her jailer. Sophia cuddled up to her mother as she tucked her into bed and gave her a head massage in the dark. She wanted her mother to soothe her for an infinite amount of time. In those dark, quiet moments of feeling ill, her mother was always there and no one else. Even Damian disappeared from view when her mother's fingers were working through her matted hair.

***

Wading in and out of consciousness, Sophia lay on her bed in her mother's arms, closing her eyes and trying to escape the aches in her bones and the headache forming in her skull. Trying to stay afloat in her bedroom seemed impossible at times. It was easier to close her eyes for good and wade into the cotton fabric of her bedsheets into an unpredictable tomorrow. There was a clock in the hallway that ticked aloud like the one at work. The ticking brought memories of Damian sitting beside her, touching her knee, in her cubicle.

But then the thought passed as her mother's fingers got tangled briefly in her hair. A strand became separated forever from its siblings and fell gently onto the highest cut carpet in the house from Sophia's head. The strand laid as supinely as Sophia did on her bed with the piece of white skin attached to where it first began its journey to the outside world. How short a hair's life can be, and how as randomly it may be plucked and forgotten!

The massage continued as if Gertrude was trying to leech out every negative thought Sophia had about her mother. Her mother was not so bad, thought Sophia; after all, she was sitting like this in the dark over her precious and only daughter, right? Who else would cook and clean for her? What right had she to curl up under these sheets she never bought or worked for? Gertrude's fingers moved more vigorously and mechanically as if her hands grasped Sophia's more forgiving thoughts—up, down, up, down went her fingers. They moved her scalp in ways that eased her headache and Sophia could only thank her for releasing the pain within her body.

Sophia felt and recognized a familiar pattern occurring. The feeling was like a massive wave of guilt, followed by jealousy, and then by hatred. Sophia began to feel this way whenever she had fought back against her mother and ended up becoming sick. Her mother did such a strange thing when she helped her sick daughter to bed and coddled her like an angel. All the horrible thoughts Sophia previously had when she felt stronger suddenly fled and she regretted her thoughts of killing her worthless, phony, wretched mother. But then the guilt became a need to have her mother and no one else. Even her father was to stay away from her when she was being cared for. Sophia wanted her mother's eyes on her and no one else when she was ill. It was heaven. Finally, the hatred came in all directions. Sophia hated the people who pulled her mother away from her. The feeling to kill her mother turned on anyone and everyone else, besides her. But once the wave of illness passed, Sophia began hating herself and her mother once again until the cycle repeated itself.

The cycle had been repeating itself since childhood. But now, Sophia could actually act on some of these feelings and not just throw a tantrum. In some ways, like her own age, Sophia felt the ability to rebel to be a freeing fact and in other ways, it terrified her more. She had to start making choices for herself as frightened as she may be. However, Sophia had to be careful or she might lash out on her family one day. Perhaps her mother never understood that the people she should learn to fear the most are the ones living under her very roof.

However, the thought of blood made Sophia shake with fear and revulsion so much that she knew she would never be strong enough to do such a thing. But could Damian? wondered Sophia. Could Damian do such a thing?

Her mother's fingers slowed down now and made little circular motions on her scalp. Gertrude's hands were getting tired. They slumped and became heavier like little pebbles hitting Sophia's head. She moved her head off her mother's lap and onto the soft pillows, indicating she was done with the head massage.

"Do you need anything else, honey? You seemed to have calmed down a bit now," Gertrude said.

Sophia turned her face away to the wall. She might betray herself in her thoughts which were too terrible to name aloud. She kept away from her mother's face.

"All right, well, you let me know if you need anything. I might check back in before I go to bed. There must be something on the television you can watch." Gertrude picked up the remote on the nightstand and clicked it on to some empty, mindless show about models. Sophia was sure that her mother deep down had always wanted to be one of those models since those were the ones in her romance novels to always get the most handsome of men.

Gertrude put the remote down after turning the volume up to its most annoying height and left the room with Sophia looking comatose and shriveled.

Sophia was at a bypass; if she did not fully commit herself to a specific plan of action soon, then she would die. It was as simple as that. The torture could only ensue so long before something in her normal behavior gives. Sophia was giving.

Her body was giving up in subtle ways. She had stopped eating as much, at night she curled up in the fetal position, and her menstruation stopped when she became skin and bone. Her mind was shutting off. Sophia laid in the bed rigid, while the television was blaring, for hours at a time unresponsively. She could only think: What was the point of living if it had to be like this every day?

There was no blossoming in a house that contained stagnant people. No amount of light in between home and work would help her to grow now. Only the rain may be able to help Sophia wash away the dirt and grime of her past experiences and presumptions about how to leave the dreadful situation behind.

The rain began with Damian and his dipped finger. The water from the pond felt like her only means of renewal. The simple act of claiming someone for their own made Sophia feel different from yesterday…stronger.

***

It was only about six o'clock at this time, still too early to go to bed. She got up and checked her email once more when she saw a new message on her laptop from Damian. He used her work address to give her his phone number. The message specified that it was urgent. Sophia messaged Damian using the number he gave her. The next words were, "look outside."

Her eyes grew large and she shot down to the floor. She did not want him to even be able to see her shadow in the window. Crawling on all fours, Sophia raised herself just enough to peek through the bottom of her window to see Damian outside waving. The moment was going too fast. There was no time to think. Quickly grabbing her phone, she messaged him that this was horrific and there was no way she could leave her house at this time. The sun would be going down in about an hour.

He replied with, "I promise to have you back in a couple of hours."

There was barely any time to think of what she could do to get out of this situation. Should she tell her mother or her father? she wondered. Did Damian feel the pain Sophia was in? Did he see how weak she looked from the upstairs window?

She recalled a moment in her childhood which was similar to this. Sophia was by her favorite fireplace where the nymphs were draping its opening. Their limbs never looked more fluid, almost lifelike. The white polish on the figures shined at certain angles where the lamplight hit. In their little beady eyes, there was laughter. They were all similar to Pan in their gleeful jamboree around the fireplace.

Closing her eyes, Sophia as a little girl heard the ring of them calling her to play, giggling all the while and tethering themselves to her fingers. One creature pulled on her pinky while another pulled her thumb, each attempting to bring her along. But for some reason Sophia resisted. She did not budge for fear on the other side of her body kept her from leaving her dining room to enter a new world. Sophia was never meant to be an explorer. She never had family members who went out in the sea adrift from all things familiar. This was her place to live in, suffer in, and perhaps even die in. There was no other land she knew and even at a young age, Sophia knew she would never leave it. Her mother was too much of a force in her life.

That little girl was never meant to grow up. She was never given the opportunity to develop her skills or abilities to progress. Her life was dictated to her from birth by the queen bee of the house who would forever make her a worker—a slave to the hive. Her mother once told her that she would always be her baby, and it was not stated in a sweet way, but rather in a prophetic way. Sophia remembered while the fireplace nymphs were pulling her away, her mother's eyes pulled her back to the home, back to her arms, back to her womb.

In a downward spiral, Sophia fell into visions of a monotonous cycle from which she could never leave. She saw each and every day as one of strenuous breakfasts where her mother woke everyone up with her rooster call and clanging dishes. She smelled burned pancakes which were held together by flour and soggy eggs. She saw her father dashing off to work each day imaging there was no home to come back to at night.

She envisioned her fireplace nymphs pulling her to lunches locked inside the school doors or the workplace doors which served as some place of solace from her mother's immediate watch. But the afternoon always resulted in her being back at home since it was the only place she was allowed to be after work ended. That time away from home was like having the bathroom to escape others, only to end up back in the mix of the office.

The endless afternoons blurred into repeated evenings of silent dinners: father was cowering behind a newspaper whose news he already knew, while mother was eyeing her daughter with suspicion about what exactly she did in the hours she was away. Finally, there was Sophia, staring down at another undesired meal in the evening's darkness. Bedtime was, perhaps, the only moment of reprieve from the brutal routine. In her bed, Sophia could hide away, shut out the cursed world, and forget her current woes.

It was the weekends that were slept away and which made the weekday seem so relentless. Sophia slept in until she could no longer fool herself into sleep. The only things she got out of bed for were food when it was not brought and the bathroom. Otherwise, she was under house arrest and the only way to cope was to play dead. The weekends were Sophia's hibernation time when she hid away from all. Her mental state became more depressed and lethargic with her limited movement on the weekends, but she was still alive. She was still alive and coping. The wheel of torture was still spinning, routine still churning, still rolling over Sophia's soul.

CHAPTER V

Sophia knew she was an adult, but her life felt like the kinds of stories where it begins fine and ends like one of her mother's plots—in rape and murder. She knew her desire for Damian was dangerous. She also had grown to love the kind of attention her mother gave her when she was ill, and to hate the difficulty it took to back away from remaining ill permanently.

Sophia was going to make Damian wait outside for her. She had to make her mother check again on her now if she was going to feel safe enough to leave the house for more than an hour.

Sophia groaned louder and coughed violently. After a few seconds, she heard her mother's heels clicking up the hallway to her room. Sickness seemed to be a cure to Gertrude, though, to what, Sophia was never really sure.

Lying down in her own bed, Sophia whimpered, "Mother..." Gertrude dropped down beside Sophia, "Yes, love?"

"I don't feel well at all," and Sophia gave a pained look to prove it for her mother.

"I know, I know. Tomorrow I'll make you some of my chicken broth, and if you don't have a fever, maybe I can add in some salted crackers too." Gertrude wiped the hair from off Sophia's forehead. She then rubbed her temples and gave her a head massage. Her hands were bowed enough to reach even the most hard-to-reach spots on her head. Her fingers dug deep as if they were violently forging new crevices in her brain.

"Your skin is so fair when you lay in bed. You're so beautiful when you're sick, my Sophie. So beautiful."

Sophia's eyes glanced at the mirror on her dresser and glimpsed her pale, washed-out face. Her dark hair exacerbated her deadly whiteness. Her blood-red lips looked like the only living part of her body. She leaned back further and further into the arms of her mother. Sophia asked herself: Would to die right now really be so terrible?

Having thought over the possibilities, Sophia knew she would rather die at the hands of this man than shrivel up without love in her life at the hands of her maker.

She slipped her dress on from earlier that day again, simply because it was the closest thing to her laying crumpled up on the floor. It still smelled of the office and dinner from that night.

Eventually, Sophia gave up thinking and headed out of her room with every bit of grace in her power to avoid making any loud sounds. As if made of air, Sophia descended the staircase, hoping her parents were at least occupied enough in their room not to step out of it for the rest of the evening. Their lights could not be seen under the door anymore, but the television could still be heard showing another documentary about the latest true crime mystery. Somehow, her mother had managed to fall asleep to this gore nearly every evening when she was not reading trashy romance novels.

It seemed safe enough to leave through the front door.

Sophia turned the knob, and with the skill of a robber, escaped from her own house without a sound. She signaled to Damian to get away from the front of the house and get onto the next block where, at least, they would not be visible to her mother's wandering eye.

Damian grabbed her wrist as they headed around the block and Sophia felt shaky, but nothing else could touch her after she chose to meet Damian. In a moment her actions would make a dent in the torture rack of routine Sophia was on, because she had chosen otherwise.

"Finally, Sophia. You made me think you had gone back to bed! Let's go," said Damian.

"Where are we going?"

"It's a place I'm sure you've never been to before," said Damian.

"Is it a social place or a quiet place?" Sophia was trying to figure out which one would be more deadly to her while awaiting his answer.

Damian took her wrists and pulled her toward him just to whisper in her ear, "It's heaven on earth, my dear."

Goosebumps raised on Sophia's skin. She told herself again she would rather throw herself onto his spear than her mother's.

Damian quickly took control back by taking Sophia's hand in his and leading her to his car. The only reason in hindsight she was able to get into his car was because she had no time to think—no time to worry.

They drove a couple of miles toward the downtown area near where they both worked. After driving through a rather narrow side street, he stopped at a building Sophia had never seen before. It was a squat building that did not seem like it

157

wanted to be noticed. It hid away from the main street and donned a plain, white facade. It looked like some kind of out-of-order boutique.

His car sat on a desolate street where only the lights seemed to count as a populace. Sophia found herself counting them and trying to squint just enough to make them resemble something living.

"Get out," Damian said.

He slammed the car door and pulled Sophia to her feet. She clung to his hands.

He seemed gruffer...colder. Sophia was afraid of him now. She tried to prepare herself for anything.

They walked over to an apartment that was squeezed in between two other units. It looked like a residential area, and Sophia was not sure whether this was a front or actually someone's home. She just looked up into Damian's eyes and leaned into him a bit before he opened up the unlocked door. Sophia's eyes went straight for the first thing that looked off about the small apartment. A single, red light illuminated the inside of the small entrance, and then she noticed the line of people. It was not a long line, but Damian and Sophia had to get behind about five or six people who were all lined up, painted by the red light that was hung above a woman who looked like she was giving out tickets.

She had curly, natty hair that sat on top of her head, tied back with a headband. Her lips were old and wrinkled. Yet, the woman had tried to cover them up with a dark red lipstick. Under the red light, the lipstick looked nearly black. The same trick was attempted with her black mascara, false eyelashes, and low-cut blouse. The blouse had long, witchy sleeves that moved with the force of each person walking by. The crepe material revealed not taut skin, but flabby folds of aged leather, and on her chest laid a large cross.

Each customer, if that is what they were, was scrutinized by this gatekeeper. She looked them up and down, snorted at some, and licked her lips at others. Sophia was mesmerized by this dark creature as she thought, what was this place?

The people in front kept going through a curtain which was past the red light above. Sophia could hear no sounds coming from beyond the entrance nor see anyone inside. She just had to trust Damian when he said it was "heaven on earth."

Damian could feel Sophia shaking, so he gripped her hand tighter as they approached the curious woman at the desk.

"Well, hello, Damian. Please come right in and I'll stamp your pass. Does the young lady have one? I've never seen her around here." She winked at Sophia.

Damian pulled out his pass along with what he said was a guest pass for her. The lady then asked for two identification cards. Sophia thought this must be some kind of bar as she took out her workplace photo identification.

"You're all set. Here. Just take off your shoes and things in the dressing room and then you can head on in. But, remember, no cameras or recording devices of any kind. You know the drill, Damian." The old woman sat back down in her seat in front of the shop, waiting for the next customer with a wistful expression on her face.

"Where are we?" asked Sophia.

"You'll see. But let me just tell you that you do not have to do anything tonight. I just want to expose you for now."

Sophia's heart lodged into her throat. What was he trying to say? she wondered. Would she have to perform here? If so, what kind of performance?

The dressing room was full of clothing items, snacks, water bottles, and other strange-looking things whose uses she did not know. Damian had taken his shoes off and was asking her to do the same. He then took off his shirt and Sophia felt like running out of there. But he said, "Don't worry, you can keep your clothes on."

There was only one door leading into the next part of the building and a sign hung next to it with what looked to be a riddle. It read:

I am an enemy of the old and lover of the youth.

The human body is full of lust, which is more beautiful and inspiring than any celestial body of the universe. Why cannot our minds match the splendor of our flesh, or match our full lips, moist and plump, after sucking on the sweetest of melons, or like the hair, long, thick and wavy that falls over Her curvaceous breasts, or His brilliant eyes that peer into one's soul and bitterly weep for the aged?

Youth is everything—it is the ripe pear before it soon bruises and withers away. I despise death, but I despise the decrepit more-so; for a failing body begins to lose its drive, the need for pleasure and what was once beautiful is now mocking itself. When a body grows old, only an ugly heap of skin remains, wrinkled like a yellow piece of parchment all over the decaying marrow of the soul.

I wish to never grow old. For this cruel, sick joke has made a Hedonist out of me. I am full of shame.

But at least I will never perish...

Damian shoved their items onto one of the racks together and took Sophia's hand again as they walked through the door.

They stepped inside, and it was all fat women, thin women, dressed men, undressed men in tight corsets, jeans, leather,

160

or nothing. One girl was being tied up and electrocuted. A man with a neon shirt reading "dungeon master" was touching her crotch with an electric stick. She squirmed underneath his touch and her body visibly melted. Soon the "dungeon master" placed a plastic bag over her head and proceeded to suffocate her. She started to panic as he ran his hands up and down the woman's body. Sophia watched both mesmerized and horrified at once. After the man let her breathe again, she fell to the ground a sobbing, sweaty mess. The master wrapped her up and soon her friend was by her side to help her. It seemed like she had gotten what she wanted based on the relaxation of all her muscles, and yet it looked like it was both a painful and pleasurable experience.

Damian whispered in Sophia's ear, "This is real BDSM. Have you ever heard that term?"

Sophia swallowed hard. "I may have heard of it, but I didn't realize it was this...this....violent."

Damian squeezed her hand as she kept taking in the rest of the room. A sign above the door read, "The Rood." It seemed to be Tudor-styled with its main common area. There were rings hanging from ceilings, straps locked into the floors, ladders made in the shape of an X, and locked cages. There was also a fireplace that took up at least a third of a room and a little doorway in the back that may have led to a basement. Moans and groans could be heard echoing throughout the building. The walls were draped in red and women graced the floors with legs wide open.

Sophia felt vulnerable and scared and she wanted to run away to think about this new world she just observed. Her gut reaction was mixed. The place was oddly fascinating, but it still frightened her.

161

This was not a normal sight at all. These people did not dance together, they did not lay each other down in bed, they did not caress or fondle. Instead, they beat, they tied and tightened, they strangled, they cut, they bruised, they shoved, and they bit. All of these savage moves made Sophia want to run out, but Damian held her tight and said, "This is art."

Art?! Sophia shook. How so? How could suspension be art? How could falling hot wax be art? How could suffocation be art? Sophia was mortified.

***

She had to tell her legs to move from where they had grown roots in the thinly carpeted floor. Her body moved forward slowly one foot, then another.

Another moan out of the abyss prompted Sophia to at least move closer to the man who brought her to this bizarre hell.

Damian stood there in complete confidence. He had obviously been here before.

"Come." Damian took Sophia's arm and led her to each instrument of torture to inspect the way each woman, in particular, was hung, chained, whipped, and beaten. He made a point to show how the men used their women, took the chains, and laid waste to everything they touched. In a moment of pride, Damian even slapped Sophia on the behind to keep her on her toes and moving forward, down the conveyor belt of pain.

With each daunting step, Sophia shrunk inside of herself to a place of safety and warmth. She imagined her covers and the sheets that folded around her body at night and not the sight of a man in front of her madly touching himself under the red lights of the room; the stranger's eyes were licking up and down Sophia's body and the closer she walked near him, the harder he worked to defile himself.

A new form of nausea worked its way up Sophia's digestive tract. She wanted to heave up everything she had just taken in from the place. Her innocent fireplace nymphs were stopped at the door. Nothing was allowed in this vicinity but human bodies—bodies that were, preferably, warm and ready for a most depraved evening.

Sophia had to sit down. She plopped herself on the only couch in the area, right in between a buxom, middle-aged woman and a couple that was probing each other's insides.

She managed to angle away from the couple and that prompted the woman on the couch to smile at her and ask, "New here?"

Sophia looked like she was going to burst into tears as she said, "Yes, very."

"Don't you worry, hon. We are all very friendly people once you get over the cultural shock." Her eyes glittered in the red light.

"Nice? All I see is fear and pain here."

"But we all desire either the fear or the pain or both! Besides, you forgot the best part—pleasure. You must be really new. Are you a virgin too?"

Sophia's eyes popped at the question. "Yes."

"Well, I'm sure that will be fixed tonight. And then all will become clear."

The buxom woman got up, laughing, when another woman offered her hand. She rose and all Sophia saw were two very naked, very meaty thighs. The thighs moved further back out into the mysteriously terrifying room. Only a woman with thighs like that could fend off the villains here, Sophia thought. The couch seemed lonely without her new friend nearby to protect her. Meanwhile, Sophia watched as Damian observed and helped with some of the proceedings in the room. Every so often he talked and laughed with people he seemed to know and glanced over at Sophia.

Damian appeared to be a frequenter of this hell. He seemed practically its spawn the way he went around graciously helping men improving their posture, beating stance, and women with their bows. He was a gatekeeper to a world utterly unknown to those who only awaken with the daylight. But when the light is shut out, Damian became the new guardian, the new God, the new sunlight in the dark. His light shown red and his voice combined to form a persuasive glow.

After an hour of Sophia sitting on the couch, absorbing the world like a newborn, Damian came to collect his property. Glaring down at Sophia, he looked so much more than a man. In this light, Damian looked untouchable. His hands and arms burst with newfound energy as if the cries and yelps of women gave him life. He seemed to desire his chosen one more than anything. But she could tell by his confidence that this was only the first night of many he planned to have with Sophia here.

She was malleable in his hands—as gooey a substance as the day she was born, even though the cord her mother bore was still there, slithering around her throat. But Damian was not interested in sharing his new play-toy with anyone else based on the way he held her neck, even if her mother did give birth to her. Then, Damian, with a small knife, grabbed Sophia and cut a sliver down her neck. She screamed and struggled, of course. But Damian seemed to know exactly what he was doing. There would be no scar, only a faint memory of the freedom she had gained and lost by crossing the line.

The knife soon went elsewhere, gliding over the mounds and crevices of her flesh. Sophia soon forgot what she was fighting for and all sense flew out from underneath her wobbly legs. Goosebumps prickled up her skin and exposed her even more to the knife's blade. Its glint was mesmerizing under the light of the room and it threatened and soothed all at once. Sophia wanted the snake-like blade to vanish so she could tend to her wounds, but Damian was in control of the situation and *not* her.

To not be in control was a familiar feeling to Sophia, one she really knew and could come to terms with even here. After all, it was either Gertrude or Damian—control in the hands of a siren or a sadist. Which was better? wondered Sophia. She made up her mind as she watched the knife threaten each goosebump that formed a head it could lop off with glee. The blood would trickle for a purpose tonight. It would run for a man who wanted to see her bleed and loved it. Damian desired her to love the pain he would bring her, the control that he would have over every bodily function, and the effort it took to make her scream at just the right pitch. He said this was art—*his* art.

***

Together, Sophia and Damian passed a woman who was being covered with heated glass jars. Her skin rose to fill the empty vacuum inside and turned purple. She looked diseased by the time the cups were peeled off her tender skin, but she writhed there in an ecstasy only she could understand. Sophia turned away from this spectacle to encounter another alien act. A man was dousing his lover in some kind of oil which made a line from the tip of her ankle to the small of her back.

She laid supinely on her breasts as he ignited her body with his own cigarette lighter. She lit up like a Christmas tree, and Sophia was waiting for a scream, but she just cackled with unadulterated joy. There were no burns on her skin when the oil evaporated. It must have been the very thrill of the fire feeding on her body which made her laugh. This woman seemed so astonishingly free.

Sophia felt distant from this woman of pleasure, but she wanted what was written on her face...ecstasy. A jealous wave came over Sophia at the sight of this woman and what she had just experienced. Sophia decided that one piece of clothing would come off and perhaps that would bring her closer to the same bliss everyone else around her seemed to be experiencing. So, off came her socks, the least offensive thing on her to remove. Her bare toes felt the cold, hard floor with its thin carpet. She flexed and stretched each toe, thoroughly enjoying the texture of the floor with her feet. Already, Sophia felt closer to the atmosphere of the room.

She smiled to herself and then looked at Damian who beamed at her slow, yet steady reaction to the whole situation. More carefully this time, Damian brought her to another corner of the room where a man with slicked-back hair, round-rimmed glasses, and a nineteenth-century tweed suit-jacket was suavely walking back and forth. He kept his dark eyes shifting from prey to prey. But it seemed like he refused to touch any of the naked women. Sophia imagined that he must have thought the proper gentleman will only take if he is given consent and consent for him meant being approached by the opposite gender first. But only a few men were like the one Sophia saw this evening. Her eyes took hold of the men in suits in the room and this man wore his especially well. His mug face, with dark wells for eyes, glared at his first victim. A little woman—petite, big-lipped, brunette, and blue-eyed—was on her knees wearing nothing but the black lingerie and heels her lover had given her. Menacingly raising his fist, he beat the little woman. She bruised nicely later, black-and-blue, in every place he touched. The beating continued on her thighs, bottom, chest, and breasts until her crying transformed into screams. Watching the two lovers was almost hysterical to Sophia at that moment because he appeared so heavily controlled, which made the woman look over-dramatic. Cold design trampled over the emotional wreck lying on the floor. This vulnerable woman's body was utterly destroyed under the fists which yielded so much force. One could almost hear the blood vessels exploding as the punches rained down on her body. Sophia shuddered.

Fear made Sophia want to put her socks back on, but, instead, she gulped and another piece of clothing came off. This time Sophia took off her underwear. Although the change was only noticeable to her as her skirt covered down to her knees, it was clear what path she was choosing to tread. Sophia was gaining confidence because Damian had convinced her at that moment to go back to their bags and take out handcuffs, rope, and a flog. He also told Sophia to strip down to her lingerie. On re-entering the club, Damian walked her around to show her off. Sophia was his property, his angel, his object, his territory, his lover, his companion, his escort, now on a collar and a leash. Sophia could feel that he was addicted to the power, the sex appeal, and the freedom the club gave him. It seemed so natural to Damian.

Suddenly, Damian said, "Let's go to the bedroom." This single room held three mattresses that were laying against one another.

Sophia was his woman, and he was her man. Sophia was submissive, and he was dominant. Sophia was a slave for him, and he was a leader for her. Her life became a document, her soul a book, all written down onto one big piece of art spread out on canvas.

They laid down together on the mattress right beside another couple having sex. But Damian only saw Sophia in that corner of the red room.

Damian said, "Call me, Sir."

"And what are your duties to me, Sir?" Sophia asked.

"I will love, care for, and discipline you."

"Thank you, Sir." She blushed and looked down again, but he caught her with his fingers under her chin once more.

They began slowly with Damian allowing the hands Sophia had craved since that day on the bus to wander around every part of her body. The healing wounds on his hands made him feel rougher. They felt the land they had conquered, but soon it became too much for both of them. Damian picked Sophia up and shoved her against the wall in the corner of that lovely, wonderful red room. He pressed himself against her hard until she felt suffocated by her already shallow, excited breath. Damian spun Sophia around to face a mirror that hung on the wall to watch herself being acted upon. He pulled her hair back and made her look. She was about to become a woman.

Sophia wanted Damian, and he wanted her. She gave him everything that night: her mind, her body, her soul because she knew he was the one man for her.

Damian bit Sophia's ear afterward as he growled, "I created you here."

"Yes, Sir." Sophia's real sexual awakening began here.

"I love you, baby," said Damian.

"I love you too, Sir."

Then, the lights went out.

***

Sophia lost consciousness for a moment. This had never happened before whenever the thought of her mother came to the forefront of her thoughts. But this time, the guilt was immense. What her mother thought suddenly came into full force and stomped the breath out of her chest. Envisioning her mother discovering where she was and at this time of night made Sophia want to vomit. She imagined her mother screaming: Are you mad? Do you want to get killed? You're in this degraded hotbed of sin? How dare you! You cannot be my child, my daughter! Is this how I raised you? To become a mischievous slut?! Well, is it?! She imagined her mother's poisonous face lashing out at Damian and scaring him away forever. She could imagine how red in the face her mother would get or how heavily she would breathe such that her tight trouser buttons would go flying in proportion to the depth of her breathing.

Black spots on a white screen made Sophia feel faint again as if her mother were jabbing her repeatedly in the eyes. Her mother must never know of this evening. She must never, ever find out about this place, what happened tonight, or anything going forward. The lines were drawn, and now Sophia's life was separate from her mother. A new leader was in charge and his name was Damian Voigt.

When Sophia lost consciousness, Damian had lain her gently down on the mattress and held her. She was only out for a few seconds, but the pain in her head was tremendous.

"Damian, am I dying?" Sophia said.

169

Damian gave Sophia his most furrowed brow and said, "Of course not. If anything, you just got overwhelmed. I've shown you a lot of things tonight."

Sophia wriggled up closer into his arms. "Damian, will you take me again?"

Damian hopped up on top of Sophia.

"Who's my baby?"

"I am, Sir," said Sophia.

"Who's my slave?"

"I am, Sir."

"Who's my property?"

"I am, Sir"

"That's right, I created you…I am your God."

"Yes, Sir."

"Good girl." Damian gave her a little kiss on the forehead before he slid his fingers into Sophia and she gasped. Her thighs were wet, and it felt frighteningly delicious. As she lifted her head up to kiss his soft cheek, he pulled her hair again and she fell down onto the bed. Gently tugging on her collar he asked, "What does this say?"

"Property of Damian Voigt, Sir."

"That's right," he said as he clenched his teeth.

"Who's my little animal?" He licked Sophia's cheeks, avoiding her needy lips.

"I am, Sir." Sophia squirmed around under his weight, moving her hips in a rhythmical motion.

He drove her crazy, and yet, Damian could so easily leave all this behind. Everything he had taught her, he very easily could put it behind him as if it never even happened.

"Who's perfect?" Damian asked.

"You are, Sir."

"And what are your duties to *me?*"

"To love, obey, and serve, Sir."

"Say it in a full sentence."

"I will love, obey, and serve you, Sir."

"Good girl."

"I am the only one who can see right through you—I am the only one who can touch you."

"Yes, Sir."

Do you like being my property?"

"Yes, Sir."

"Good."

To Sophia, Damian was, walking, living, and breathing perfection: her God, her love, her life. As soon as he stepped into Sophia's life, she had become fiercely attached to him. What a burden it was to be in love, Sophia thought. What a sick person one has to be to fall in love. She fell so deeply in love that being together until death seemed too short. Any time spent wasted to her felt like she was closer to death and losing him.

Sophia began to feel like a pressurized explosive device was set to go off soon. She thought that for the first time in her life she might lose something of value. The guilt began to mix together with the utter bitterness at having to eventually lose such a gain. She clung onto Damian's chest even tighter now.

"Turn over on your stomach," Damian growled.

Sophia turned immediately. Obeying was an easy task that Sophia had become expert in.

Damian pulled the belt off from around his waist. Pulling its two sides taut, Damian made his belt snap and jolted Sophia out of her obeying haze. She did not even have time to hide her face or brace for the immense wave of pain radiating from the small surface area of belt making contact with her bottom.

Mercilessly, Damian beat her over and over. She grew more confused with each thrash of the belt. How could someone do this to one they love? Sophia wondered. Maybe Damian does not love her? Maybe her mother was right, and he just wants a toy. Did Damian not know how much this belt hurt at that moment, how much his belt stung with each bite, or how much the spot burned before the nerves stopped reacting at all?

Sophia could feel droplets of sweat on her back from Damian's forehead. They were rolling toward the site of massacre down below. They cooled her back for a time while her mind reeled with questions.

Taking a break to catch his breath, Damian squeezed her cheeks between his hands and pulled her to him, sucking the rest of her life away from her with a kiss that ended with him throwing her face away from his hands. He was treating her like a leper.

Damian turned from her and began pacing, rubbing the sweat from the back of his neck. Like an animal in a cage, Damian became angrier. His blond hair fell over his face in thick pieces that were wet with his sweat. His chest heaved as if he could not get enough of the air in the room. His footsteps shook the floor beneath Sophia and reminded her that he was still there in the darkness—planning his subsequent move.

Sophia touched her bottom and pulled her fingers back up close to her face. They felt wet and she examined them in the dim red light. She was bleeding. Tears welled up and she cried at the trauma her body had experienced.

"You hit me," Sophia whispered.

"Yes, I did." Damian was still pacing and staring down at the floor.

"Why?"

"I have to separate you from her somehow."

"Who? Mother?"

Damian shot her a look of revulsion. "Yes, god, even the way you call her 'Mother' is disgusting. You're mine now. Got it?"

Sophia winced. "But…but I'm hurt, I'm bleeding…"

"I know. You need to be shocked. That's the only way to snap you out of yourself."

Her hand reached back down toward the newly-formed welts on her bottom, but Damian seized it before she could touch the wounds.

"Don't. Deal with it," he said.

Sophia could not understand what he wanted with his violence. She held her hands together with an expression of mercy in her eyes. "Please tell me why. Is this BDSM? Is this what your art means to you? Beating me?" she sniffled.

"It means I want you to myself. I'm your master, got it?! Not her. She doesn't own you anymore. If this is going to work between us, then you need to submit fully to me. I expect your body, mind, and soul. Part of my art is shaping you into my tool. I cannot use you the way I please until you let her go. Get rid of her. I'm exorcising you tonight. No more clinging fear to your mother is allowed when you're with me. I plan on beating your dependence on her out of you because I want you. Don't you understand?"

"No!" cried Sophia. "I can't leave her. I'm not strong enough. I'll never be able to escape the noose of her umbilical cord! But I love you, and I want you to save me. Damian, please care for me…" she crawled toward him on her knees, her backside aching with each movement of her legs. The skin pulled taut on her bottom and she cried louder than before. The couples on the other mattresses next to theirs left to give them space. "Take me back, Damian. She's always with me, weighing on my heart. I hate her, I really do. Yet, I can't leave you now. You know that." She bowed down as low as she could go—inhaling the carpet's filthy musk. "Do with me what you will."

Damian placed his shoed foot on Sophia's head and wrenched out his belt, while Sophia cowered below him.

Eventually, he grew tired of his tirade. He no longer cared to hear Sophia's cries. Damian grew limp with exhaustion and threaded his belt back through his pant loops at an agonizingly slow rate. Fingering each loop with his hands that had been damaged by retaliation, Damian seemed to be relishing his belt making its way close to him. He treated his belt as if it were another obedient pet.

Laying there on The Rood's mattress, face down, Sophia wept.

Rather than dwelling on the present moment, Sophia recalled when she was young, she wore her father's shirts to bed. The hem tickled her ankles and kept her safe. When night came, Sophia closed her eyelids gently with her cotton shirt riding up as she tossed and turned in her new big girl bed.

Now, Sophia's feet hung off this strange mattress as she lay in Damian's arms. She planned to wear his shirts to bed in the future—the hem would gently rub her thighs and keep her safe. She had imaged that when evenings came and the shirt rode up her stomach where Damian's hand laid it would cause Sophia to feel *whole*.

But now Sophia could only hope to return home. There she

could crawl away into a crevice of her mother's dark house like an insect, and only emerge again when all grew quiet. When Damian beat her she had tried to find the ecstasy of the other bodies in The Rood that had shown on their faces. But all Sophia could feel was pain and fear. She wanted to shout out for her mother to come and take her away from Damian, if only until he calmed down. Even prying through the window to her bedroom seemed a better solution than staying here trapped in his cold world. Damian would never run his fingers through her hair or give her hot tea when she was unwell. She thought that he would beat her whether she was healthy or sick. Perhaps, thought Sophia, this is exactly what I need...

Once she could start to feel her backside again, Sophia attempted to take the pieces from the night that were good enough to be representative of her lover. His caresses, his warmth, and his desire were pieces she had tried to glue together into a whole.

To be whole was a new experience for Sophia. She always knew she was missing something, but the exact reason and what it was were a mystery before tonight. Sophia was craving real affection—not the kind of affection that comes as a result of being ill. Sophia was missing a person in her life who desired her, and her alone. Damian, it seemed to her, is the missing piece. But with that knowledge, Sophia could never go back. She would never separate from Damian again on this earth—she could not.

While the threat of Damian leaving was swept into the background of her mind, Sophia remembered the days when she played in the mud, the days when her friend and Sophia felt the grass beneath their feet until they froze. On those days, she was willing to get dirty—she was allowed to let go. Now, those days are committed to Damian. Sophia orgasmed with him, and at that moment she felt dirty, primitive, child-like, and *free*. They were two sweating, heaving bodies experiencing the dirt.

CHAPTER VI

Sophia's gut twisted and she curled up into a little ball in her bed at home. Dreams of death flooded her mind as she lay on her back, feeling naked and vulnerable; she moved onto her side and curled up hoping to be unseen by all.

Thinking back to the days in childhood when her sickness had made Gertrude adore her, Sophia felt a deep desire to run back to her now.

She wanted to run back to the time when Gertrude slipped away from Sophia whose eyes were only open in dreams. Skipping down the stairs to the kitchen, she told her husband to continue his phone call more softly because their darling was sick, and she went about making Sophia some broth.

Gertrude told young Sophia broth was meant to embody her warming embrace, her tender words, and her loving work to make the ill well again. It meant these things to Gertrude, but to Sophia it meant even more. Whenever Sophia grew ill, she did not have to attend school, did not have homework, did not have chores, and while her mother was making the broth she had the time and the space to be free from all responsibility. There were no obligations even to exist.

Sophia spent the week in bed. Everything was done in

bed. Gertrude would not allow anything to be done without her help. She brought Sophia breakfast, lunch, dinner, and anything else she desired. All that Sophia could do was to prop herself up on a pillow and watch the television. Akin to a drunkard, Sophia's dark eyes glazed over in front of the television as she wasted away in bed. The broth lost its taste. The bed grew uncomfortable. The world lost much of its shine—her mother its last ray of light.

But thinking about herself now, Sophia was no longer a virgin, and it happened on this night. Sophia shut her eyes as if trying to hold the moment with her lids. She had had sex, and she came home alive. No one had raped, robbed, abducted, tortured, or killed her. In fact, the people there were all kind. But there was pain experienced in the club, not completely unbearable, but it was still pain and fear. The fear experienced at The Rood though was easier to tolerate than the fear of the unknown. This kind of fear happened suddenly and was controlled. Sophia could even let herself give the fear up by trusting Damian. She felt like releasing her fear and trusting him actually made him stronger. He took her fear and eliminated it by shocking her out of it.

This form of loving another was the first time when her anxiety began to dissipate significantly. She felt freer. She felt more like an adult. She felt the way she figured she was *supposed* to feel as a woman.

After tossing from side to side in bed, Sophia decided to get up and write her memories down in a journal. But then she envisioned the walls of her room coming down around her as she realized she was back in her mother's domain. Her mother was sure to read whatever lay around in her room. She could never, ever write tonight, or any other night, down if Damian was the subject. Sophia promised to commit the night down to her memory until Damian would finally take her away from her home.

The loop of these thoughts had gone on in her head for about an hour until they finally made Sophia fall asleep.

She dreamt she lived in an attic. This attic's atmosphere grabbed a hold of her clothes and left musky fingerprints. Every piece of oak depended on another to withstand the world's changing moods. Dormant corners slowly decayed in the dark, while slivers of light graced the four-paneled walls with every sunrise. A diamond-shaped window was the jewel of the room. It was made of stained-glass, contorting each pure ray of light that entered the attic. A quiet hum of crickets entered the serene room. The crickets' tiny legs pushed the dust from outside through the cracks in the room. This army of dust fell gently down onto her mahogany desk, planning to win by the sheer quantity of their numbers, fallen brothers, covering the surfaces of all things once.

The dream then morphed into thoughts of summer. She envisioned herself speaking to a stranger, saying:

"I don't know why I remember that sizzling summer. It was a summer full of sweat and just like any other, but I walked far more. I brought myself to muscle fatigue as I trudged further up the hill. A thin layer of hot wetness coated my back and made me stick to my book bag. My life was kept in my bag, and by that I mean, my books. As Sisyphus pushed his life uphill so too did I on summer days.'

"I don't know why I remember the Walnut Road apartments. Each one stood tall with their brick skins out in the open waiting to be weathered and deemed 'uninhabitable' by the buildings progeny. Someday, it would run down and the little stone-carved images framing the doorways would crumble. But I felt comforted knowing I will not be there to see it happen.'

"I don't know why I remember passing by a scene I knew I would never forget. On my way home to Walnut Road. I passed a man trying to open his afternoon beer. He kept hitting the cap against the elevated sidewalk ledge. A young woman walking in front of me was beginning to turn to pass him and enter into the complex, we both were stopped by the sound of a "pop" and a very delighted man. The woman laughed and said, "All right!" while the man cheerily sipped the suds from the lip of his bottle—leaving the cap on the ground. For the next few days, I remember walking past the bottle cap until my urge to pick it up became too strong. I held that cap in my hand before placing it in my pocket and never looked back again.'

"I don't know why I remember my roommate sleeping on the couch apart from her boyfriend. She told me she had 'commitment issues' and felt like she needed to have the ability to run away at any moment. Why? I don't know. But for several nights, I saw her wrapped in a thin blanket on a much-too-small couch, holding onto a pillow instead of the one who loved her. A tiny trickle of drool always graced the pillow and not her lover's chest. Yet, his door was always open. There were times when I desired to push her back through his door or even take her place. Who could deny the offer of constant affection and love? Yet, as the 'third wheel' in the relationship, I could do nothing. I could only watch and wait for some element of her character to change. It was only for one summer, on Walnut Road, where bottle caps and lovers were abandoned."

Then the dream became one about a mysterious man.

Sophia's body was not responding to his looks, for they were old and predictable. But his hands touched her…hands, calloused hands, that were not her own. His hand glided up from her hips to her breasts. They fondled and squeezed, caressing what they *owned*—her body. Pushing his body into hers he forced her muscles to unwind. Moistening her lips, she kissed his fleshy, soft cheek while feeling the grainy sand of unshaven hair on his face. The pounding rhythm of their bodies made her shake uncontrollably. She cried out—blood rushing from her senses to those parts which gave her such bliss. All the worries that filled her mind with fear fled as if a light had been cast down upon their heads. Discovered and uncovered, she gasped as the feeling overwhelmed her. She may faint. She eased her trembling limbs into her lover's arms, and a delicious warm buzz lulled her back to sleep…

***

Sophia's subsequent dream was about her college days when she had brief reprieves away from her mother. The only worthy remembrance Sophia had from the time were college students who smelled like coffee and cologne…and more often than not like cigarettes. The students dropped condoms and chewy bars that were scattered across The Rood's floors. Piles and piles of trash littered the floors, and Sophia walked around in it ankle-deep. She was searching through the trash to find Damian. He must have been somewhere underneath it all. Pushing aside a great swath of chewy bars and condoms, Sophia found Damian with another woman. This woman wore purple lingerie and false eyelashes, and she wore her hair down to show off her vitality. In a moment of searing pain, Sophia ripped the belt from Damian's pants and beat both of them to a bloody pulp. A splash of red now covered the chewy bars and condoms which would never look the same again to Sophia.

Forgetting his betrayal, Sophia imagined the base, raw power of Damian's kiss as he melted into her and engaged the untamed animal within her soul. Quickly, her brain deteriorated, while every muscle in her body cried aloud for freedom from the lustful longing. On fire, they both pressed into one another. The flames licked their faces clean. She missed him the moment he released her. "Say you love me," she said, "tell me you're all mine." What about him and his love for her? Sophia wondered. Does he know what love even is? She thought that she must know because the most natural feeling came from sleeping with him. Her head resting on his chest made Sophia feel safe. She always kept her legs at a ninety-degree angle under his, her arms wrapped delicately around his torso, and her head rested on his firm chest. Sophia dreamt of a sea of blankets weighed down on them—strapping them in for the night. The blankets made them feel warm and ready to drift off into the still night as if all was forgiven, but tainted condoms and chewy bars were still left by his bed.

***

Sophia's dream mutated into a scene where her entire body melted as Damian took her into his arms. Her legs and arms trembled and would not cease. She wanted him more than ever, but she supposed a million little kisses would have to suffice—kisses with the power to beg for more. "Please," they whisper, "please." Sophia experienced a total loss of feeling and a complete fall from grace. Her love of him had brought her to the edge of death and back. Sophia owed Damian her soul.

Sophia turned over in her bed and tried to imagine what an Eden would look like. She thought:

I am Eve. I love myself. I dance naked behind closed shades to Mother Nature in all her beauty and grace. I am walking perfection in my body, mind, and soul. My skin is plump and ripe—just right for picking. You chose me, I chose you. My Adam of divine creation is a whole of experiences and choices. I want you to teach me all you know. I cannot stop thinking about you. I tried to hold you and hope that time would stop. I wanted you to become a part of me in order to love me back, reciprocally—equally. I wanted to feel your skin fuse together with mine. I hate that I cannot wake up without thinking of you or fall asleep without thinking of you. I only feel whole now when I am with you. Is this dependency? I miss my own island, a place where fantasizing kept me awake enough to be productive. But now I'm broken...useless...obsessed. I hate it and love it all at once. You have reduced me to the most uncomfortable frame of mind. I am tangled in a desperate struggle within myself to keep living in a world of scholarly endeavors and a world of pleasurable delights. "Balance," you say, "everything in moderation," but I cannot allow myself to be cold anymore. You have cracked open my guard and now you must play a dangerous game with my vulnerable need for love.

I never want to leave your bed, but every morning I must. As with death, I fear loss, but I ignore it until the morning comes and steals you away. I loathe the sun for that reason. It breaks us with all the passions which were built up and released at night. They evaporate with the first rays of light that peek through your windows. They illuminate your face and tease me. You look so delicate, soft, and warm—so young, so innocent. But the sun wakes you, you hold me closer to your palpitating heart, you look upon my face and gently whisper, "You are beautiful" into my ear. Alas, sun, did you hear that? He is not yours, he is mine! Mine! He is *my* ray of warmth, *my* sun, *my* amour, the one who will follow me around until night comes and I can touch him again. His physical form will comfort me until the sun comes back to take his body from me. I am tortured by your presence because I always want more: more of your body, more of your love, more of your smile, more of your laughter, more of your warmth, more of your soul. I love you.

His body became transparent in her dreams. A mask enshrouded a stranger's face with Damian's own perfect mold. His warm, taut skin encapsulating the muscles underneath that stranger's body. My love, ripping out his own soft, blond hair to shield his shivering brother. My man, a being, deprived of his own skin, by my mind, and tagged onto another…just to keep him with me, always.

Sophia envisioned herself taking hold of Damian and weeping. She ripped the flesh from his bones, held herself to him, and then covered them back up with his flesh. She wanted to be as close as physically possible to her idol. She focused on images of her nails with blood underneath them. They had the look of ominous claws. The tearing was ceaseless, and it must have given Damian so much pain, yet not a sound was heard. Nothing stirred but her bloodied fingers and the will of her muscles to rip a man apart just to build him back up again.

Peeling and peeling on, Sophia could not stop herself because she felt such a hunger to be near him when she felt so terribly far from him this night. That evening her dreams made her admit to herself she could no longer sleep alone when someone who loved her dearly was out there in a world she wanted to explore with him as her guide. But the fear of losing Damian was enough to kill her now. Her allegiance was pledged. The knife had entranced her. All fighting was futile.

Sophia dreamed she looked down at her own hands that were once clean and asked herself if what she had done was worth it. Her thought was, "I'll do anything to keep him." Her devotion ran down into her fingers that ripped through Damian's skin and into his marrow. He must know the power he wields over her. He must have discovered it last night when they made love. The sex they shared would be their undoing. But she feared it would turn into real death if either one tried to break away. There is no mercy to those who love. Sophia believed true love was an impenetrable state which could only remain positive if the other accepted to stay. If Damian left, then love would turn into the most vengeful beast. True love could give life as well as take it. The venom from a rose's thorns was like love being misused. Sophia was determined to play either role of a rose.

***

Once the sun lit the room, Gertrude woke up in her half-empty bed again. Her husband had gone back to work. He came and went like a phantom. In fact, the only reason she knew he had come back home last night was that the lights were not on when she awoke.

Lying there in her bed, Gertrude recalled their first argument, back when her husband used to put up a fight. She remembered the way he tossed up his hands in frustration and begged for forgiveness all in the same gesture. There was nothing in his movement that made her more disgusted. He lived like a little bug, always scuttling to and fro from work, chomping on the scraps of food she made him. He was a small man.

Their first argument began when her husband was out late hanging around the office with his coworkers. Gertrude called his office twice with no response. He had missed dinner, and Gertrude was furious.

She locked her husband out of the house. She would only allow him in if he confessed his sins. The initial, preplanned words that crawled out of his mouth were: "I'm sorry I didn't call you back—I just thought it would make things worse."

"Well, you could have *at least* warned me you wouldn't be home until midnight. Do you realize how stupid I felt setting up the dinner table for us and then eating by myself?" Gertrude's cheeks sunk further down into her bones as she shook with anger.

"I know, and I'm sorry. I'm not feeling well...I was frustrated. I love you. Please, let me in? I haven't eaten since breakfast."

Gertrude was still fuming and was about to tell him to walk back to his office in the cold alone to sleep there. But her heart kept sinking the more she thought about tormenting him for not calling. She could not possibly be this weak. Gertrude unlocked the door and let him in.

But her husband was not there. Peering out around the corner, she found him sitting on the steps, waiting. He turned around, immediately stood up, and held her waist on bended knee.

"I'm sorry," he said.

Lightly tousling his hair, Gertrude's thorns disappeared. She bent down to kiss his head and turned to go heat up his cold dinner.

The first argument was the most romantic moment Gertrude had ever had with her husband. At that point, her heart had not grown apart from his own. She wanted to make him miserable, but only to a point. She wanted to wear him down but never break his fine, weak frame. She knew she was the power behind the household and its goings-on.

The woman in charge had to make sure the husband was bringing in the majority of the funds and that the daughter was, at least, doing her end of the chores. As for herself, she made it a duty to make the meals and take on the other chores around the house while the other two were away. This house was hers, after all. It embodied everything she wanted and was meant to be. With its perfectly round pillows and textured carpets, this house was made for the designer. It was made for the seamstress with its brilliantly sewn curtains and bedspreads. This house was created for the artist which adorned the watercolor paintings she had made over the years. The walls avowed the dreams that Gertrude had left behind once she realized a child was on the way from the bug she called her husband.

She often thought: How could this beady-eyed little man impregnate me? Me!—the most complex of creatures who could have done so many creative things with her life. I could have been a painter or a writer or a fashion designer or an architect. I could have done it all! But why and how did this man change my whole path?

The years Gertrude spent on this question stopped her from doing anything but working breathlessly all over the house. She felt that the only thing she could do now was paint the walls a different shade every month, rather than create another painting with her watercolors. Once her painting stopped,

Sophia had noticed her mother's consuming habits on the rise, like that her television set now shouted out about the latest atrocities in the world, and her pile of romantic novels from the library stacked up higher than ever. Gertrude's eyes were either attached to the television or to her books. Oftentimes, both lulled her to sleep alone in her bed.

Bedtime in her room entailed dimming the lights down, turning the television to a constant murmur—with only murder pricking up Gertrude's ears, and holding the latest steamy romance on her stomach as she laid down to read. Every night at ten o'clock her book laid open on her shallowly breathing chest as she slept. All night the television set shifted the lighting in the room from bright white to dark shades of varying hues.

Gertrude's husband came in at some time to turn everything off and crawled into bed as far away from his wife as possible. He always left the book floating there on her chest rather than risk waking the sleeping beast. Her breathing was always slow and death-like. Sometimes she woke up with nightmares, but these were rare and extreme when they happened. When Gertrude jolted out of sleep, her book always fell to the floor, and she ended up being more upset that she lost her page than that her dream was frightening. Besides, she always feigned the cold-shell look where nothing could actually scare her. Gertrude was invincible and wanted others to know it.

III

PART THREE

CHAPTER I

Hearing dishes clanking meant it was a new day for Sophia. She launched out of bed before realizing where she was. This was not Damian's domain; it was Gertrude's.

Gertrude lived as the Madonna of the house. She gave life, and she could also take it away. Her entire world was in that house, a house where all created order derived from one source.

Sophia remembered the many days of her childhood, especially when she turned twelve, when the mornings brought only despair for her, when she imagined what was going on outside of the doors of her home—which she no longer got to see while bedridden. Her state remained a mystery to her until her mother chose to reveal its limitations. The length of her time in bed remained under the guise of "let the illness just take its natural course" and the hours of the day seemed to her to dissolve into sunlight and darkness. Sophia could barely understand where she was awake or where she was asleep—the only difference was that one felt like a quieter space, one where her mother could not reach her. That was what darkness began to mean to Sophia.

Today, her energy immediately diminished after recognizing that fact and she got dressed without haste. Then, she wondered:

What have I done? I can no longer sleep alone in peace. My mind cannot leave you and your sweet name by the wayside. All my thoughts encompass you from the time I wake up to the time I fall asleep. What is this? Love? I cannot stop thinking about you. It's torturous; love is torturous. Call it being "irrational," but I depend on you now to make me feel whole. Where is your soul? Let me find it, please.

Damian would be impossible to keep from her mother for long. He was making Sophia appear too giddy around her parents. She started smiling, which made her mother suspicious. She had to hide all emotion in front of her mother to avoid her finding out about Damian. Otherwise, she would be cut off from him indefinitely.

Now Sophia's days began with feeling like she was suffocating and like she was only allowed to breathe by the evening when she was planning to be with Damian. The valve in her throat was tightened at breakfast with her parents. The tension built up, the pains grew more intense, and her mind uselessly obsessed throughout the day with strenuous stress that could topple, stress that could tame, and stress that overwhelmed the senses.

A sense of being constantly overwhelmed haunted her when she walked down the long hallway to work. Every cubicle was draped with artificially-colored walls with "freshly-made" what-have-yous. Florescent lights made the faces of her coworkers hard with shadows and old age. She wheeled around with her nose shoved into a pile of papers. Her heart was picking up speed now as she attempted to place imaginary blinders on her face and seek out only the things she absolutely needed to complete her job: last week's signed report, tomorrow's unsigned letter, and today's voided document. She would much rather work by herself.

Sophia imagined a day in her future life, having arrived home overwhelmed by the monotony of everyday life, as she lay all of the groceries down. Her love would be home in an hour and dinner must be ready by then.

She imagined that her stomach churned as she opened a book on her dresser. Flipping mindlessly through the pages, she came across a note and pressed flower. The note was from her love and it said: "Relax."

The valve in her throat was released for the day, she decompressed, the stress vanished and she was left with a warm sensation. She was reminded of all the comforts Damian brought to her life. She went through all the dull processes that made up a day, just to live for those dreams where she lay in his arms.

Shaking her head, Sophia kept imagining what every day would be like living with Damian rather than her family. The days seemed brighter just thinking about it. But then Gertrude shouted upstairs, "What is taking you so long?! Come down for breakfast and stop dillydallying!"

Her screeching startled Sophia who jumped up and ran downstairs to the kitchen. Breakfast was laid out—some cold eggs drenched in day-old butter.

Sophia looked outside the window, which allowed only the smallest rays of light into the kitchen. There were shadows growing the further away from the window one got. The corner of the stove was dark, the doorway into the kitchen was hardly lit, and the cabinets on the opposite wall were swallowed up by the shadows.

Although it was autumn now, Sophia contemplated spring. That season, in particular, always coaxes her into a dance with its breathy winds, its green grounds, and its blossoming flowers. The sky is blue and lets the sun heat the coming day. But within a few minutes, clouds form overhead while the soft winds become blustering eddies. The rain comes in torrents, crushing corn stalks under its tremendous weight. The fat, pink worms crawl out onto the sidewalks and try to slither to the other side. They make mankind self-conscious about his weight because he steps on their little bodies. Sophia thought humans are such heavy creatures, and yet the wind can rip the umbrella from our hands. Seasons have the most weight, strength, and power. The moods of Nature, Her seasons, change chaotically in a dance of their own. These moods play out on earth and all of the organisms on it are swept up in its wildness. But spring can be cruel because it rips away all warmth from life.

Sophia finished up her breakfast thinking about spring. She figured spring washed away all dirt and mess created by winter. Winter forces most things to hide and wither, while spring cleaned up after it.

Meanwhile, she watched Gertrude walking rapidly ahead of her husband while his ailing feet could not catch up. She left him for dead. Sophia saw in her body language that she did not love him anymore.

Her poor father never got any love from the cold woman that he married. She kept the house running, but what was she doing it for? Sophia pondered. It was clearly not for her family's benefit. Gertrude worked chaotically. In fits of rage, she wrangled the dishes and mop as if to show her family she was the constant victim of some kind of abuse.

She felt abused by her husband who was never home, and she felt abused by her daughter who worked and supported herself with her salary. Meanwhile she, poor and miserable, Gertrude was trapped in the house all day to work on something no one recognized. She demanded recognition for all that she did—relying on self-care methods to reward herself. But no one told her that she could not go out and get a job for herself. No one was chaining her to the bed or the kitchen to work as an unpaid slave. She alone perceived her bondage and despised anything and everything that touched the premises of her domain.

***

At today's meal, Sophia could not help but smile foolishly down at her soppy eggs. She noticed her thighs pressed tightly closed in delight. Everything felt delicious down there. She was budding into a real woman now. Aware of her body in so many new ways, Sophia felt more powerful than ever, and she wondered if her mother experienced such love.

A radiating sensation traveled from her groin to her stomach up to her breasts only to travel back down again. It reminded her of the fulfilling orgasm she had last night for what felt like days. In fact, sitting there at the kitchen table with her parents made that night seem like ages ago, or that it simply had not happened at all. But Sophia knew this heightened awareness of herself could have come only from the actions of last night.

Adventure now abounded in her life. A powerful fear still kept intruding at odd times of the day, but so far Sophia was able to beat it back. After all, the only important thing in her life now was Damian. She lived to serve him. It was imperative she make it to work to see him today. She noticed already the impact his presence had on her.

She longed for him, and once he was near to her, she latched herself onto his arm, like she had done last night when she held onto him walking through The Rood. She felt safe looking over his shoulder at what the other lovers were doing. He remained her rock, the only one she had wanted to be with that night.

She mimicked his expressions and colloquialisms. This morning her mother's scolding made her smirk like Damian had in the face of something she had feared. She gave a face that told her mother that she was unafraid and even that her scolding was now more amusing than frightening. It gave Sophia strength.

When Damian gesticulated while talking, so too did Sophia. In The Rood, Sophia moved her hands like Damian had as he had caressed her body. He had told her that he wanted to be caressed too. He said: "Touch me softy before you bite." She obeyed.

When Damian discussed business, so too did Sophia. Yesterday, in the office, Sophia had only spoken about papers that had needed to be signed. She had handed a pile to Damian who then gave his thanks and asked about how his filings were going. Business was then the only topic in the office between them once he knew he had her.

When Damian bent forward to kiss, so too did Sophia. Sophia responded to his kisses on the mattress at The Rood. She bent her head forward to meet his lips, and sometimes he had coyly pulled away before she could reach him. Their games made her giddy.

However, the games subsided later because Damian had told her at some point among the chaos of last night's adventures that many cultures did not believe in death.

He said, "Death for many is just a long sleep from which a person may eventually rise again."

Sophia could not digest such a notion, although it did make her feel like she could hold onto Damian for a much longer time than she thought. His death was impossible to fathom. Sophia was not ready, and would never be ready, to separate from her lover. It became clear last night that every time he touched her with those perfect hands, it would feel like the first time. She felt a warmth to which her straining fingers gripped onto and refused to budge. Here, where so much could go wrong, Sophia was determined to utterly dissolve every relation she had to this world just to hold and cherish him—no matter how he treated her. She wanted to breathe in his air, and hope that maybe one day they could become one, single entity. Or if they could not, then she would never allow death to separate one another on earth.

Paradise on earth was only possible in his arms. When he gripped her firmly at the venue last night, Sophia felt grounded. She was placed by Damian back down on this hallowed ground to be consecrated with the dirt and the water that flowed from his hand to her forehead. He was the man of influence—another Satan who knew too much about love and was banished by the wholesome, clean women. Women would not touch him, for they knew deep down that he was mischief. But Sophia would gladly be touched by someone more powerful than herself. She oozed and bled for such a man to take her.

Last night Sophia quaked in fear at his revealing of himself. But today, with the morning light poorly entering the kitchen of her family home, Sophia felt a thrill. Her mind tingled with pleasure at the experience she just had. She was sure that no one in the room had ever had a similar experience. Her mother would be furious if she only knew and her father would only look baffled at his sweet daughter's risky behavior.

To hold this secret experience over her mother's head was the first taste of control Sophia had ever had. It was delicious. If Damian was near right now, Sophia imagined this as being the appropriate time to lick his chest and bow down at his feet in front of her parents. She envisioned doing this right in front of her mother with her backside sticking as high as it could go up in the air at her. It was the ultimate plan of rebellion. Even at the age of a young adult, Sophia thought she brought this childish behavior up to the standard of an adult. Damian could take on the task of staring right back at her mother with knowing eyes that he was in charge of her now—not Gertrude.

This was *freedom* for Sophia. She would be taken away by her knight and take her revenge beside him. No one could harm her now. Her virginity was lost along with her need to be attached to Mother.

Still...a tiny voice in the back of her mind made even her strongest thoughts waver. Uncertainty was back there somewhere and she found herself plotting against her escape from the trenches. But Sophia dug in deeper, shifting her weight on her chair at the kitchen table as she stared back at her eggs.

Lifting up her fork, Sophia pinioned her egg to the plate and imaged her mother being strung up against the wall by knives—dozens of knives like the one Damian skirted up and down her body last night. The eggs could not move away from her fork, nor could her mother. Sophia was in charge, and would only let go when she chose to eat up her meal. The eggs were torn apart and lifted up swiftly to her mouth. The thought of being a giant and mashing bones between her teeth was a bit too much for Sophia to handle, so she left the eggs alone as if her mother was hanging by her clothes against the wall until she shriveled up like a grape. That was easier to imagine. Her mother would beg for Sophia to let her down, but she would refuse every time.

***

"Eat faster, or you'll be late for work," Gertrude nagged.

Sophia stabbed her eggs more viciously this time.

"Don't scratch my plates."

Sophia knew what her mother was: she was a manipulator, a heartless woman who did not know what love was. Sophia almost felt sorry for her; she would never know what true loss would be either.

Putting her fork down, she pushed a bobby pin into her hair making sure the frail wisps were firmly pulled back. She noticed every unplucked hair on her stomach, chin, arms, and legs. Her body was a well-kept garden that without order would grow chaotic. That chaos approached with a new fervor. But Sophia cut down the great stalks before they grew too long with her black straws withering from their severed stems, collapsing into a bed of fallen sisters, never to rise again. She had complete control over these meddling weeds and to end their tyrannous reign was her immediate goal.

Yet, more-and-more her heart quickened at the longing for truth. Sophia desired an answer and each path to truth seemed to taunt her searching mind as one idea after another she felt like she was closer to an answer. She had a desire to understand her mother with a longing twice as violent as in her childhood. For she was utterly consumed by the search

199

for truth. Her behavior was controlled by her need to know as well as her consciousness. She awoke with the need and fell asleep with it too. Her very being was teeming with questions about her mother that no one else noticed.

But Sophia wanted to understand *why* her mother was so concerned about her dishes and not about her own daughter. Why did she fully throw herself into washing the dishes and not in her husband's happiness? Sophia wondered. There must be some reason for her lack of feeling toward her own kin. But this concern about her mother could only arise when she was at enough of a distance from her mother to be able to observe her. When Sophia was no longer stuck in bed and under her mother's power, she could see her mother as she was.

"Hurry up already. Look, your father is nearly finished, and here you are with one whole egg left! I mean what do I have to do, force-feed you?" asked Gertrude.

She had always been a nagger, but today was especially annoying.

"I am eating as fast as I can, Mother." Sophia looked up from her plate and glared at her mother.

"Well, hurry up! I've got dishes to wash. I don't just sit around here all day twiddling my thumbs!"

Sophia felt like she was having her back broken in half with a cane. Her mother's voice was, unsurprisingly, the cane. Inflicting pain on the closest members of the family was Gertrude's true pastime. Sophia thought that her mother must have thoroughly enjoyed harming those she was supposed to love by seeing them sweat and bleed and suffer.

"Mother, I am eating at the rate I want to. If you push me, I'll just eat slower." Sophia put her fork down at that moment to emphasize the threat.

Exasperated enough Gertrude rolled her eyes and grabbed the arts section of the newspaper her husband was hiding behind.

"I have an ungrateful child. How? Lord knows..." Gertrude snapped open the newspaper, ready to completely ignore her daughter's existence, but Sophia felt the draw to break the cycle of being ignored.

She spoke up.

"You know, I'm still here, right?" Gertrude's face shot up over the paper. "Yes, and...?"

"Well, I'm not something that can just be ignored, and then I'll leave the house every morning and forget how you treat me," said Sophia.

"How I *treat* you? How about how you treat me every day? I wake up in the morning basically alone, I get up to get the place warmed up, and get breakfast ready. Yet, here you are taking your sweet time with the eggs I made for you, and complaining on top of it! You're a young woman now, but you still act like a heartless child, Sophia. I mean really. I work tirelessly for the both of you, with nothing in return." Gertrude had left her paper halfway up to act as a simple barrier between Sophia and herself. It kept down the level of hatred being spewed with the paper taking some of her venom.

Sophia swallowed hard. This would be the first time she would continue to talk to her mother in a moment of heated confrontation. But she was determined to feel out her freedom.

She said, "Thank you for all that you do, but you're crushing me with it. I can hardly bear it anymore. I feel like I'm suffocating here in this house with always having to feel grateful toward you."

"Well, having an abundance of gratitude in life won't kill you. You should be grateful. I made you and raised you basically alone." Gertrude shot an irritated glance at her husband, who sunk visibly lower in his chair.

"But I am so sick of still being treated like a child."

"Then stop acting like a child."

This quip stung most of all because Sophia thought that this kind of discussion and persistence was the most courageous thing she could do. Being told that sticking up for yourself is childish was not something Sophia could handle at the moment. Her mother had diminished her will to continue the conversation.

Nothing came out of Sophia's mouth now—only a long, painful silence. Meanwhile, Gertrude had lifted up her newspaper again, smiling into the pages and contenting herself with the knowledge that, once again, she was right. Her daughter was still an ignorant child who required the guidance of a knowledgeable, wise parent. She was the real leader of the house, after all. Her daughter would never understand until her age and experience caught up with her mouth.

***

A quietude formed in Sophia's mind as she absorbed the vitriol her mother spat in her face. For the first time, there was a bubble that formed where only Sophia's thoughts could linger; she thought of her mother apart from her, as another adult, as a woman. She thought: How could a human being fall so far into a well of bitterness, just sitting on the bottom and letting the water come up over her head?

Her mother held deep lines from all the frowning she did throughout her life. There were no lines of laughter. She was utterly unhappy, sitting there with her red knuckles clutching at the edges of a newspaper she did not even care to read. Her fingers donned callouses she formed while sewing and the backs of her hands were dry and cracked from constantly washing dishes with harsh soaps.

"Mother..." Sophia could not make her voice louder than an unsure squeak.

"What?" Gertrude lowered the right corner of her paper just to glance over at Sophia.

"What do you want out of life?"

Gertrude's furrowing lines worked dramatically on her face as she tried to comprehend what exactly her daughter was asking.

"Are you feeling well, honey?"

"Yes, I'm feeling fine. I'm serious, what do you want? Money? Fame? Comfort? What?"

"I think you might want to stay home and get some rest. You seem tired."

"I'm not tired! I'm trying to ask a question. I'm just curious. Have you ever wanted something, *anything*?"

"Well, of course. I wanted your father and you, and we have this expensive house now too. What more could I want?"

Sophia looked down at the table, disappointed that she seemed further from the truth than earlier.

"You could want to teach sewing to other people or spend your time preparing interesting meals."

"You think I really have the time to do all that? I don't and I won't ever have the time with you two still needing me, especially you, missy. Now, please, just finish your eggs."

"You don't have to take care of me anymore though. I'm not five years old."

"Excuse me, but do you remember how you were feeling yesterday night? Terrible, right? I thought I'd have to carry you to the hospital myself at one point. You *need* me."

Gertrude gave her pleading eyes that also held a hint of pain in them. Sophia did not want to press further, but it was so hard to get the real answer from her mother. Although it was true she soaked up anything and everything her mother could give her when she felt ill, now she wanted her mother as far away as possible. Damian was meant to be her champion caregiver now.

"Yes, mother, I need you. But that doesn't mean you can't go out and do what you want in your own life."

"Ha! Right, like I could go out there and leave this place to rot without me," said Gertrude. "No, no I am a part of this house and a part of our family unit. I am not going to abandon this family for my whims. I've spent too much time here. The world is all right without me in it."

"What does that mean? You only need to take care of yourself, not the world. You don't seem to want to do anything that will make yourself happy."

"Since when did breakfast at our table become the time for interrogation? Lordy! I'm fine just as I am, and I don't need my daughter telling me what I should be doing with my life. I made my choices, okay?"

The newspaper barrier snapped up again, and meanwhile, Sophia's father had slipped out the door on his way to work. He did not want to be dragged into the middle of this family feud. According to Sophia, he must have assumed they could probably both figure it out without killing each other.

Sophia had lost the quietude in her head as her subsequent words destroyed the space for silence. The words "should" and "choices" and "life" spun around and around in endless sequences in an echo around Sophia. Sophia's quest for knowledge fell to the floor after hitting a wall, which embodied her mother's soul. It was a high wall and one which bore many cracks, but Sophia's petty attempts were too meager to do damage to the facade. Gertrude had held firm and closed off all communication as soon as Sophia felt a new crack forming in the wall, just like a house centipede who has found a new home in an undesired location. Sophia scuttled along with all the speed she could muster to get those questions answered honestly, but to no avail.

The day was won by an unhappy woman who had stood by her own unhappiness.

Sophia could not fathom falling so deep in the well of despair. Her whole life was ahead of her, and now Damian had entered it to make it even better. She promised herself at the table that morning to never become her mother.

The newspaper crinkled enough to make Sophia look up from her now-empty plate and grab the mug in front of her.

Gertrude's eyes flared as she laid them on her mug being taken into her daughter's hands. Sophia could now see clearly that she was the object of hatred in her mother's eyes. Gertrude's mind rattled with: "That's mine!" She watched her daughter ignore the lid that slid open with the lipstick stain left on the side, which indicated it was her mug—tiny drops of coffee ran down onto the table.

A feeling of disgust forced Gertrude to leave the scene before she snatched her coffee mug back and spit in it. Upon Sophia exiting the kitchen, Gertrude headed back toward her mug. She lifted it to her lips and let the hot coffee run down her throat, allowing it to warm her breast that contained her beating heart.

CHAPTER II

The morning was filled with rush-hour traffic and early-bird wake hours. Sophia noticed that the men of downtown wore black and fitted suits, the women wore pastel blouses and pencil skirts. Their marksmanship when lunging through the correct bus doors was expertly done. The smell of gas from the buses seeped into everyone's clothing. The echoing voice of the driver who counted each call as one less from the whole. Twenty more calls until the end of the day, the driver thought. Everyone exhaled on Friday morning—the weekend was nearly upon us. The seat imprints were fading—losing all color and shape. Just as everyone changed with each passing work week. The professionals all had more wrinkles, more gray hair, more pain, less rest….all so they could run their homes in comfort. The professionals worked so that the streets could be cleaned, the post got delivered, the pencils were made, and the jewelry was sold. Everyone loved the commute amongst such energy and buzz in the city, but so many hated their jobs. The commute was full of fresh dew and morning sun. The job was often windowless, time-consuming, and energy-wasting. But for those few professionals, the day was spent always on the commute.

Sophia looked forward to her work, though. She would meet Damian at the main doors to the office because she knew that neither of them could wait to see the other. She began to feel like she was living a double-life.

She kept thinking about how Damian was becoming an addiction. Thinking about his very name gave her a tremor to the bone. She felt dependent on Damian because she knew that the end of the workday meant a departure. Whether that end came in the solemn evening or the dreary morning, they would have to separate. She would have to return eventually to her mother's lair, and Damian would return to his own home. Her lover was allowed to freely walk and talk to whom he so chose, but the half that was stuck on him was never satisfied. She wondered: How ghastly is free will in that of her beloved?

Sophia wanted to latch on like a parasite and never let go. She wanted to be united to him all of his life. No task could ward her off his track. Only Damian's eyes had an appeal to her.

Where did the spark go from other people's eyes? Sophia wondered. Where did it flee to? What constellation does it dwell in now, quivering in fear from the horror that mankind has relished in for so long? Where did that spark go? Where did the dreams go?

Sophia could tell immediately whether someone had a passion for life or not. Those men were very few and spread thin across the earth. But when two sparks make contact they ignite, and so Sophia looked upon humanity as she had never seen it before. Her world became a vibrant whirl of traits—mostly ones that encompassed ambition, drive, and stubbornness. Sophia was the queen of all of those characteristics, and she wore them rather well...but whoever becomes hypnotized by them must beware of the burning light. Sometimes, it may extinguish the smoldering ember.

Damian was an ember and Sophia held the fire. She wanted to consume him. Sophia wondered: If he was not a killer, then was she? Sophia felt nauseous at the thought of her being the predator rather than the victim. Perhaps, this was a sign she was not strong enough to be one anyway.

The bus kept lurching forward, stopping, and then lurching forward again. Its usual crowd of people packed themselves onto the bus. A homeless woman was bundled up in one seat and her trash bag of items was loaded onto the seat next to her. People passed by with loathing in their eyes, attempting to stare down this perpetrator who was taking up a full seat with her garbage.

The men gave glances with their stern eyebrows, but the women did it with their pursed lips. All noticed the taboo, but no one spoke up. The homeless woman continued to sleep there without noticing the upset passengers. After all, what did she care? They had homes.

Bags on strangers' backs kept hitting Sophia in the face and she had to look after herself. If only she could carry a helmet or some sort of hard stick to poke away her bag hitters. The bag carriers were especially deadly when the bus suddenly halted at a stoplight, causing the mass of people standing to fall forward and grasp anything that could keep them upright, including the seats, hair, other bags, poles, handrails, jewelry, shoulders, and hands.

In those moments of emergency, Sophia crouched down behind her bag. She would rather someone fell or grabbed her bag than her face, and it seemed that the further back on the bus you were, the harsher the sudden stop felt. On more than one occasion, of those dangerous bus rides, a tire blew and the bus driver hopped off to make a phone call somewhere while the rest of the bus riders remained clueless as to what happened.

Everyone ended up looking at each other in confusion while some people kept manically checking their watches, looking back and forth, and deciding they did not have time to wait. They subsequently became the first to hop off the broken bus. Those early leavers signaled to the rest of the commuters that something was wrong, and after a few more minutes it seemed like everyone had to get off at once. Pushing and shoving became acceptable for those few minutes of chaos where everyone decided en masse to leave. They all felt like the bus had betrayed them. The way to work often was doubled for everyone regarding time and all of them knew that no amount of grumbling and swearing got them there any faster than their own two legs. However, that still did not prevent the swearing coming from under everyone's breath which had become louder and more pronounced on the bustling rush-hour streets. This was just a regular day in the city. It was ever-present chaos that had become a part of Sophia's routine.

**

The city moved speedily along as if without a hitch. Tanned tights in high heels strutted through one yellow crosswalk light after the next, just making it before red. Belted up trousers walked determinedly in tapered shoes that were buffed and shined. Traffic lights in this environment were recommendations which only the old and foolish abided. Moving along the paths that dictated their lives, these were the professionals of downtown life—the backbone that elegantly walked the same paths with the most efficient moves. No time was wasted, at least, not until the work began to commence.

When work did start the water cooler became the designated area for most of the employees to stand around and chat as they forgot their purposeful race to the job. Their racing was only to get out of the elements and not to get started on work early. It rained often in the city and the sign of water falling from the sky was no longer an exciting prospect. The adults bolted for shelter. The streets were full of people adversely reacting to the weather. It was no wonder that the weather was such a common subject to discuss when the workday began.

Sophia was among these souls on the streets of the city—only today she was lost. The bus had failed to get her to her destination, and she wanted to cry. A welling feeling filled her, tears brimmed in her eyes, but on the cusp of falling Sophia breathed. She was not a victim here in this world. Besides, the city made everyone anonymous, and the more average the behavior was, the more anonymous a person became. As long as she did not cry, then no one would notice her sorry attempt to figure out which direction to walk to get to her office.

Placing her right foot in front of her left, she chose a plausible direction based on the street signs. She knew her office was too close to justify looking at her phone to see exactly where she was in relation to her office. It was more embarrassing to be seen aimless in this busy city than to seem purposefully busy walking toward a destination. The only option was to walk straight and turn around if the sites were completely unknown to her.

Sophia found her thoughts focusing on the good things. She tried to feel gratitude for the building that could shelter her and the idea warmed up her body in this chilly city atmosphere. She thought:

We are such passionate creatures…

I am the baby. I have yet to begin my journey. I have struggled to make myself the best person that I can be. But I cannot live among people who do not care about what they are watching, absorbing, or feeding on—I cannot sit by while my heart strikes like madly wild bells within my body. But hope gives people the chance to take advantage of the life they have and feel both the greatest sorrows and the greatest joys imaginable.

We cannot hide behind our fears forever…

I always thought the sickening stomach I got when I looked at the people on the bus made me abnormal. No one else looked as distressed—until I thought that those people must be missing a Damian in their lives—a newfound need and desire. They were missing the air to breathe that would leave their eyes swimming with laughter.

Today, Sophia had wanted to shake awake everyone on that bus. She felt like running up to the man in front of her on the sidewalk and laughing joyously in his face. The rush of freedom was overwhelming. Her life could start over right here and now in the downtown city streets, where the drivers that passed forgot her existence within seconds. The anonymity kept her feeling safe in the morning streets. But she knew her every movement was being imagined by Damian. To him and his thoughts, Sophia was naked—to everyone else she was clothed in anonymity.

There was nothing out of the ordinary to the unseeing eye, but Sophia knew. She knew that the seasons would forever look different in her life now. With Damian in the world, her general outlook toward life expanded. Her blossoming was occurring right on her way to work, and no one important to Sophia was even there to witness it. But there she was turning into a blossoming flower stretching out toward the sun.

Sophia felt gratitude as she walked forward. The buildings were starting to look utterly unfamiliar to her, so she pivoted on her left foot and headed back to where her bus had stopped earlier. This now would become another reason as to why she would leave for work early.

Along the way back, Sophia overheard a woman come up behind her and slowly pass her on the sidewalk with her phone pressed deeply into the side of her skull. She dropped down on a sidewalk bench up ahead of Sophia where her head dropped down and she began crying.

Sophia thought it an unfortunate thing to witness a breakup. Her heart ached for this woman as the pumping echo of Sophia's anxiety rose about losing Damian in a similar manner.

The woman with the phone cried, "Please stop, you're killing me! No, please, just come here—come here…" It was as if someone had slaughtered her in front of Sophia with the blood gushing from clenched fists covering her face as the city-dwellers quickly walked past her.

People tried not to notice this yelling, fuming conflict. She cried, "You haven't changed!" Sophia just kept listening, thinking, and walking more slowly toward her office.

The woman's palms sweat and the moisture was left on her covered forehead, while her tears covered the rest of her face. She was all water, so perhaps Thales was right and all matter is made up of it.

The fight was over in minutes and Sophia kept on walking.

Perhaps she should have gone over to her and asked her if she was all right. But she did not. Sophia stood further down the sidewalk until the weeping woman left, her dark curls bouncing up-and-down behind her, her empty soda can rolling around on the ground beneath her feet.

***

This woman made Sophia aware of the differences between them: for while Sophia dreamed, this woman had put on stilettos this morning; while Sophia ruminated, she had caked her face in makeup; while Sophia discovered, she dyed her hair; while Sophia loved, she dressed down for work; while Sophia tried to embrace living fully, she got drunk during breakfast to escape living fully; while Sophia looked at the positive in Damian, she partied to put men like him down; while Sophia expressed herself to him, this woman cut herself off from him.

This woman survived a breakup and would do so again. Turning left, she walked into a cafe, wiping the tears from her eyes and fixing the smudged mascara running down her cheeks with a napkin. The barista took her order for the largest latte Sophia had ever seen and this woman then pulled out her laptop, which looked like all the other laptops in the little bar window. All of them were lined up in a row: one, two, and three. Each one of them an exact replica of the other. Sophia walked faster to pass by the cafe window and leave a world that held nothing for her behind.

A breeze overtook the city, and Sophia's body hit the icy wind like a bird flying into a clean windowpane. Her skin contracted and shriveled up until tiny bumps formed. They looked like welts, all purple and red. Pale complexions can never hide anything. The thin, blue veins on her hands were shrouded by the skin around them. Sophia watched each trail pulsate—placing her fingers ever-so-gently on them—they suffocated. Her hand noticed the deprivation of blood and it tried to contract, but Sophia's mind would not release its domineering hold over her own body. This was the windowpane bar that Sophia wished to sit behind with her hollow beverage and her painful thoughts.

Her fingers curled around her wrist as she headed down what seemed to finally be the right street to her office building. Sophia felt her pulse quicken as her feet moved faster. She was alive, and at that moment forgot what Damian's body felt like. The pacing of her steps increased to a run because she had to find Damian and hold him close. How quickly the mind forgets another's touch!

Sophia knew she would never need another man simply due to the fact that she never remembered his touch for more than a day. The sensations would fade away as swiftly as the night devours day. In his arms, the need for anything more faded away. There was nothing more out in the world than what was given to her right up against his chest.

What must Damian think of holding her? she pondered. Would he forget how her hair felt beneath his hands or how close her waist was brought toward his own when he held her tight? Was he even thinking about her now before work?

Curiosity overcame her fear, which made her less anxious than before. The sidewalks felt like they were getting longer, which made Sophia more determined to run into Damian at work. The streets rolled on and on, in an endless sea of asphalt and foul-smelling paint. Leaves fell down from their hiding places in the trees and blocked Sophia's path. Her willingness to crush newly fallen leaves diminished as she aged. These were her feelings toward the world now. She had a need to preserve and protect all that was new and precious.

Perhaps this gentleness was a form of femininity Damian brought out in her. She felt akin to the newly fallen leaf, with its casting from the tree and its fall far down onto the ground. Or she felt like a worm that crawled out in the rain and sizzled in the sun or a baby bird that fails to fly properly out of the nest and dies on its first day of freedom.

She could only be kind to the living that were failures.

What a strange line to cross, thought Sophia...a strange line that shifts away in slow motion, where death's grip falls closer to one's throat. A clock on one of the city's buildings dawned its face to invite Sophia's eyes to wander, and absorb so many pretty people all in a row, each bearing special talents that nobody knows. Yet, Sophia could see the tame grow tamer, and the quick grow slower. The woman who had an over-the-phone breakup was a person who made herself into a worm or a fallen leaf or a bird that failed.

Maybe Sophia should have saved her. But she was different from Sophia because she *chose* to fall. Sophia and the birds and the worms did not choose to fail.

The city harbored those failures in its clutches. Downtown began to look like a more kindly place to Sophia. She loved knowing at what stops everyone got onto her bus, she loved knowing all the shops right around her workplace, and she loved listening to the faint music escaping the earbuds of a fellow commuter. Seeing the autumn creep in and cover the older buildings with fiery foliage made it even more of her home. Yet, every summer the streets thinned out as people took their vacations and left the competitive environment. The buildings became empty, and the trash bins overflowed with broken lights.

City dwellers noticed the changes and they just looked at it as a given as much as the seasons changing. Life moved constantly in the city. There were many chances to fail here, which is why the failure rates were so high and the people hid away from the sunlight like the rats that shared their homes with them. Walking these streets gave Sophia a reason to scope out where she could hide away. Besides, she still felt sick and weak being this far away from home.

Being far away from home still sometimes made Sophia nauseous, seeing the reel of memories play from her past when illness kept her mostly stuck at home.

Moving her feet around in bed, young Sophia had tried to regain the feeling she had been losing in them over the past week.

As soon as a stirring of any sort occurred, Gertrude knew and alighted to her daughter's room, thereby making herself a part of the morning view.

Sophia looked up. "Good morning, mother." She rubbed her eyes that had sunken into her pale face.

Gertrude picked up a folded corner of Sophia's comforter, pulling it back up to its proper place around Sophia's neck.

"This is all my fault. I was ill when I had you, my womb was just not ready for such a fragile creature. Or, perhaps, my weakness made you so fragile. Those doctors should have warned me." Gertrude was not looking Sophia in the eyes, but her hand had touched Sophia's as she was speaking.

"No, mother, you didn't mean to make such a delicate child," said Sophia.

"But I did, either way. I should have sued that hospital when I had the chance. I mean, look at you! You are so pretty, yet

217

you may not even last to the end of next week!"

Sophia winced and sank further down in her bed.

"I have sacrificed so much for you already, dear. I'm not sure how much more I can take. Could you cave in a bit? Maybe we should start seeing your primary care physician again?"

"No mother, that's okay. I promise to get better soon and no longer be a burden."

"Please, honey. You're not such a heavy burden. I just don't understand what is wrong with you."

The conversation dropped off with that guilt-ridden note, while Gertrude picked up the breakfast tray to take with her down the stairs and get it ready for lunch. She grumbled under her breath all the way down about her sacrifices no one had noticed, and all of the bad luck that had rained down on her family. As Gertrude turned around the corner toward the living room, she stopped in front of a cross that was hung above the entrance.

"What have I done to you, Lord?" she said, moving through the doorway to watch her favorite crime show on television.

**

Ambling along the sidewalks, Sophia found every dirty alleyway inviting. The dirt looked less offensive than usual since it offered up an extra layer for Sophia to hide behind and panic in if she needed to. An alleyway never twisted here, they were always straight and narrow, like a mouth yawning before closing its jaws tightly together again. If only she could go missing without being noticed. But by the next few feet, Sophia was swiftly passing by the opportunity.

Few things made Sophia stay on this path toward work, back home, and then back again. In fact, the only thing which made sense to her any more was sleeping with Damian. For he was the only way out of the alleyway she had just passed by. Her most challenging moments at home felt so soulless. How did that come to be? she wondered. Was it too abstract or concrete to think about? Where did all her motivation go to defy her family? The only time Sophia lit up any more was when she daydreaming about having sex again with Damian or even simply laying in his arms once again. Sophia felt safe with him. She trusted him with her life. His pale, white skin covering his thick muscles which were strewn around all of his bones made her feel safe. His every breath made her feel surer of herself. Sophia thought: I am *whole* with him.

Staring down at her feet, she watched how they moved in such a straight line, and yet, she imagined all of the minute balance corrections they were making as she moved forward. Her body was so intelligent. But it was drowning due to her own concerns with matters that had no bearing on her body. Sophia moved slower and with less purpose when she was contemplating alleyways and running away to hide. Her body was unable to move in its most natural way, and it was stifled by being forced into positions that kept her crippled.

Sophia wished she could grow an impenetrable shell around her thoughts. She wanted to wrap her mind up in a hard, rounded exterior that would prevent all suffering and disease from puncture wounds. Living in a guarded way was her mother's doing. Sophia was aware of the cause, but currently unable to fix the problem. Rather, the spark behind Sophia's eyes began to flutter and flicker. Words fell short of her hearing them, and to deny their entry was easier than to try to understand them. Abduction, kidnapping, rape, murder, death—all of these criminal acts are cropped out of time and are pelted at her naked body. Unsightly bruises become welts and she imagined peeling off her own skin, one flake at a time. Renewing herself every month, she was whole for a few weeks, and no more...

Sophia's office building was looming and growing higher and higher in the distance. For a young woman, this place brought her esteem she had never previously tasted. But her new social ranking had not set in yet. Sophia still felt like the useless, troublemaking child her mother made her out to be at home.

There was one more street light that needed to change before Sophia could finally make it to her office, and in this time she caught a whiff of a passerby's cologne. A mix of timber and fresh air made Sophia turn her head around to catch more of the smell up. She fantasized about putting an office highlighter between her legs like a spreader bar. Meanwhile, the only thing ringing loudly between her ears was the word: flesh.

Damian moved so fast, and Sophia got swept up in his constant motion, that he was spinning a world up of crazy dreams and infinite time. But she felt so *alive* in this slow world. Sophia was allowed to take contemplative walks to nowhere. She could really see the wet receipt on the ground with the soiled ink spreading across the page, or the great blobs of snow falling down onto the street and matting people's hair.

The deep breathing as she walked down the street kept her calm and tame. Her feet propelled her forward into the cold air, but she no longer felt numb from it. It bit and she cringed, crawling further back into the womb.

Sophia's louder thoughts kicked in to perpetuate her toward something—her purpose? What is my purpose? she wondered. What would build me up enough happiness to last?

There was no future with her mother there, standing in front of the gates to her freedom. Her freedom meant becoming an independent adult who could fall in love and start a life without her family stamping out all growth. Nowhere on earth would Sophia be able to even be with Damian or fulfill her own goals when her mother was mobile, living, and breathing. The only thing Sophia could think about was going back home by bus and eating dinner, but after her arrival home things became foggy. Strangely, Sophia never saw anyone in her house aging either. Her mother would always remain able and ready to scold her daughter. Sophia, in her imagination, always had fair, taut skin and a mind in upheaval all the time. Her hair forever remained dark and her breasts always petite. Only her eyes she imagined growing dimmer as the years faded away. She was sure her eyes had sparkled at birth like jewels, but they had already become dulled from her imprisonment at home. Sophia could conceive of eyes growing old.

Her eyes went from her feet and the sidewalk cracks back up to the office building. Sophia was headed toward the door with the large, golden street numbers written right above her head. Of course, to her anxious mind, the next thought was if one of those numbers were to fall on her head, she would be dead in an instant, crushed by the number four. Her obituary would have some line in it about how four must have been her unlucky number, and as the people who knew her would disappear, the only thing remaining would be a silly joke. The girl who died from the number four.

CHAPTER III

Arriving at the main lobby of the office, the first thing Sophia saw was Damian, and her initial reaction was to run right toward him and hold him tightly. But instead, the emotion jostled her so much her legs sank into the lobby floor and she felt more like crying. The change in environments was jarring. Thin wisps of hair tangled around her ear. The fuzzy ring had left her numb and her pupils dilated as she stared at the sunspot frolicking on the building wall. Damian's voice cut out after a while and he did not resume talking again. Their minds both became quiet to the droll hum of the dial tone from the security guard's phone highlighting the vast expanse of ocean in between.

Finally, Damian lifted Sophia up by the arms and asked if she was okay.

"Yes, yes. I'm fine. It's just I was overwhelmed by seeing you here before I even got to our office." She waited patiently for his response, thinking that maybe the floor had a better answer for her as she stared intensely down at it.

"Well, I'm glad you're happy to see me," he chuckled, grasping Sophia's hand and walking with her to their floor.

He said, "I just want you to know we are going out to lunch."

The lack of option actually made Sophia less anxious as she

nodded in assent beside Damian.

Inside the office, a ring of coworkers were chatting before they got down to their own work. Sophia overheard their surprisingly philosophical discussion:

"You are not an island unto yourself, you know," said Amber.

Tyler wrinkled up his forehead in disbelief as he said, "Of course you are! We were born alone and we'll die alone."

"What a harsh view of life, Tyler. I would say that we should be looking at the world full of beauty and help humanity rather than hurting it. For example, I am getting rid of all the plastic in my house now to prevent more from going to the landfill and harming the earth," said Grace.

Amber just had to add in, "Yeah, me too!"

"Good gracious, I'm not saying to not be kind to each other, but I am saying you will not die without another person in your life," said Tyler.

"I can see that," added Jeffrey.

Amber shot him a nasty look as she shifted her hefty body toward the perpetrator. "Well, I'm glad you're not my neighbor. That's all I'm going to say."

The circle broke up while Damian and Sophia gave each other a knowing look and moved into their own cubicles for the day's work ahead.

Sophia launched herself on the pile of papers for the day, attempting to squelch all of the thoughts she had. But her mind kept wandering back to the conversation her peers were having just a moment ago.

She thought about herself and whether she felt like an island. Deep down, Sophia wanted to survive independently, but she felt certain circumstances had made that ability cease to exist long ago. She felt like she depended on both her mother and Damian now. They both controlled her thoughts and her whereabouts during the day. Strangely, she also felt a draw and repulsion toward both people. But perhaps other factors could have made her feel like she did now: old, tired, depressed.

One owner cried out "stay with me," while the other commanded, "come with me." When Sophia went to one the other voice grew louder. At the same time, her body became so conditioned by the dichotomy that once the alarm grew for one, she went into a panic. The sweats, chills, heart palpitations physically took her away from the one leader she was currently with. Her physical withdrawing was the only way for Sophia to breathe, otherwise, she suffocated waiting for release from her current captor.

Sophia was a captive. In a world formed by sex and death, Damian became the former and her mother became the latter.

Together, they helped Sophia make sense of the things she had seen in the past days, from people dressed in suits twenty-four-seven who worked for the government, to a broke college student who had to open beer lids off the stone ridges outside of his house, or a young mother of two little kids who were each constantly swinging on her tired legs. Alcohol motivated much of it. Drink lubricated the divide for many between sex and dying, blurring the two until neither hurt so much. The world of adults was drowned out by an intoxicating fluid which was used to dull all of the pains from the day.

But Sophia desired Damian to work in a society that did not keep him from producing his best. She hoped that he could find happiness in his work just like she did with her papers. In the future, she imagined finding her perfect balance between work and play with her lover by her side.

Sophia knew now that she was an adult and she wanted to be around those who desired to better themselves. She wanted to converse with someone about the possibilities, and not the limitations anymore. She had had enough.

No longer would she desire the tea from her mother's teapot or the care she gave to all sick creatures, no longer would she seek out a hole to bury herself in at night, and no longer would she want to get lost among her parents' things as another antique lost in the ruins. Sophia felt, from a distance, she was nearing the word "I" and moving further from "us" and "we." If the idea was correct, she knew the decision to leave the nest would be the right one.

Still, Sophia felt the world was laughing at her for her optimism. But laughs are meant to be relished, and not used by some coy college girl amused by pictures of her discarded boyfriend. Laughs are meant for moments of pure exhilaration, not chatting with your friend before class on a sunny day. Chuckles, giggles, things of that nature are acceptable in modesty, but not laughter. That is sacred.

It was lunchtime and Damian took her to the office building's cafeteria.

Every now and then, Sophia had moments of intense nostalgia. She *felt* a memory from her childhood. Her last one was on one of her babysitter's walks: the suburbs, the green grass, the peace, and the playfulness of the day.

Those were the more positive moments she remembered, but then there were times of illness. Lying in front of her own television, the lights blinking and sounds blaring, Sophia rotted away. Her mother had always turned it on after she woke up in the morning in order to "stimulate her already weak mind." But Sophia lay there without taking anything

225

from the outside in. She had to turn inward to escape; it was the last place to hide.

Maybe if her father was at home more often, then he would be able to see what was really going on. What was really going on? Sophia had devoted hundreds of hours to this question, thinking over and replaying each interaction she had with her family. The answer had to be buried in her family's past actions somewhere. How many possible combinations are there before an answer comes to her? she pondered.

The possible solutions changed daily for Sophia. Yesterday, the family's instability was her mother's fault. Today, it was her own fault. Tomorrow, it will be her father's turn. One or all of them were at fault for keeping Sophia living differently than all the other kids at school when she was growing up.

Yet here she was now, still daydreaming, eating poorly-made cafeteria food in front of their "Good Eats" slogan for sustainable food "made from scratch." The plastic might have been, but the food was not, Sophia thought.

***

"Reminds you of elementary school again, doesn't it?" asked Damian.

"Yeah, it makes me want to eat my lunch in the bathroom stalls as opposed to here," said Sophia.

"Did you really do that as a kid?"

"Sometimes." Sophia could not admit to him at that moment she still found the stalls a peaceful place to be.

Damian poked around at his food, thinking about what they would do next.

"Sophia, I want you right now."

Sophia stopped chewing as her stomach knotted up tightly.

"Where....where...at work?"

226

"I know, but we could use the bathroom?"

Sophia giggled, "I don't think so."

Damian looked back down, disappointed, at his food. If he had really desired to go have sex in the stalls, then he would not have backed down as he did.

"I'm sick," he said.

"What's hurting, love?"

"No, I think I have an ailment of the soul," said Damian.

"Well, you're not alone then." Sophia kept her face down, staring into the plate in front of her.

The two sat there across from each other feeling the weight of what they had just admitted to—a weakness of some kind.

"Why are you ill? You seem so strong to me."

Taking her hand in his, Damian said, "I can't feel much of anything. I lay on my back at night like I'm already in the grave. I want to love and be loved, but I can't be bothered with the time to lay there and do nothing. I just feel a pressure to take and conquer as quickly as possible; there my whole pleasure lies. I will always desire you, no matter how long it takes or if I have to follow you to hell and back."

Moments passed as Damian waited for Sophia to respond.

She swallowed before saying, "Well, I sleep on my side all wrapped up like an embryo. I never did come out of the womb. My whole world is still so small. Sometimes I wonder if I'm actually breathing on my own."

Damian reached out his hand to grab hers. "I'm expanding your world. Going to The Rood with you made me feel so fulfilled...Sophia, I can only feel when you're beneath me."

Sophia's brows furrowed as she looked up at Damian. "When I'm *beneath* you? What do you mean?"

"I mean, that demeaning you in public is the only way I

seem to know how to get pleasure anymore. I need you to succumb to me and my desires." He started stirring the spoon in his drink. Not making eye contact with Sophia, Damian had seemed to think it would make this conversation easier.

"I do worship you, Sir…" she said as her head lowered, remembering how awful she had felt by the end of that night at The Rood.

"I know you do, baby. But I just feel numb. I feel numb when I don't have power—like just now when you told me 'no' to sex in the bathroom. That makes me feel, I don't know, impotent… Do you understand what I mean, Sophia?"

"But I thought everything was fine. I can give you more, I promise."

"Thank you, little girl. That means a lot. I just wish I knew how to keep myself from being numb all the time. I also wish I knew how to eradicate anything left of your mother in you." Damian slurped the remainder of his drink.

"I wish I knew how to do that too. But she comes back to me in so many different ways. When I'm on the bus her voice will warn me about inhaling secondhand smoke from the other passengers. Or when I'm at work her voice will tell me to scurry around the office even faster, especially in front of our boss—to give off the appearance of working hard enough for a raise. Then, at home, her voice literally calls out to me from the kitchen where she tells me to do more around the house. If it's not about chores, then it's about men—and how evil they are. But I can't believe her now…not now, love. Still always, though, I am labeled "the guilty party." She calls me innocent only when I am sick. Damian, don't ever treat me well when I am sick. Don't even be kind to me when I'm half-dead. Beat me, if you must, but don't coddle me."

Damian nodded his head in assent. "I will never coddle you when you are ill. I want you healthy and strong. I want all of your energy to be focused on serving me. I will always require your utmost attention and obedience. Do you hear me?"

Sophia smiled. "Yes, Sir. Thank you, Sir." She felt more at ease knowing that Damian would support her mental healing. He was prepared to mend the scars of a coddling mother. She thought she could now not recover without his push nor without his love.

Though a doubt overcame her that had to make sure: "You still love me though, right?" asked Sophia.

Damian was quiet for much too long before he said: "We each need to find happiness and respect ourselves before the sickness will fade. I want to love you, Sophia. I really do, but right now I'm spiritually sick."

"You're sick?! What about me?! I've been sick my entire life! I've been beaten, shamed, and ridiculed by my mother—and now *toyed* with by you! Where can I find peace and health? Damian, *make* me well again." Sophia felt she had to choose between him or her. There was no other choice for her to make.

Damian leaned forward and laid his forehead against hers. They closed their eyes.

"I promise to *make* you well again, love," whispered Damian.

She winced as his words kept echoing in her head because the sad truth was brought to light as she remembered that her life was never really her own. She felt it never could be her own—not at this point. Sophia retained the thoughts of a child and not the thoughts of a woman. She felt like she would never amount to anything.

Sophia said, "You know, I had a history teacher in high

school who gave a lesson on how the people in the Middle Ages believed life was just a 'vale of tears' to suffer through until death. The origin of the phrase is unknown, although some think it comes from a hymn. I have been hoping that this suffering of mine would end once I became an adult, and I would prove my history teacher wrong. But now, I'm twenty-two years old and I have nothing. Is life just suffering, Damian? Can you really save me from it?"

The tears rolled down Sophia's cheeks as she spoke. He was the only savior in her personal hell, and yet even he had an illness of the soul.

"No, Sophia, it isn't. You have me. I'm here, even though I have been eaten, chewed, and spit back out by society. You know, I constantly have people ripping power away from me: the government, the police, other people.'

"But I'm my own man. I can handle myself and I don't care to protect anyone else but you. In exchange, all I ask for is your complete obedience."

Sophia gulped. "I'll try, Sir. I mean, I'm really trying now. I can't live without you…" She got up from the lunch table to sit by his side. Taking his arm in hers, she rested her cheek on his firm shoulder. For a blissful moment, she felt calm.

Damian softened as he grazed his finger across Sophia's cheek. She sniffled.

"I am not a leader," he said. "Leadership in the culture today means appeasing everyone by wearing different masks. I have one face, one vision of how the world ought to look, and one life to live it that way. I will not dumb my ideas down for another or change the message of my life to accommodate more people in general. That's how I lead, dear. I plan on being blunt with you just as I would anyone else. Understand?"

Sophia reached underneath the table with her foot and rubbed his leg. She wanted to connect with him. He was *her* leader. "Yes, Sir." She choked down a small sob. This was her savior, she thought. Damian would lead her to salvation without trembling. Therefore, she thought she must not tremble before him. She had to be strong.

"Good. I'm glad you've agreed to my requirements. I will rescue you and show you that life can be more than suffering. Life can be full of pleasure. If you only follow me, obey me, and remain with me, then I will show you what life could offer you, little girl."

Sophia's mouth curled up in a small smile as she blushed. But then she became serious as worries took the place of security. The only words she could use to verbalize her fear were "but you truly do love me and only me?"

Any answer apart from "yes" would make Sophia scream in agony. Damian was quite aware of this and the utter power he held over her.

Damian squeezed Sophia's hand and got up from the table.

***

Sophia would not let go. "Damian, wait, please. You don't have to love me now, just tell me that you'll bring me along wherever you go?"

Her eye contact grew weaker as her anxiety mounted. If Damian did not agree to take her along, then surely she would not survive long.

Damian nodded, "Of course. We will both learn, and heal together." Moving away, he walked slowly back to his cubicle from the cafeteria, leaving Sophia alone at a long plastic table with two meals that had barely been touched.

Sophia ran through the conversation again in her mind,

tracing each word he used for any hidden meaning or message. Her own words came back to her in small packages, even though she really wanted to shake Damian and tell him: "I want someone proactive, active, and reactive—anyone but passive! I want to be with a man, not a child. Don't tell me you're always numb—you have one life, so live it! Don't just sit passively waiting for your life to hand itself over to you—you have to take the initiative to go forth and conquer! Conquer me!"

Loving someone, to Sophia, meant telling them the truth and sharing one's passion with the other person. Being infatuated with someone must be the most crippling emotion a person could have because then neither truth nor passion may be shared. That other person must remain in the dark until they pick out a piece of you they may express a liking for, and only then could you reveal some of yourself. To love is much easier. Damian would learn how to love Sophia quickly, she thought.

Still sitting as if stuck to the lunchroom table, Sophia focused her vision on the girl in front of her. She was sporting white sneakers, though not completely white since the worn and dirty shoes sealed her small feet into the dark. She wore ankle-high socks—white, plain, and bunched up around her ankles, keeping them warm from the chilly, autumn air; the gray floral pants, tight, with large pink flowers dispersed all over her legs; the dark pink sweater, much too large for her slender figure. It looked cozy and warm and the neck dropped low. Her dark, brunette curls were at the length of her petite neck. Dangling earrings softly framed her face. Dark, tired, bags laid underneath her eyes with the glow of her laptop illuminating her overwhelmed face. Yet, this girl looked calm, marching relentlessly toward the end of her work. Completely enthralled in the page on the screen, time was irrelevant and yet she kept progressing forward. "I've been here since...," but she does not stop. There is a continuity in her poise and diligence. She was a combination of atoms, brought together in a burst of passion, and moving forward ever since.

Then she sat up and walked back to her cubicle on the other side of the office to a place where Sophia never lurked. The other side was much too far for a girl trying to stay on top of all the documents in the office. The white-sneakers girl made Sophia want to be like her. She wanted to see if her "better half" would survive in the world longer. Which one of us will crack first? Me or my happier, ambitious other half? wondered Sophia.

She promised herself to keep tabs on this girl for the rest of her career in the office. Sophia would probably work here until she died because she worried even more when she was without work. It was as if she were attached to a set of pulleys and every time she stopped walking forward, she would be dragged instead. Her life was intertwined with her work, and if she stopped it would mean death.

Sophia thought it was hard to fit love into this pulley system she had created. She did not want to hurt Damian in any way. But her work kept her preoccupied to the point of exhaustion, and that was the only way she currently knew how to live. Work until going home simply meant sleeping away the evening to arrive back at work the next day, much like her father.

For the first time, she felt she knew what her father was doing—surviving. He had created his method, and now Sophia was forming hers. She decided on working until she got lost in the papers and felt physically and mentally fatigued by the end of the workday, and only then allowing herself to dream about Damian. He was so comforting to be around. His laugh was contagious and his smile made her sigh. His touch brought goosebumps onto the surface of her skin. The little bumps made her body shiver and ache with desire.

She wished she could have seen him when he grew from a boy into a man. Maybe that would have helped her to develop more fully into a woman. Her semi-metamorphosis created more of a crippled butterfly than anything else. Her wings had never expanded properly, and there was a strange hole in her thorax. Her legs wobbled, while one of them must have surely been torn off at birth.

To live crippled and sick in the world was deadly, and Sophia knew it. She needed a practical man who could serve as her guide through the darkness.

Right now, Sophia saw that her work came first over her love for Damian. But she wanted this to change if he would only take her hand and be a leader. She would march with him anywhere else but around here. She would go anywhere but here where there was constant bitterness and an unbearable silence surrounding the problems in her home; where all they talked about was nothing and hated learning; where her mind raced for answers, but nothing ever escaped her mouth; where all of them sat, the vibrations escaping from their mouths that meant nothing. Sophia felt suffocated, alone, and in pain at home. They never meant anything they said. They were opposed to learning.

Silence can expand. Sophia could feel it. Silence lingered there among her family members, their brains straining to say something "to their kid," and then it expanded and revealed the faces of fear.

**

Sophia rose from the flimsy table in the cafeteria. She bent down to grab the two plates still full of food. Everything had to go to waste, including her body and mind.

Sophia was forced to focus all her energy at home on surviving until the next day. But she would face that like a machine. She promised herself to work until her life was her own. Her butterfly wings had to dry out and expand, that was all.

"Oh! I'm so sorry, sir," Sophia said. While thinking about her wings, she had crashed the plates into another man waiting in line to grab his lunch. He turned around to look at Sophia and she felt like she was staring Evil in the face. He was a six-foot-tall man who wore shiny, black lace-up boots, dark-stained jeans, and a button-down shirt wrapped around his thin skeleton. This man looked relatively normal until Sophia got to his face. The soul got sucked right out of her as she looked up into his snake-like eyes. He wore thick, red-rimmed glasses and whenever the person next to him had spoken about something cynical, he flashed his sharp-white-toothy grin and laughed. His laugh stained his cynical comments, rendering them as nihilistic pieces of propaganda.

But this man had a method. His few discarded pieces of "wisdom" landed on one's subconscious and spread. In a plague-like manner, areas of the brain were violently shut off. One by one, the people around Sophia in the cafeteria exposed to the virus were smiling back. These people began to nod in agreement with him. This devil: he must not win over her mind. Sophia squinted hard, attempting to force out those noxious words of his with her mind. She repeated to herself an incantation against his vile phrases. Slowly, she could feel his propaganda start breaking up. The words he spoke began to disentangle themselves into a harmless jumble of words and then letters. Unwinding, it loosened its hold on Sophia's mind and coiled into itself before burning away into nothingness. Now, the only one who was not a nodding, smiling automaton was Sophia. The man's pitchfork tongue sticking out of his thin lips could tell she was the *final* victim. Slithering over to her, he hissed: "Why do you disagree that at the essence of human existence there is a *lack*—an ungraspable desire which can never be attained?" The rest of the people in line have stones for eyes. They bore right through her. "Well," Sophia gulped, "I believe people can fill this lack and we can be perfect." The devil showed his toothy grin and just laughed and laughed…

Sophia dropped the plates and dashed out of the cafeteria, miserable and breathing heavily. Catching what little breath was left, Sophia thought that if she ever lost Damian, life would be worthless. She could not live among cynical monsters like that man in the lunch line.

Back at her cubicle, Sophia placed her legs under the desk, and both feet flat on the floor. Her hands came to rest on the desk just to make herself feel grounded. This was one predictable world she could handle living in. Breathing in and then out, Sophia closed her eyes and remembered being told in her last year of college that "at the heart of human existence there is a *lack*." This was the same religious mindset that essentially said, "Nobody's perfect." The notion that there was something better to be had which humans could never reach was preposterous and irrelevant to them. Today Sophia demanded a new definition of perfection, one which does not mean "stasis" and which allows one the ability to learn from his or her mistakes.

Sophia desired to be perfect, and someday she believed she and Damian would be perfect together.

It was the kind of people who remained concerned with humanity, those who created their own worlds which replaced this one. Every single day Sophia was trying to figure out this puzzle. It made her head hurt because there was just so much to absorb in life. All of those topics that also concerned others made her desire something else, something "higher." Yet, she believed that that "higher" is right here on earth. But that is so hard to believe in and live by. Sophia had a few coworker friends, a few family members, and one lover. Sophia woke up every day with her head spinning and fell back asleep with her stomach in knots. She lived between a world of stress and fear and a world of jitteriness and desiring. Were her professors right? Sophia wondered. Does human existence consist of a lack? Why was she always setting her sights on a purpose? Why could not she ever feel at ease, other than when she was sleeping in another's arms? Sophia had so many questions she had yet to answer. Yet, when she had gone home for the day from her classes she was always more depressed than at college. She thrived on the stress. This was what college had done to her. She became an optimistic student all her professors spit on. She got up, found food, worked, worked, worked, and then went back to sleep. Sophia's life as a college student was one of constant movement, and on some days Sophia could not tell whether she loved it or hated it. She had just wished she had a home…

CHAPTER IV

The bus commute back home was becoming too short because Sophia needed more time to shift from her adult self into her child self rapidly. If she walked into that house as an adult, she would surely suffocate even more than she already did.

The sunlight during this time snatched Sophia's sight as she quickly covered her face with her hand to protect her eyes from the autumnal rays. Another pretty young woman was sitting next to her and had to do the same thing. Sophia noticed and looked at her sideways, she smiled and they both laughed at how ridiculous they looked. It was as if it was a scene out of a Jane Austen novel and this other woman would never realize how much Sophia relished that moment of shared humanity.

The bus kept moving and the sunlight kept changing around the bus. The evening sun reminded her of her favorite season, autumn. But every time it came around, her anxiety increased tenfold. She stepped on crumpled leaves, forgot her umbrella at home, and refused to go outside without a scarf. Why did she worry? Surely it was not due to her most valued season. But maybe her fear was a matter of the night's encasing the day in darkness. Her anxiety increased with the encroaching feeling of mutiny by the night. She tried to avoid letting her fears animate the objects around her, but it was difficult. For even her fear took on a life of its own.

Upon getting home, a new quarrel arose with her mother:

Gertrude foisted open the front door as she saw Sophia approaching to remind her that the appliances were only to be used between the hours of seven a.m. and ten p.m. "You, miss, had run the dryer at six forty-five this morning."

Sophia had to breathe in the insult and exhale a "thank you for reminding me, I will avoid using appliances out of that time frame."

"Also, when I ask you to take out the trash, your bulk recyclables should *not* go in the trash. The recycling bins are out by the bicycle racks.

"It would be nice if next time, you didn't pull my recyclables out of the trash, aggressively circle my name, and write in red marker that there is something wrong with me," said Sophia, growing bolder.

Gertrude scowled. "I did that out of frustration because I actually care about this earth."

"Well, what about me?" Sophia passed her mother by crouching under her arm that crossed the doorway and ran up to her room.

***

Sophia's ceiling had pockmarks all over. The white, textured layers looked extremely hard and unforgiving this evening. Every bump retained some light and an ominous shadow from her lamp down below. The cool ease with which each bump took on both the dark and the light made Sophia feel stronger as if she were the one who could handle both sides coolly. There was a shift in the atmosphere of her room—a tightening, a closing in, some kind of end.

Sophia feared being forgotten in this room that never aged. She could wither away in these sheets and the light would only play over her ceiling. In fact, she imagined that even the ceiling would laugh at her trying to accomplish something with her short life.

Then, the tears came and Sophia sat up on her bed. At first, a warm, salty tear entered her mouth. It was comforting to feel in those first moments when the levee started crumbling, but the crack gave way to the water pushing against the gates. That is when the tears became as overwhelming as the sheer amount of liquid. Running over the snotty puddles forming underneath the tip of her nose, the tears let themselves drop from the height of Sophia's chin down onto the sea of blankets beneath her body. A large and rounded spot began forming where the drop fell and conspired, larger and larger the spot grew and soon Sophia sat amongst her own moat.

Her tears felt refreshing, and her mind focused only on releasing as many tears as she could that evening. Allowing them to flood any other emotions out through her eyes, Sophia grew calmer.

Sophia thought: I am still that little girl staring from my swing at the landscape beyond the playground fence—only now I sit behind a desk in a law firm, looking out at the next cubicle beyond.

From my seat, I can pay attention to the smallest changes. My attention to detail is refined, which is why even small parties are too overwhelming for this small flower. Famous explorers throughout human history had a love for the unknown, but I love the known. I love that birds will always be birds and that the sun will rise tomorrow, and my scenery outside will not vary much. I love feeling a sense of permanence in my life because the seasons cannot promise it, my coworkers cannot promise it, my family cannot promise it, and even my lover cannot promise it.

Having some semblance of permanence is all I have ever wanted in my life. Pushing paper around all day at work is permanent. My joy comes from knowing that at nine o'clock in the morning I will be at my cubicle sifting through this paper or that paper. I will know who needs what done and when. I have lunch every day from noon to one o'clock. I go home at five o'clock without exception. My mother could have thrown a plate at my head that morning on my way out the door, but I will still be at work where my coworkers need me. No matter what I do the papers will be there in their neat stacks waiting for me to sort through.

My mother has her own routine, only her routine is self-sufficient. She does not really need or want anyone to wash her dishes, fold her laundry, or redecorate any of the rooms in her house.

She does not love me. I am not a part of her plan. Her job is harder with me around...to have to take care of a sick child. She cannot love me with the way she looks at me on most days. Her face scrunches up like she smells something putrid, and her face turns away from mine when I enter the door. I have brought the outside into my mother's domain. I have cigarette and gutter rain lingering on my coat after I walk through the door. I look worn out. I wear an expression of anxiety on my face that repels anyone who looks at it.

Yet, all my mother can do is look away. She turns away from her daughter as she goes out to beg and plead to a crowd that does not even see her. She is the dead among the living. Even though she says, "we need to have this conversation, in my opinion," what she really means is "do or die."

My response to her was always "yes, Mother," implying that one of us will "do" and one of us will "die." A prophecy is what my mother wanted, and subsequently needed, to make her life move in any direction. It is as if she was waiting for a push forward by a spirit or a ghost or a god to lead her to do something right. In no other way would my mother move. She is waiting for an afterlife where she is king of all. Usually, at the beginning of the week, I found my mother on her knees, praying and whispering to someone she could not see. The whispers involved lots of lost phrases and forgotten promises on both ends—my mother often forgot what she said and her God forgot to deliver.

For years now a shift in the direction of my life has been impossible. Nothing can truly change the trajectory I am on unless I make the first move. I must overcome the power of this overpowering house. I must move my mother out of the way of my path to lightness. She must rest elsewhere, rather than on top of my frail lungs.

***

By the time Sophia was twelve, she had weaved together the story of a "perfect family" that fell apart when she was born. Her father was bringing home the money, while her mother was taking care of the home. But when she became pregnant with Sophia, she got sick. Her womb puckered up at her daughter's conception and wanted to spit her out. But little Sophia stayed. She fought for as long as she could, digging her baby nails into her mother's womb until the doctors had to pull Sophia out themselves. Her mother nearly died…at least so she says.

My mother never told me her story, thought Sophia as she continued to stare up at her ceiling. Where did she come from? What were her parents like? How did she get here? The only story I had heard was a brief summary of how she met my father. One day, my mother was outside on her parents' farm, feeding the horses. When she suddenly felt faint. My mother told me she had not been fed dinner the previous night, because she had forgotten to pick the apples that day for the neighbors' party. It caused deep embarrassment for the family, and she suffered the consequences for it. So, she fainted from hunger right there on the farm and my father passed by on his way to deliver some medical supplies to her family. He became the hero when he revived my mother and she has depended on him ever since.

Sophia felt more determined than ever to take the sharpest kitchen knife and plunge it into Gertrude's heart. The blood and shock would last a much shorter time than the pain of never having done anything at all. But the thought made Sophia dizzy with fear.

She thought of more reasons her mother deserved to die. Sophia thought that freedom was the outcome of such an extreme act and that without death there would be no independence. After all, her mother saw her as no better than cattle to be slaughtered at the right age—cattle without agency, cattle without mind, cattle without opinions, cattle without need... To be her mother meant to hate work and money. Her mother's paranoid view entailed seeing a machine that kills and strips one of all value. Cattle have no value—unless they are dead. Sophia was not allowed to have any agency or value in the Weber house, and to be a woman in a system like that renders her as powerless—naked in the face of the machine.

Her mother also fed on that suffering and grew by telling her friends to start a revolution, namely with the recycling. She bullied and harassed those people she saw as the villains until they were forced to change their "unsustainable ways."

To be her mother one must be blind to mankind's psychological desires, thought Sophia. Her mother ignored the fact that people are allowed to *choose* where they want to put their trash. Gertrude refused to acknowledge that what she was doing was wrong. Sophia promised herself, laying on her bed that night, never to become her mother.

Sophia wanted her life to be filled with love and achievement. She desired her work to make the office run smoother, and her coworkers to love her for it. Yet, her mother scowls and gnashes her teeth. Work and money for her are gained by means of "blood, sweat, and tears." There is no joy in work for Gertrude. Carrying a burden is what work felt like for Gertrude, and other people must feel an equal amount of the weight.

All Sophia had was work. Work brought her self-esteem, love, friendship, patience, strength, virtue, the ability to express herself, and *grow* as a human being. It is not just some time-wasting form of enslavement or a burden, but a gift that allowed one to feel a sense of permanence in life. To be her mother one must preach death, but to be Sophia one must preach *life*. Sophia chose life.

From now on Sophia was determined to control the situation just like her ceiling with its two tones of light and dark. Nothing would keep her from drastically changing her path for the better.

Moving onto her side, Sophia dozed off as her arm fell limp, dead, tired, and exhausted. She remembered she was painfully human at that moment with her arm squished limply under her side. If only she could become an extraordinary human being, Sophia thought, something above and beyond the contemporary—immortal at all costs. Then, her arm would never feel achy and tired.

Shifting onto her back again, Sophia was left to stare at her pockmarked ceiling. Remembering her brief ride to college from home, Sophia was given another lecture on the dangers of college boys and sexual diseases. Gertrude could scare her about sex, but by that time Sophia knew she could have all the sex in the world at school. Only college classes made her too sick to her stomach to think about chasing boys. She remembered a philosophy professor who she will call "Mr. Chasm" smacking his fist against his desktop to help voice his opinions to his paying audience.

Sophia recalled him shouting: "I command you all to look upon the face of suffering!" The phrases rang through her ears. She winced, trying to recapture the flames that had been snuffed out with her professor's fallen hand. Presently, not a sound was heard—not a word spoken until her professor pointed toward the door. His phone rang. Students packed up their low-lying hearts, stuffing them into their book bags, and trying not to press their sticky fingers together too hard. The *deed* was done. The students crawled from Mr. Chasm's class— faces drooping, feet dragging—cynical buzz words nixing all other more pleasant thoughts, while Mr. Chasm just blew his nose, turned off the classroom lights, picked up his jacket, and left the room. His black shoes scuffed the hallway floor and the sound of screeching echoed infinitely onward.

The imagined scuffing of shoes rattled Sophia back into her bedroom with the glaring ceiling mocking her for all the things she had to deal with in life. The shadows played off each nub like broad smiles. She lowered her head and breathed deeply. Sophia's mother was an obstacle, an enemy, a wall. But how to get over it? she wondered. How to overcome such heights? Murder would mean jail and never gaining freedom...but was that the only price offered to Sophia? What if death was the only way to get away from her mother?

Sophia contemplated grabbing her final paycheck from work and running away with Damian. But her mother would hunt her down. There would be a private investigator, cops, and the news. If she ran away, she would be found and then bound up even more under her mother's weight. Was there any way to silence someone without killing them?

***

Killing her mother would make Sophia lose her mind. Even now, the thought of permanently silencing her only brought back intense reminders of her mother massaging her head and buying her gifts when she was ill. A rush of nausea kicked on the anxiety over even stepping out the door away from her mother.

No, Sophia could never, ever leave her. If she killed her own mother, it would be the end of herself as well. Freedom would have to come another way.

There was one bus ride back home from work that Sophia would always remember. It came in a flash of inspiration—what if she jumped right off the edge of the sidewalk in front of the oncoming bus? Then, her mother would receive a call from the police after they had picked up her phone from the ground and found her number. Her mother would rush to the scene sobbing and realizing she had made the biggest mistake of her life by not letting Sophia go free.

It was almost a challenge the sidewalk was giving to her. It had the yellow rim and the raised edges cautioning her away from the end, but what did those matter? Could they force her away from the edge like an electric fence? Or was the only thing keeping her from executing such an idea her own will to live? Until then, her will to live did not seem very strong. Her mother may only see her mistakes if something drastic occurred.

Sophia remembered inching a bit closer to the ledge, but as soon as a car honked at her she jumped back. Her heart rate increased and her breathing became labored. The next thoughts were about people noticing her thoughts, reading the large exclamation point or emergency signal flashing over her head. Sophia rushed into the nearest office building, asked where their public bathrooms were, and hid in the stall until she regained her normal breathing again.

That was the last time she thought she could overcome the sidewalk's yellow line. Nothing in her soul would allow her to move past that line. Freedom had to be attained another way. Perhaps, she never really believed her mother would understand her daughter any better if she was dead and gone.

There were now three possibilities Sophia was working through: her mother's death, her own death, and Damian's survival. The first two came to naught, but Damian could be her savior here.

At lunch earlier that day, Damian had talked about how sick and tired he was of people taking away what was his. Even that man he punched took what did not belong to him. He had a right to what he fought for or made with his hands. Sophia thought that she should also get to keep what she worked for—Damian's love.

247

Sophia needed his touch, and his arms around her at night. She did not want to admit her addiction to him. But after pondering about this need, she discovered he was the final goal for her freedom. Sophia's work and everything else was a means to this end. She did not care much for money or fame—only his protective arms keeping her worries at bay until morning.

Damian must come and save her tonight.

Tonight Sophia would finally do something drastic. She would finally change the way the river flowed. The path to freedom was so close she could almost taste it. Whether the change would be internal or external, it was about to come like a prophet in the dawn light.

Life would arise in this wretched room, underneath the rippled ceiling, and the undulating curtains being blown by the fan. Sophia could no longer lay in wait for change, movement, motion. All life was change. She was ready—for now she believed that life was made for the intimate.

Sophia bolted upright and took out a notebook. Tomorrow she planned to burn the thoughts she committed to the page today. In it, she scribbled out her fantasy about what she thought would bring her the most amount of pleasure. It was making love to Damian in this bed, this prison of a room, right beneath this ceiling with the pockmarks.

CHAPTER V

Breathing more slowly, Sophia rose back up from the floor of her room at the call of Gertrude screeching, "Dinner!"

Sophia's heart speed picked up and she began gasping for air. These episodes occurred more often since she had become locked in her bedroom. Coughing a few times and catching her breath, Sophia forced her heart to slow down. The race was aimless. It was over anyway; her mother always made it to the finish line before she ever could reach it.

She trudged her way down the steps, counting each carpet-cushioned step as she went to try to slow down her mind. Meditating on each fiber under her feet as they crumpled up underneath, she imagined each fiber being her mother's head.

"Finally, the princess arrives down for her meal," said Gertrude. She berated Sophia with these types of "jokes" from time to time.

Sophia winced and took her seat. There was another fuming speech forming in the recesses of her mind. But this time she attempted to fill her thoughts instead with Damian and what he would do to her tonight.

Gertrude saw the faraway look in Sophia's dark eyes and she felt threatened, so she dropped her fork with a clatter onto the floor.

"Gosh darn it! Now I have to get another. My work here is never done, is it Sophia?" bellowed Gertrude.

"No, it must not be," Sophia said.

"I know, I know. But when you help me out, I give you things for it, right? It's like you still get an allowance for things that normal adults have to do for nothing."

"Yes, I suppose you're right."

"Of course I'm right!"

Sophia stuffed her mouth with food to avoid saying anything in return. Her gagging was the only thing reminding her she had to stay in control.

Gertrude came back to the table with a new fork in hand and said: "What's that on your neck?"

Sophia choked.

"Let me see it. Come here. Are you ill? What is this right here?" She poked at something on Sophia's neck, right where Damian had kissed her the other day. Sophia recoiled, realizing what had happened.

"Nothing, it's nothing. I accidentally hit myself with the back of my brush while I was brushing my hair. I was in a rush this morning to get to work."

Gertrude seemed to have accepted that answer, but perhaps after reading all of those romance novels she suspected the truth.

"Well, it could be something more serious. If you're ill, then I suggest getting up from this table right now and getting into your bed. I'll bring you some warm milk and a heating pad," said Gertrude.

Sophia could tell this was not going to be let go. Her bruises were proof of something—illness or no. It was difficult to surmise what the goal was though at the time. Without dwelling, Sophia got up and pushed in her chair deprived of finishing her dinner.

This is what Gertrude did best, Sophia thought. She found some kind of possible guilt in her victims and exploited it mercilessly.

One time she complimented Sophia on her dress which was not new. She had seen her wear it many times to work, only this time Gertrude had seen a hair stuck in the shoulder of her dress that was visibly lighter than her own.

"Oh, that dress really flatters your figure, honey. I never noticed before how nice it is." She turned up her mouth into some sort of a smile that screamed of deceit.

Sophia quickly looked down and around her body to make sure her dress was not partially stuck in her underwear. But that is when she noticed the small, blond hair sticking out of her dress on her right shoulder. An animal could not have made it up there and they did not have any pets. It was then that Damian's sweet face came into the picture and she knew he had laid his head on her shoulder, smelling and licking the side of her neck before leaving work.

It was astonishing to Sophia that Gertrude could have seen such a small discrepancy and use it to her advantage so quickly.

She had to come up with something quick, yet all she managed to say was, "thanks."

Another time she came home to a smiling mother. Sophia knew she had found something. Gertrude said, "Look what I got in the mail."

Gertrude laid out a letter that had been stuck into the mailbox by Damian even when she had told him not to even think about it. The only words it had on it were "Let us go."

How could her mother have deduced from that that we were talking about her? Sophia wondered.

Sophia gave a blank look at her mother and said, "I don't know what that is."

"Hmmm, well that's odd. Our last initial is hanging right outside on the front door, right near the mailbox. It would be a big mistake if someone did not know it was our mailbox that she...or he was putting this note into."

"Accidents can happen to people who are not aware of their surroundings. Perhaps the mailman dropped his own personal note in our mailbox without realizing it. I would just return it to him tomorrow afternoon since you'll be home."

"I will ask him. Now, how about some dinner? I made your favorite lasagna dish."

Lasagna in our household was a keyword for "I've got you. I've found you out."

Sophia's throat tightened and her body recoiled; she knew Gertrude would ask the mailman if he had seen someone put this into her mailbox. Maybe he saw Damian and her whole secret would now be in the hands of her mother. The relationship would then end for good, and Gertrude surmised as much.

No one was allowed near her daughter because they were sure to abduct, rape, and kill her. She spoke of it as if this were a prophecy. At least that is the story which was frequently told to Sophia. She would be harmed outside of Gertrude's motherly hold. But her arms went too far, her eyes were too dark, and her thoughts were too grim. Sophia was afraid for her safety, but less so when Damian was near her.

***

The lasagna was lukewarm and hard as a rock at the edges.

Sophia dissected the black bits from the edible parts on her plate, her fork and knife scratching against the disposable plate being used tonight. The disposable items came out on occasion, despite how her mother ridiculed others about their waste, when her mother was too exasperated to deal with the loud dishes, and this time Sophia knew it was her own fault for causing the distress.

The hickey Sophia had forgotten about was growing noticeably hotter on her skin, as if she could have felt the bruise forming and sinking deeper into her own flesh. She was now branded with a revealing kiss. Her mother must know.

"The color compliments your dress," Gertrude said. She was acting like a dog that could not let go of a stick it found out on its walk. She bit down on Sophia's bruise and held on. "Hopefully you can find a matching outfit for it tomorrow at work. Do you have anything that's eggplant-colored?" Gertrude gave her best showman's smile.

Sophia coiled further into herself, afraid she would explode if any other gasket were loosened. All of the words and opinions maddeningly swarmed inside her skull, bashing the sides of her brain until there were areas inside which mimicked her hickey on the outside.

"Stop it." Sophia looked up at her mother to gauge the reaction. Gertrude was sitting at the table with wild eyes.

"Don't you ever tell me that again. What right do you have to complain? Here I am cooking and cleaning for a *whore* who doesn't even care what happens to her own mother."

Sophia looked over at her father who was simply shaking his hands at his wife's comment. There was not one attempt to change the word which had already been put out into the open. Her mother knew there was someone in her life, and she hated it.

"Mother, how could you. I just—"

"You just what? Do you remember all of those times when you were sick and near death in bed? What did your poor mother do for you then? Huh? What? She fed you on a platter, she massaged your ungrateful head, and she walked you to the bathroom, and brought you a bucket when you were too weak to get up yourself. You are ungrateful. And now, you show up at home with a hickey on your neck that I washed and cared for. Who did that to you? What is his name? You know I will not tolerate any boy in our home. You are a sick girl who needs help. You are not able to be in a relationship with someone I've never even met. You are forbidden to see him ever again, and you're lucky to still be alive." Gertrude slammed down her fork and stomped off upstairs to her bedroom. The conversation was over before it even began. Her mother would never change.

Sophia knew this was the moment where she had to pursue the path away from her mother, her father, and this doomed house. With her appetite shot to bits, she looked at her father lost in his newspaper—sinking into the inky words on the page which focused his thoughts on anywhere but here. Slowly shaking her head, Sophia got up from the table and left it quietly, not making a sound.

A shower would perhaps help her to clean off the word her mother used. She wanted that black filth to fall down her body with the water and wash away down the drain. Hopefully, the word would not clog down there with all the hair and soap scum. She desired the word to disintegrate, along with all the other dirt covering her thin body.

Sophia's wrinkled fingers did not allow her to feel her soft lips as she gently rubbed them underneath the shower head's tender kisses. So she moved her hands down her face and her breasts and her thighs to see if she could feel herself. She did not feel like a whore. She imagined that whore's felt slightly hairy from lack of upkeep and they had raised skin all over from previous misuse. Whores must always smell unclean even under flowing water. Their hair is always greasy, and their eyes never sparkle. Their teeth must be gnarled and stained, while their backsides remain rough from the whip. Whores did not have the luxury of a wealthy home in a city with a clean office job.

Touching herself all over again, Sophia felt her situation must be different. After all, she had parents to care for her when she was sick. Is not that what her mother said? She just happened to be controlled by them and her fears were more on the inside than the outside.

The shower felt so good to the soft, pale skin that just barely stretched over Sophia's body. Falling water gave her a new womb to cry in. If she could purge herself of anything poisonous internally she would do that too. But Sophia was afraid that the raised parts would always remain scars. There would be no movement of that which was a part of her.

Sophia thought, then let Damian make new scars to cover the old! Distort my old skin with the new, adorn it with fresh peaks to bury the old valleys. Renew a sense of my own self-worth. I'm not a whore, I'm a martyr. Give me the scars that mark a new owner, like a family crest that has changed hands. Deliver me to a god that I can see and hear and taste! Make my doomed existence end and give birth to a new life that leads to a singular devotion to the one I love. Promise me, Damian, to take me home with you. Promise me to build upon these scars until I no longer recognize myself. Change my shape, change my heart and soul. I am ready—there is nothing left for me here.

***

Closing the shower door behind her, Sophia felt a new resolve. The water she let sink in deeply, her open pores only had to absorb the rest. She walked dripping in her towel toward her bedroom, imaging that with her shed towel she shed her skin as well. The towel lay there and the mirror took its fill of her body. Her eyes went from the top of her head all the way down to her feet, scanning up and down for any signs of the dirty word her mother used. It was gone, or perhaps it was never there. But the hickey still lay bare, a splotchy purple-green color on her neck. The bruise shone more like a jewel on her skin than an injury.

Sophia felt that the bruise made her look more mature without marring her youthful skin.

Tiptoeing over to her door, she peeked out and saw that her parents' door was closed at the end of the hall and all of the lights in the house below had been shut off for the night. The time for sneaking around was over for the Weber household. But not for Sophia; tonight she would disrupt all the house's rules restricting her and her newfound life.

The small pebbles came up to hit her window once again. She had been prepared for this. Earlier in the day, Damian was determined to come and see her tonight. It was now or never. The risk was palpable, and the house even felt like it was attempting to fortify itself against intruders. But Sophia was prepared; she wrapped herself quickly in the robe that lay open on her bed, ran up to her windows, and waved at Damian. Then, she launched herself down the stairs as quietly as could be, opening the front door with robber-like abilities. Damian stepped through the door in a second and followed Sophia back up to her bedroom.

The lights were still all out in the house, and as the evening progressed, Sophia knew eventually both of her parents would be fast asleep.

"Come along! Oh, god, I've missed you, Sir!" Sophia got on her knees and bowed down deeply at Damian's feet.

Damian pulled her up by the arms suddenly and held her there, making her feel his heart beating away heavily inside his chest. They pressed into each other hard in order to become like one body trapped inside the doomed house. The house must not notice an intruder.

Akin to the Trojan horse, Sophia masked his body with hers. She tried to shield him from the harm she experienced in the house her entire life by covering him in her soft blankets in bed.

"There all tucked in for the night," she giggled.

Damian smiled and pulled her in with him. "Yes, all tucked in, my little girl."

Sophia fell in love all over again with him. She yearned for their relationship to take on an even stricter "Dominant and submissive" model. She needed structure, and lying in his arms and on his chest made Sophia feel safer than ever before. She heard his heart beating, saw his smile taking shape, watched his warm green eyes glimmering, and felt his strong arms holding her. Surrounding her body with warmth, she was adoring of its presence.

Sophia thought: When I am all alone, the restrictive chain unwinds itself from my throat and I am able to feel relaxed again—free. I become free to eat, free to travel, free to explore. But I cannot love. After a while: I feel lonely, depressed, hollow, numb, yet free. So how can I figure out the key to loving another, whilst still being able to breathe? Damian thinks that because I am free, I can serve. By being a submissive for him, I accept the rules and restrictions allowing me to be ultimately free.

I imagined Damian reaching his suntanned hand out for mine and I gave it to him effortlessly. The spots of sunlight slipped through the leaves of the trees onto the sandy ground beneath our feet. As we listened to the sound that the crunch of the sticks and sand made under our feet, we briskly walked to the pond. The drizzling rain hit our bodies as if begging to be noticed by us. I felt the soothing warm drops sink into my skin and it filled my insides with warmth and comfort. I turned my head up to look at my Master and his face looked purposeful and strong. I knew I was safe and his forever. When we arrive at the edge of the large pond, he asks me to get down onto my knees. I comply. Slowly he smiles at me and dips his finger in the icy water. Lifting his dripping finger up to my forehead, my Master writes "Property of Damian Voigt." I shiver. My baptism began a new chapter in my life...the one I had been waiting for since my first baptism into the church I never chose. But this life is of my choice and my true calling: sex, life, love. I can only truly relax when I am having sex with my love because that is when I feel the furthest from death. I feel so alive that my worries subside and my entire focused energy becomes blindingly aware of my body. Every slap, every bruise, every chain, every bite, every muscle that forces me to the ground is highlighted in my memories. My mind revolts, whilst my body begs for more—harder, Sir. I wanted him to force himself on me so that I have no control—no say in the matter. My life was literally in his hands, and I trusted him as I have never trusted anyone else with it. I wanted him to be mine forever. I gave him consent by the way my body responded under his muscular hands as he turned me over his knee and spanked me until I fell onto the blue, carpeted floor. Then, sliding off his belt from his pants, I crawled away only to be pulled back under his legs. Repeatedly, he whipped me with his leather belt while my knees stung from the rug burn. My backside became a bright red color and he proceeded to lift me up and throw me onto the bed. Pinning my bruised wrists down, he forced my legs open and placed himself on top of me. Breathing heavily he whispered in my ear all of the things he was going to do to me. I tried to struggle under his weight to no avail. I gave in and he took me, used me, and made me into his pleasure. I loved it.

***

We fell asleep together, exhausted after giving ourselves so completely to pleasure.

Sophia's thoughts were a hazy vision of what she gave and what she took with her to paradise. Digging my swelling feet into the clumps of dirt below, I exhale. Shaking follows as my thoughts linger on his arms…

Yet, a deeper voice echoed from inside Sophia, whispering, "Empty, empty vessel, jumping overboard, S.O.S."

My plummeting expression groping in the dark for his lips. Ah, love! What if I let you go for another? Sophia wondered. Surely, sentimental hauntings would raise alarms in the creases of my brain. I would always remember the ease of each morning awakening by your side, and the warmth of your cotton shirt touched with the smell of soap from the local grocery store. Breathing seemed so easy and smiling too hard to suppress each time I saw your face.

I gave what was mine to you because I believe we are soul mates…or perhaps I did not believe in them before and I just saw you as close to such an ideal. All I do know is that alone in my parents' house whenever I cook or clean, our life together overwhelms me and I have memories of you.

You have long, blond strands of hair and big green eyes. Your noble nose gives your smile a sweet look. I envision mentally letting you go. I have barred myself the access that I always thought I would have with your body. There are times when I wish I could crawl back sniveling and weak. I would beg you to kick me, hurt me, and pound me for returning to Mother.

I would say, I am so sorry, Master, for my sass-mouth. It is so dirty from not having been renewed by you for such a long time. I keep forgetting my place, and I need to be punished to be reminded. I want you to spank me until it stings so that whenever I sit down I will remember who is the boss, who makes the rules, and who created me to obey, Sir. I am your beloved baby, and I must love, obey, and serve you, as you must love, care for, and discipline me. If we do this together, we both benefit and are pleasured together. We do what feels right and natural and that is how our relationship became a loving one. I want you to have a wonderfully restful night, Sir. Dream all about holding me again in your arms, pushing me around, commanding me, punishing me outside and inside your own domain. Dream about making love to me by the pond and "baptizing" each other in it. We are free to create our own rules and our own world.

In the morning, Sophia imagined, I would jump out of bed to serve you coffee before you even woke up. I would run to the kitchen to make a cup of coffee, kneel beside the bed, and whisper, "good morning, Master," in my God's ear. You wake up with a slight smile on your face and take the hot coffee from my little palms. You take a sip and frown, "...you forgot the sugar, little one." Without a second thought, you spring up from bed, grab me, and toss me over your knee. I get fifteen really hard spankings on my backside before you let me go get the sugar. I pour some into your coffee and then bend down and kiss your feet while saying, "thank you, Master, for disciplining me properly. You are fair and kind for only giving me fifteen spankings. I need you to guide me, teach me to become a better submissive for you. I am grateful for your discipline and training, Sir. Your effort will not go unrewarded." Slowly, I spread my legs apart on the floor in a new position you taught me and wait for you to finish your coffee. As soon as you decide I waited long enough, you made love to me right there on the hardwood floors. From now on let us live that way together.

Sophia moved closer to Damian's neck. She felt like moving right in and settling there permanently. She wanted to bite and suck, bite and suck until she became a new appendage Damian never knew he needed. He was no longer on his own. If she could poison his veins with her venom, she would. His power lay in physical strength, but hers lay in her mental strength. She willed it to be so, that Damian fall in love with her and never leave. She would bow down, even if she had to dig a hole and jump into it just to bow down further before him; she would lay there quietly and still as long as he wanted her near; she would wait outside his door for days just to get a touch from his glorious hands.

She rubbed her face deeper into his neck, and suddenly

Damian woke up and grabbed her by the neck. She forgot to breathe anyway from the shock, while he raised himself up and lowered himself right next to her cheek whispering: "Do you know I am so grateful for every moment I have with you, dear? I want you again, and again, and again because each time I know will be unique. Thank you for giving yourself to me."

The grip on her neck became softer as Sophia closed her eyes with happiness. "Thank you for taking me, Sir. Don't ever let me go."

"Never. A beautiful little flower like yourself will wilt if its roots are not strong. I adore you," said Damian.

Kissing each other softly, underneath the ceiling that now had no light to mock her with, everything became pacified in her room. A new era began to change the little torture chamber of a bedroom. Sophia and Damian twined up together, binding all that was a part of them to one another, all the while losing track of where one body ended and the other began. Their dreams helped to create a fog that further blurred the lines of their bodies so much so they may have even shared the same dreams.

CHAPTER VI

There was a particular dip in Gertrude's bed. It was from her husband who was out again on a night shift at the hospital. She did not mind though, because she often went to sleep before him anyway. They never had the same schedule. Still, the dip in bed seemed to sink lower as if inviting her to take over it all to herself. Those were the sheets where they consummated their marriage and conceived Sophia. Each edge of the crisp, white sheet had yellowed with their sweat. Their bodies sunk deeper into the mattress with each passing year as if gravity were pushing them down into their graves.

I do not want to die, thought Gertrude, and yet, and yet... perhaps it would be restful and quiet... I would not have to deal with my daughter's rebellious behavior or my husband's cowardice anymore. Who knows, death could very well be a charmer. Death may reach out its skeletal hand to touch me and gracefully place me down at the pearly gates. The sunken holes where his eyes used to be would point in the direction I must follow, with his boney finger pointing ahead as well in case I missed his eyeless sockets. Curtseying to him, in case he could not hear, I would step up onto a fluffy white cloud toward my final destination. I imagine the white light

263

is snow reflecting the sun off those blindingly bright gates. Then the Lord would greet me in heaven, reminding me of all the sacrifice I had put myself through to get here. A crowd of admirers who have watched all of my struggles would stand behind him in awe.

Stepping through the gates, rose petals would fall around me from the flower-bearers' baskets. I imagine myself laughing carefree like when I was a little girl. My kitten would wrap itself around my feet and not my sister's. I am the martyr. I am one of the Lord's chosen few. I raised an insolent, sick girl up from an early demise and into adulthood. My whole life was…is devoted to her and she has the gall to go out with a man. Well, I will never accept him into our family. That man is an enemy to the security of our house. Tomorrow I will make sure she breaks it off.

No child of mine, of God's, is meant to be soiled by another. The planet is full enough of sinners as it is. The planet has become an overpopulated dump. Mother Nature must hate us, as she is being kicked, beaten, and suffocated by her own kin. I am actually surprised that the Lord has not come down to bring plague and misery. We are long overdue for a good plague to wipe out the diseased species and allow the new and innocent to dominate the earth.

Someday, my life will be right. Someday, God will hear me and my prayers. Someday, the just will find justice.

When that day comes I will be there right in front, holding my Bible in the right hand and my cross in the left. No words from others will reach me but God's voice. I should have married myself to Him from the get-go. Instead, I had to learn the hard way that no men on earth are as good as my God. He leads me to the truth. Men on earth are mere flawed shadows dragging at the Lord's feet. He must be tired of carrying all that weight. I would serve Him kindly. I could wash His feet and clean His clothes. The community serves only one man, only one God. Yes, I belong to heaven. I belong up there where my sacrifices get recognized and count for something. I want to be there.

The only thing I would leave behind on earth is a necklace of mine for Sophia and the house for my husband. In heaven, there will be no pain, no sex either. But I suppose I have learned by now that men on earth are mostly disappointments anyway, and the men of my dreams are only written in fiction.

She stared up at the ceiling from her side of the bed, spread out her tired legs, and picked up her book from the nightstand. It was another steamy romance novel from a new series about cowboys stealing women out in the Wild West. Those cowboys were all well-endowed and their tight jeans assisted in showing that off. The words on the page helped to take Gertrude away from this abhorred life she led and into a world of real men and planned romances. Nothing, in the end, was allowed to go wrong in those tales, nothing. The hero took the woman and she gave in to his demands without being harmed—only pleasured.

If only I could live such a life, thought Gertrude. I could have power over the entire scene and my pleasure would be the only thing that mattered. Who cares about the man? Who cares about the setting? I just want that pleasure and I want it now. I would get it even if he had to bleed.

Her wrinkled thighs banged together in bed, getting the sheets stuck in between her coiling legs. The sensations of Gertrude's body were still alive. The thought of power at all costs is what made the story take on importance for her.

The book's climax ended when the hero saved his lady from a burning barn where she had been waiting to make love to him. They kissed as he was running out of the red swinging doors when, suddenly, it exploded and the hero had to jump on his favorite horse with his woman to get away in time. It took no time before they arrived safely to a beautiful western-style ranch where they ended up marrying—everything was drenched in sunshine.

Her sinewy hands went limp as the book was laid open on her stomach. Gertrude's head laid toward her right shoulder and a bit of drool had slid out from between her crescent-shaped lips. They were thin and crinkled even though she had never smoked. Something else had sucked the life out of her mouth.

A gentle rise and fall of her chest made the book move wave-like with each breath. The lights typically remained on all night. Gertrude's husband was the one to turn them off when he arrived home later in the evenings.

All of life lay in that book for Gertrude—all of its thrills and excitement, along with its formulaic stories that only allowed good things to happen. There was no risk of sickness, rape, or murder. Romance novels only permitted happy endings. It was *safe*.

Gertrude dreamed of holding onto a cowboy's large shoulders, nibbling his ear, and wrapping her legs around his masculine hips. She could feel his hands cupping her breasts and standing there between her legs without letting go of her gaze. They roughly play together out on an abandoned field, but Gertrude changed it in her mind into a playpen built for only pleasure without pain. She was not allowed to be hurt or betrayed inside this dream world. Her cowboy tried to speak sometimes in her dreams, but she always put a finger to his lips and silenced any desires he had to share. A silent plaything was all she had ever wanted. But he had to be warm. For sweet warmth was the only comfort and pleasure another human being could give her—not thoughts nor wishes.

Since her marriage began, Gertrude had lived for these romance novels. They filled her evenings when the television had nothing to offer by way of tragedy. Reality, to her, consisted of deception, rape, and murder. But fantasy: that was all power, play, and pleasure.

Romance novels let her live with her other imagined half, her gorgeous twin who made love without fear. In the real world, her love was frustrated by a husband who was never there, never with his wife. She was not even really attracted to her cowboy in reality. He bumped into her and they made a solemn agreement to marry after they put themselves back together from the initial bump. Her husband was a calculated man, as was she, but there was something missing.

Love was not a household word. The word only tumbled out of Gertrude's mouth after she had read a risqué scene. Love was a byproduct of the romance novels that circulated in and out of the Weber house on a weekly basis, specifically after Gertrude went grocery shopping. The library staff all knew her name and recommended the latest novel from her beloved genre.

To escape her lonely life, she plunged her nose in these books as keenly as her husband did his newspapers. This world was too dangerous and the people that filled it were cruel. The only way Gertrude could survive was if she fought and defended her body against the brutality of others. Her home was her palace and the moat was dug deep enough to keep out even the sneakiest pestilences. Her family must remain behind the thick doors, Gertrude thought, or they will surely perish. Loving in this world was impossible, which is why she thought her romance novels were but a dream. Gertrude would never feel as the characters did about each other and about life. The novels would always remain distant dreams in a white-washed and worn reality.

***

Getting deeper into the book's plot, Gertrude's mind grew foggier. She dreamed about chiseled abdomens and legs of steel. There were conversations tossed back and forth between herself and her husband that accidentally were mixed into the book she was absorbing, such as when she saw her husband dressed in only blue jeans and a cowboy hat. He also looked younger and more physically fit in her head than he ever did in real life.

"Why did you choose me?" she asked her husband.

"Because."

"Because why, dear?"

"I bumped into you on the sidewalk. Remember?"

"Yes, I remember. But did I look pretty to you? Is that why you wanted me?"

Her husband paused before deciding on, "Yes, you were a looker."

"Do you remember anything else about me?"

"Not particularly. We just seemed to need each other."

"Yes, I needed you. But did you need me?"

Now, the conversation ceased and Gertrude remembered a day when she talked to her husband about whether or not to let their daughter go to her first dance at school:

"Dear, I'm afraid she'll be plied with drink and abducted

right from the school gym!"

"Oh, honey, that's ridiculous. They have parents there watching all the students."

"No, no, no, no. This world is not safe for a young, sickly girl."

"Okay, then she won't go."

"Right, exactly. She will not be permitted to risk her life for a silly, insignificant dance. Besides, I don't trust those parents with their own kids."

The moat was dug further around after that conversation, as the light into the kitchen grew dimmer, and the ceiling's shadows longer.

Gertrude twitched, thereby waking herself up and shifting the book a little more over to her left side, as her right was beginning to get sore. She lifted the book up and watched as the line from the book's spine left an odd rectangular dent in her wrinkling skin. She kept her eyes on it with pleasure, for a simple object like a book had power over the shape of her skin. She followed the outline with her fingers and at each sharp curve her finger felt the lines converge. A delicious feeling gurgled in the pit of her stomach as if clapping at the amusing tracks on her stomach. Her fingers moved down a bit further and found a new line, one she forgot was there. There was another line, and then another, and yet another all expertly sliced in straight lines. Gertrude began to remember each one, she had a line there from her appendix operation, another couple of lines from her hysterectomy, another few lines from her gallbladder removal. Her stomach was a battlefield of scars.

She had been to doctors for surgeries more times than she had had birthdays. Doctors made better cowboys than her husband, who shed off his job attire as well as his feelings once he walked through the front door. Back when Gertrude was younger, she made surprise appearances at her husband's hospital just to find some spark again in their marriage. She got a thrill whenever he was still in doctor mode, helping a patient get from the hospital bed and into a wheelchair. But then the flames of jealousy hit, and she was later found by her husband huddled up in his office with the largest medical textbook she could find, diagnosing herself with a million little things that all required surgery.

Doctors were better than cowboys, thought Gertrude. Cowboys rode around and saved troubled damsels, but they did not operate. They did not cut their buxom women open and peer inside at what was wrong with them. Gertrude needed a man with a scalpel. She needed a man who was not afraid to slice her skin open and release what was lodged inside. Gertrude loved her sickness and she wanted to share it with her doctors.

Picking up the book in her hands again, the chapter was talking about a conflict between the cowboy and his newfound lover. The cowboy wanted her to come away with him to live on a dirty, old ranch, while his love-interest wanted a rich, new one. This conflict spoke directly to Gertrude. Her own goal in life was to find a rich fortress and hide in there all of her treasures. Her family would be there, her pricey furniture, her hobby-related items, and her clothes, everything that gave off the impression of supreme wealth. That is another reason why doctors are even better than cowboys, thought Gertrude. Cowboys are poor and, sometimes, criminals, while doctors are loved by society and have a lot of money. Her husband knew what she wanted, at least in terms of wealth and prestige—he provided that for her. Perhaps that is what he meant by them "needing" each other.

There was one more foggy memory that overtook Gertrude and it was of Sophia tripping and falling on the ground outside of the house when she was three. She wailed after getting up and looking down at her bleeding knees. The sidewalk gravel had gotten stuck in her flesh and the rest had ripped off pieces of her delicate, new skin. Gertrude rushed to her, crying and screaming more loudly than her own child. The scene was awful. Gertrude felt as if she had fallen herself and that the world was still moving when it should have stopped and taken care of her. Immediately Gertrude picked up her crying toddler and ran to the car where she drove to the emergency room. Apathetic faces met her and some troubled looks encountered Gertrude's frightened eyes as she ran in toward the front desk asking to see a surgeon right away.

"My daughter might lose her legs! Don't look at me like that! Do something, idiot!"

"Ma'am, we're going to ask you to calm down and tell us what happened."

"Can't you see my daughter's knees?! She just fell on the gravel outside! Now, help us!"

A doctor overheard the yelling and came to take Gertrude quickly into an empty office and clean Sophia up. After some antibacterial wipes and bandages made their way onto Sophia's legs, Gertrude was thanking the doctor with all her heart and soul for saving her child's legs.

"Thank you, doctor, really. Toddlers should really be surrounded by soft things only, don't you think? May I also take a lollipop before I go?"

On the way out of the hospital, Gertrude recalled eyeing

another hospital she would take Sophia to after a few days to follow up on her knees. It was this kind of parenting care that made Gertrude believe she deserved a more grateful, adoring family.

***

Lying in bed, full of lasagna, Sophia kept turning from one side to the other as if trying to help the food through the curves of her intestines.

She reached out for her glass of water to wash the pile of slush further and further down. Perhaps the water would help to curb her desire to throw it all up again so she could become light as air and float out of this still horrid situation.

Another speech, meanwhile, kept inventing and reinventing itself to a sleeping Damian.

Sophia stood tall and she spoke with all the passion she could muster to Damian, saying:

You know what, Damian? I just realized I am a child. I wake up every morning mesmerized by humanity and all its endeavors: like the fact that people fill their days with song and dance, or that universal love, truth, justice, and beauty is contested by philosophers on a daily basis. In a world full of scholars and artists who rule their own perspectives. I have my own views. It is the perspective of the third person: the observer, the taste-tester, the awe-inspired critic, and lover of life. I am one who engages with pain and joy, only to experience the highest extremes of both and wish to share them with my brothers and sisters. It is this childish wonder that inspires me to constantly remind mankind of his place in nature, of his character, of his potential, of his limits, of his beauty, of his ugliness, of his grace, of his mortality, or of his utter perfection in the cosmos.

Sophia imagined Damian taking her in his arms and making love to her right on the pavement behind their workplace. He made her want to live, and that also meant to love.

Beneath the covers, a warm pocket had formed around Sophia's curled up body. It was a pocket she never wanted to leave. There was comfort for her in the warmth she perpetuated. It reminded her she was alive, although barely. But her breathe ceased when she heard several pebbles hit her window, followed by a whistle from outside. It only happened once. Sophia rolled over to find that Damian was no longer in her bed. She crept out of bed and peeked out of her lowered blinds to find Damian down below.

"What are you doing?" Sophia said.

"Liberating you. Let's go!" Damian waved for her to come down and enter the darkly lit streets of the city.

Hopping around trying to get on some socks she found on the floor and her robe, Sophia quietly opened her bedroom door into the black hallways and carefully descended the stairwell. The fuzzy carpet tickled her feet as she took them two at a time, racing to get away for good.

The house door seemed to desire her to stay in with a doorknob that felt extra secure by its resistance to turning. But Sophia pulled hard, no longer caring whether the noise woke up her sleeping parents.

Sophia put out her hand this time for Damian to grab as he ran with her toward the woods near her house. Instead, Damian grabbed her hand and then moved up to her neck as he whispered, "quiet," in her ear. Sophia tried to stifle a giggle.

It was dark outside and Sophia could hardly see Damian's face, but she knew it was him. She could feel the dried blood still crusted over on his hands. Her heart was beating quickly as Damian proceeded to pin her to a tree. Sophia begged him to pleasure her—she got down on her knees on the muddy ground, kissed his feet, and pleaded for him to make this as painless as possible. But Damian would not have any of it. "You act like a little animal, you'll be treated like one," and he pulled her up by her hair, throwing her back against the tree. Using rope, he tied her hands behind her and shoved his tongue down her throat to keep her from screaming.

Flipping Sophia swiftly over his knee, Damian hit her hard with his belt again and no one could hear the lashes. She shouted "Thank you, Sir!" against her will. Her body and mind racing together, each half crying for release in hot ecstasy muddled with fear. She loved watching his face contort into a pleasurable, animalistic smile. He licked her face as he beat her. Finally, she mumbled thank you enough times under the pressure of his hand over her mouth that he pressed her up against another tree, ripped off her clothes, spread her legs, took off his pants, and had her in the dark to the point where every pulse or movement rang throughout her body in a delicious, ebbing pain. Only after the adrenaline rush did Sophia feel nauseous and weary. Her body had been used, violated, and tenderly held all at once. Sophia was penetrated by her God in the dark—where their shadowy passions lay like ivy twisted around the trees until she and Damian choose to redeem them again. Sophia and Damian would resume their modest nature in the daytime until darkness washed over them once more and the desire for destruction overcame them.

There is a pressure boiling up—rising. The highest flames reach Sophia's heart so tactile and close. She laid a hand on her chest to try to cool the swelling heat. Sophia wiped away droplets of sweat that stung her eyes on the way down.

However, the more she left her previous life behind, the more she pined for her mother. Wrenching away her heart from any feeling of nostalgia, Sophia wrapped her silent cries inside Damian's arms. No matter how violent he became, Damian's care was now more vital to Sophia than her mother's. Sophia *needed* him to live, even though she was constantly fighting with the tormenting recollections of those soft fingers massaging her hair and those deceptively warm meals in bed. She needed someone to push her around to show her she was not fragile. Damian's violence, she believed, was actually an act of devotion—of *love*. The lashes from his belt were a form of repentance and salvation for a girl who could never stand up to her mother. The physical pain was much easier for her to endure than the mental manipulation. After all, Sophia would not break like glass if she was dropped. Physical pain caused callouses, and callouses meant resilience that Sophia did not have to focus on for them to grow. Her own skin would create tougher layers and soon the belt would no longer seem as shocking as it had on that first night. Over time, Sophia's skin would thicken and diminish all the mental scars endured within the Weber household. Already, Damian had succeeded many times in shaking her out of those visions, but they seemed always to creep back in at night, and she believed a descent into anxiety and fear would be worse than a rise. Descent rests low in the stomach, she thought, coiling around eel-like, emitting pressure on the body surrounding the creature. Sophia shifted around in her bed trying to find a more comfortable position. But like a foolish boy blowing up a balloon to the point of bursting, she could not find a way to lay still in peace.

She saw her mother for what she was—a lonely, tyrannical, bitter person—but she still could not leave her behind. The bond was too strong, and only death would sever that bond for good. Sophia knew she would never stop needing her mother.

"Purity" was a word that turned into "putrid" whenever Sophia saw it, on her bookcase or a mug in the kitchen. Gertrude believed in angels and heaven and purity. In the event the Lord did come down to speak to her, Sophia would ask if he would take Mother with him too. Perhaps then, "purity" would no longer turn into "putrid" for Sophia.

Sophia was being torn by her ever-changing emotions. She wanted to know when she would die, but could not bear to know when at the same time. Her childish fingers showed no sign of age, and even the thought of death was a distant mirage of fuzzy dark figures in musty corridors without end.

Yet, when she awoke by Damian's side the next morning to see a few gray hairs on his head, Sophia shuddered.

***

Gertrude took up the whole bed with her body that night. However, it was not too long before Gertrude shot up from sleep for the first time since her childhood. She had had a nightmare.

She screamed, "Her ashes! Her ashes! I cannot find them!"

A wave of nausea rolled over her, leaving her forehead sweaty and her throat tight.

"Help! Help me! What have I done?"

Gertrude looked over to where her husband should have been but was not yet. With a flip of the covers, she uncovered herself and ran to the bathroom. The floor felt cool and she lay down on the tiles to stop the sweat from dripping down.

In every painting decorating the walls of her bedroom, she saw a crumbling house. One painting she had made when she had first married her husband. It was of a sea of serene waters enclosing identical little houses that littered its coast. But now the blue of the watercolors appeared darker, the waves higher, and the houses more vulnerable than they had ever seemed before. Next to it hung a painting of a cottage in the midst of a forest. The green hues softly meshed in the background and in the foreground the cottage's chimney was emitting a heartwarming smoke. Gertrude squinted and a fear emerged of stones falling from out the cottage's exterior walls. One of the walls was weakening and the whole cottage would soon become fodder for the forest and its wildlife. Fear was settling in Gertrude's body before she had even acknowledged its presence. Yet, another painting that adorned itself above her bed was of a baby Sophia. She was wrapped in a garb Gertrude found appropriate to the stature of her home: a white christening gown. The laces of the little bonnet Gertrude had tightened around Sophia's head secured her chin. But, tonight, Gertrude discovered a crack in her canvas cutting through the wall of the house baby Sophia sat in. The thin crack slashed near to her white gown. Gertrude thought she must figure out a way to stop this crack before it pierced her baby's frail arm.

She envisioned a moat filled and overflowing, growing into a tsunami crashing down over her domain and demolishing every last wooden piece of the house down to the ground. Her fortress was writing out its own ending on its walls over the years, and Gertrude had never even noticed it.

There was a tiny fracture in the wall between the bathroom door and the corner of the wall. She looked at it from the cool tiles of the floor. Its spidery legs grew out and no one knew what it was letting in. Abduction, rape, and murder in many forms could be slithering through those cracks and descend on her entire family in this crumbling abode.

The faintness abated while the thoughts of death raced through her mind. Gertrude began seeing images of her daughter dying in so many brutal ways. Everyone on the television had Sophia's face superimposed on theirs. She was at once the killer and the killed. Sophia was the predator and the victim. She was the sinful and the innocent.

Her daughter was in danger and she herself was too. Perhaps, this was a sign from the Lord that both of them had to attack the other in order to live. As she envisioned the red and blue lights of police cars and news cameras showing up at the scene before she did. Sophia would be lying on the ground drenched in her own blood just like when she was a toddler, only her knees would be saved this time, and this time it was her heart that did not make it. Gertrude watched herself scream as a murder weapon was pulled out from behind a trash can in the alley of this miserable city.

Gertrude was committed to winning, and yet...she saw, horrified, her daughter's shrieking face as she must have pleaded with her murderer, clutched at her chest, and fell on her knees in defeat. Gertrude tried to stop her gruesome imagination from continuing to torment her. But she failed and within this blurry vision, she saw that Sophia had been mortally wounded. Dropping toward the ground in agony, Sophia had lost her life, but she had also escaped from her mother. Sophia may have succumbed to a physical wound, but she had not let her mother's scars be the cause.

Seething, Gertrude wanted to run up off her bathroom floor

and into this dream world, shaking her daughter. No longer would she be kind and sweet when her daughter was ill or in need. Now, she would shake and smack and tear at her to wake up before it was too late.

Her daughter was not *supposed* to die, thought Gertrude. It was a thing that was never allowed to happen. The massages and soup were meant to keep the house from crumbling. Her defenses were there so long as her other keepers of the estate were there. Gertrude would never let her daughter go. She had to have her in her home, always. Her daughter was meant to be the prize piece of the home, dearer than the dining room fireplace. Sophia was to become the next owner of this estate after her father died. She was never to be emotionally or physically hurt as her mother was. Even though her daughter was sick often, Gertrude was determined to keep her alive.

There would be no men, no loud noise, and no chaos in this house to ruin her daughter's wellbeing. If that meant that the moat had to be dug deeper or the walls higher, then she would do it. Her daughter would be raised on rich land, not on poor land. Her daughter was too good for cowboys or dances or the hot sun. Her skin must remain pale and taut, her beauty untouched as much as her soul must remain pure.

Gertrude half-closed her book and fingered the dent the book made on the left side now of her stomach. She was used up, old, and not as beautiful as she once thought she was. It was a hard life that had made her an old rag. Her family had never shielded her from anything. She was lucky she had even made it to this age unscathed. Yet still, she had only become sick recently. Sophia, on the other hand, had been sick from birth. Gertrude would not let her catch her disease; the brunt of the sickness remained hers alone.

Her disease would be the only thing to lay with her in that dip in bed and drive her deeper down into nothingness. Slowly gravity was reducing her to dust in her own bed. She refused to ever let the world do that to her baby. Sophia's sickness was minor; Gertrude's was great.

Opening back up her romance novel, Gertrude read until her eyes felt heavy and her heart rate dropped down to a ghostly pulse. Sleep came over her once more, only deeper than before, where her restless mind could finally be overcome. The lamps remained on and the television droned, but Gertrude's book kept riding the wave on her chest.

When her husband finally came home, he had to scoot her over to her own mattress dip. Her body fit in it like it was the outline of a crime scene. On her stomach, the book remained leisurely undulating up and down and up and down again. Gertrude did not toss, but rather lay there on her back with the book in place all through the silent hours; her hands lay squarely by each side like a soldier. She was unapproachable even in sleep, a tower unto herself.

The only thing that seemed off to her husband when he finally got into bed was that her book was dog-eared and pointed to the word "ashes," and her hands were cold as ice.

THE END

About the Author

Kaitlyn Bankson was born on 3 January 1994 in New York. Kaitlyn studied literature and philosophy throughout her education which shaped her creative voice. Her published works include: *Metamorphosis: An Anthology of Poems; Unveiled: An Anthology of Nonfiction; Urgency: An Anthology of Short Stories; Marginalia from the Snake Pit: A Novella;* and *The Paper Pusher.* Kaitlyn's unique perspective and raw prose bring light to matters that are often left untouched. Readers can see more of Kaitlyn's work at www.kaitlynbankson.com.

You can connect with me on:
- 🌐 https://kaitlynbankson.com
- 🐦 https://x.com/kaitlynbankson
- 🔗 https://linkedin.com/in/kaitlynbankson

Subscribe to my newsletter:
- ✉ http://eepurl.com/glJhKf